Praise for
THE LAST LIST OF MISS JUDITH KRATT

"As the keeper of the family treasures and the family secrets, Miss Judith Kratt is a Southern eccentric in the tradition of Faulkner's Miss Emily. But Miss Judith does not wallow in the past or embrace the dead. Instead, she works to protect the living. *The Last List of Miss Judith Kratt* is a universal and timely story that exposes the dangers of nostalgia and the value of assessing both things and people in a clear-eyed, honest way. It's a thoroughly captivating story, and it's beautifully told."

—Tiffany Quay Tyson, author of *Three Rivers* and *The Past Is Never*

"Andrea Bobotis has written an amazing novel, one which interrogates, with such controlled and beautiful writing, what it means to be Southern. Utilizing a unique form and a carefully crafted mystery, Bobotis is a writer capable of deep truths, and this novel announces her as a major voice."

—Kevin Wilson, author of *The Family Fang, Perfect Little World*, and *Baby, You're Gonna Be Mine*

"The droll voice of Andrea Bobotis's heroine, Judith Kratt, might charm you—but don't be fooled into thinking this is simply one woman's trip down memory lane. *The Last List of Miss Judith Kratt* is a multilayered story about family, race, loss, and loyalty, featuring a complex cast of characters led by a woman who learns it's never too late for growth and change."

—Cynthia Swanson, *New York Times* bestselling author of *The Bookseller* and *The Glass Forest*

"Andrea Bobotis is a new, original voice as Southern as they come! In *The Last List of Miss Judith Kratt*, she unravels a complicated web of dirty Southern secrets. Using masterful writing and a perfectly calculated reveal of damaged history, she ends up weaving a tapestry that is so much *more*."

—Leah Weiss, bestselling author of *If the Creek Don't Rise*

"Capturing the unique, singular voice of a once-genteel South that hid its deadly secrets and brutal crimes behind facades of grand houses, Andrea Bobotis gently leads you down a garden path of one family's shameful story, only to leave you gasping at its devastating, inevitable destination. If William Faulkner were still alive, I'm pretty sure he'd wish he had written this book."

—Emily Carpenter, author of *Burying the Honeysuckle Girls*

The LAST LIST of MISS JUDITH KRATT

Andrea Bobotis

Published by Sourcebooks Landmark, an imprint of Sourcebooks
P.O. Box 4410, Naperville, Illinois 60567-4410
(630) 961-3900
sourcebooks.com

Library of Congress Cataloging-in-Publication Data

Names: Bobotis, Andrea, author.
Title: The last list of Miss Judith Kratt : a novel / Andrea Bobotis.
Description: Naperville, Ill. : Sourcebooks Landmark, 2019.
Identifiers: LCCN 2018033669 | (trade pbk. : alk. paper)
Subjects: LCSH: Heirlooms--Fiction. | Family secrets--Fiction. | South Carolina--Fiction. | GSAFD: Mystery fiction.
Classification: LCC PS3602.O265 L37 2019 | DDC 813/.6--dc23 LC record available at https://lccn.loc.gov/2018033669

Printed and bound in the United States of America.
VP 10 9 8 7 6 5 4 3 2 1

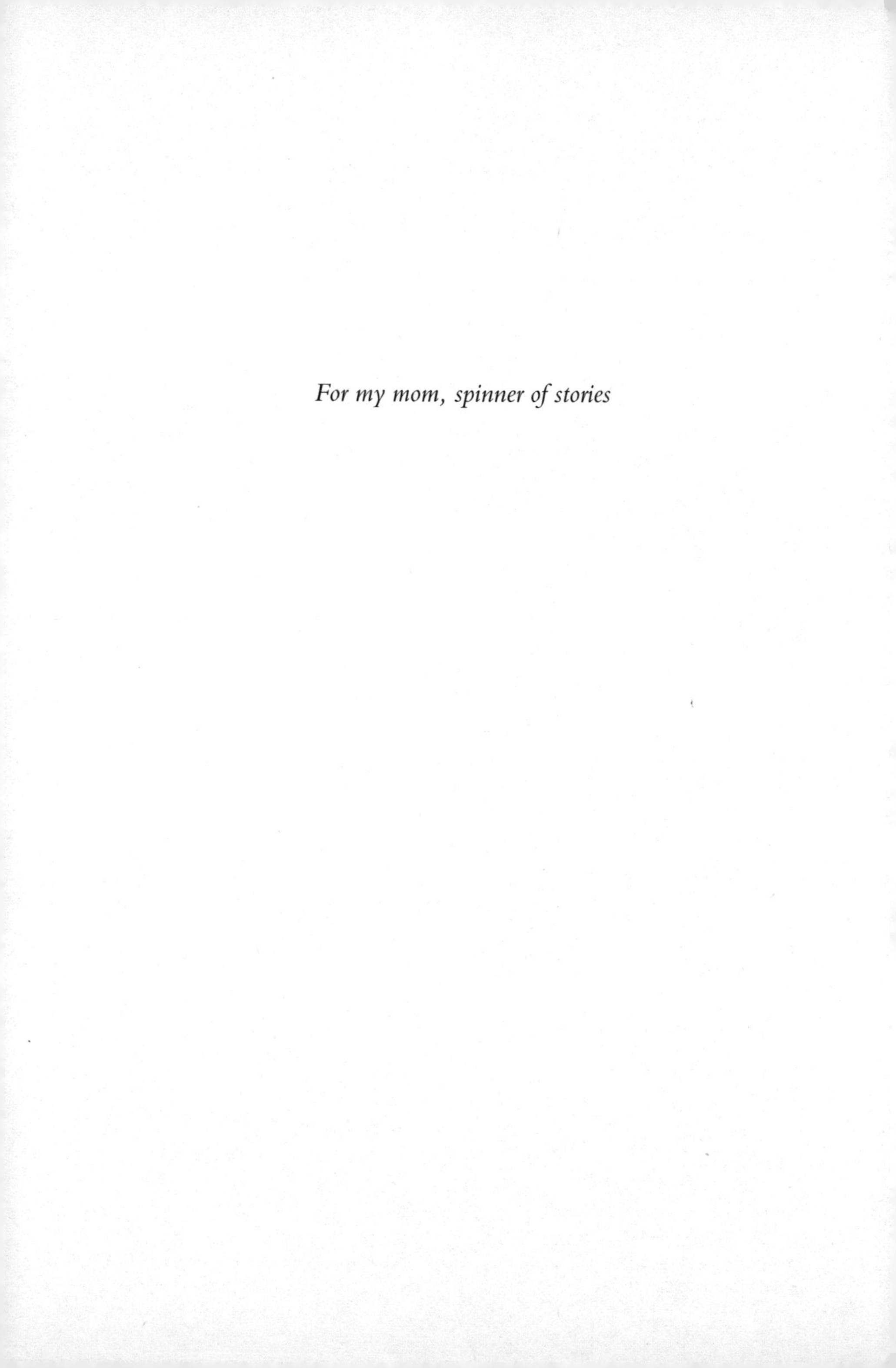

For my mom, spinner of stories

Murder Stuns Distinguished Family

Quincy Kratt, age 14, sustained a fatal gunshot wound to his person in the early hours of Friday, December 20. Young Mr. Kratt was a scion of the cotton industry in Bound, South Carolina. His father, the influential businessman Brayburn Kratt, is one of our local captains of that industry. The principal suspect in the shooting is a negro called Charlie Watson, who is employed by the Kratt Mercantile Company and whose whereabouts are as yet unknown.

York Herald,
Saturday, December 21, 1929

ONE

May 1989

Whenever I hear a train's horn in the distance, that bruised sound, I think of Quincy. He spent half his days down at the depot, true enough, but it's the nature of the sound that reminds me of him, how it's at once familiar and remote. How upon hearing it, I feel obliged to lift my gaze and weigh the horizon, but how it leaves me with less than I had before, eyes reaching toward something I'll never see. After all, where that train's headed, stretching across some unseen field, is anybody's guess. Same could always be said of my brother.

That afternoon, the train's horn made me wonder: What would remind my brother of me? I thought it might be a good question for Olva, who was sitting with me in the sunroom, both of us warming our old bones, I on the cushioned seat and she the uncushioned (her preference), our feet sharing the wicker ottoman so that, now and again, my foot accidentally nudged hers. The sound of that faraway train settled in my ear like a teaspoon of water, but Olva, eyes closed, was humming a cheery little something, and every few bars, a smile surfaced on her face.

When I asked the question "What would remind Quincy of me?" her smile fled the room.

Perhaps it was unfair of me to saddle her with the question, especially since she was ignorant of its context. The train's horn was another reminder, an urging. I opened my mouth to tell her I was planning to write an inventory of the Kratt family's heirlooms but closed it again. I suppose I wanted to savor my idea, unspoiled by others' opinions, for a bit longer.

And she had not yet answered my question about Quincy. I had expected her to say something like "Miss Judith, do you mean back when your brother was alive? Or are we referring to his present-day ghost?" Because Olva is always willing to humor me. She didn't grow up with brothers and sisters and so has a limited understanding of the vagaries of siblinghood, the way devotion is splintered with contempt, but she also has the knack for answering all manner of questions, even the type that might require her to put words in a dead brother's mouth.

I saw her face tighten around an idea, something twisting its way from her mind like a screw digging its patient way through a plank, when, all at once, her face released, and she resumed her humming.

So I asked the question again.

"What do you think anyone—not just Quincy, it doesn't matter who—would associate with me?"

Again, her humming faltered, and just at the verge of my being able to identify the tune.

"Maybe it's the scent of rose water," I suggested—just for something to say, not meaning it. "The kind Mama taught me to make from scratch. The one I let you borrow when we were teenagers."

Olva gripped and released the arms of her chair. Her eyes

took a slow tour of the sunroom before finding mine. "Why, it's this house, Miss Judith," she said. "When people think of you, they think of this house."

A little *oh* rose from my mouth, a bright note of satisfaction.

Olva never lets me down. She was right, of course. I am inseparable from this house, its six thousand square feet sitting on four acres, not to mention the adjoining five hundred acres of our family's land that spills out to the west and north as far as the eye can see. When people think of me, surely this great structure assembles before their eyes. I would not be put off if my name called to mind phrases such as *triangular pediment*, *columned portico*, and *Palladian window*. Then again, most people in these parts could hardly be expected to possess even passing knowledge of architectural vernacular. If the words *Colonial Revival* fell out of your mouth in their presence, they'd go looking for a big white tent under which they'd hope to find everlasting salvation, courtesy of fire and brimstone.

"Olva," I said, looking over at her. She had closed her eyes, as if trying to gain ground on a nap. "Olva," I said, louder this time. "Invitations to this house were hard to come by, weren't they? Back then, I mean."

Her eyes opened softly. "Yes," she said before closing them again.

Olva was right. Invitations were in limited supply. That is, unless you had some standing in town, or unless my father, Daddy Kratt, requested your presence. His requests, hard and brusque, arrived at the arches of people's ears like orders. Any invitation to our home was pretense for an interview, in which Daddy Kratt would appraise how much you might help him build his empire in Bound. Lurking outside the study, I sometimes eavesdropped on these interviews, feeling relief, a gentle uncoiling in my chest, that I was not on the receiving end of Daddy Kratt's abrupt questions. You never knew when he might choose to speak. Words dropped from his economical mouth with no warning, and if people made the mistake of attempting small talk, they were always taken aback by his reply, even if they anticipated it.

My father might have been frugal with his words, but he spared no expense for this grand house. Built from sand-yellow brick, it was like the sun itself, or so Daddy Kratt made it feel, with the whole of Bound orbiting around it. He modeled much of the house on the famous Biltmore mansion, right down to the copper showerhead in the upper bathroom. So you see, when I am long gone from this earth, I will not be dissatisfied if my name invokes little more than the plumbing. Yet I suspect I'll be remembered for more, starting with the other handsome items that populate the Kratt family home: the mahogany secretary in the hallway, the peach R. S. Prussia vase on the mantel, my grandmother's pie safe in the kitchen. I could go on and on.

The furniture was practically begging me to share my news.

"Olva," I said, and I didn't have to look over, because I knew she was listening. "I am planning to write an inventory of the items in this house."

I waited for Olva's reply, which didn't come. The silence held a faint whistling.

"Olva, I am planning to write an inventory of the items in this house."

"A fine idea."

How right she was! It makes good sense to put down a record of the things in this house, seeing as Olva and I are its last human fixtures. Such evaluations require a long perspective. Having been on this earth seventy-five years, I stand that test.

I turned to her. "I can anticipate the question in your head."

"Can you."

"You are wondering for whose eyes this inventory is intended. Seeing as I have no heirs. A reasonable question."

"I imagine so."

I sat up taller as I came around to my point. "By virtue of my inheritance, I am"—I searched for the word—"I am the *keeper.* Not just of the Kratt family's valuables but of its stories, too. I tell you, Olva, I woke up seized by the idea. Given its intensity, I was half-surprised not to find a hole burned through my pillow."

"May I ask what the urgency is?"

It was not a question I had anticipated. I thought about the piece of mail I had hidden from her earlier in the week.

"The timing is right. That is all."

As I set out to write this inventory, I am amused by the thoughts that take residence in my mind. The distant train, for instance, with its whale call, fills the house so resonantly in certain moments that it feels nearly like a thing, and I would not be surprised to glance up and discover the sound sitting in the corner, having materialized into a noble mahogany armoire.

Years ago, the train's arrival was the highlight of the day. When it signaled its approach, boys out hunting would hotfoot it back from the fields. Shops would shutter, and mothers could be seen ferrying picnic baskets to the depot with their young ones in tow. The turnout was a more accurate measure of our town's population than any census could pinpoint. Men, women, and children would gather to watch on the depot platform or the wide knoll facing it, and most likely, not one had any real reason to be there other than to marvel at how the train, one moment hammering toward town, could in the next be easing into the station, as if the weight of their scrutiny alone had subdued it.

The depot was one of the places where my brother, Quincy, collected his information. He didn't work for the train company or any of our local businesses, but I guess you could say he was a merchant in his own right, selling the secrets he learned about people. In return, he earned a little money and the racking dread of everyone around him. Never seemed enough, though. I suspect he would have traded it all for a single slap on the back from our father. The railroad inundated us with goods, but for Quincy, recognition was always in short supply. It was a shame. He never did have a head for letters or numbers, but he sure could get a read on people.

I have occasion to think of Quincy frequently these days, as many of the things in this house call out his name. And it is good to remember him, even if it causes discomfort, because don't memories have duties just like everything else in this world?

Here was another question for Olva.

I turned to her and asked, "Aren't memories a little like furniture of the mind?" We were still sitting in the sunroom, watching the late-day sun unburden its remaining light on us.

"Yes, Miss Judith," she replied and left it at that. She was tilting her head back and forth in the way she does, considering a procession of ants ticking along the footboard.

Olva and I share the belief that the world reveals itself to you if you take the time to sit and wait for it. Waiting, I've found, is not most people's area of expertise. Olva is a blessed aberration. Just this morning, she studied a praying mantis for upwards of an hour, admiring the feline strokes of its arms and that long body curved like an ancient sword. As I watched her, it dawned on me that the measured way she tilts her head, combined with the giant spectacles that burden the bridge of her nose, sometimes give her the appearance of a praying mantis. I told her as much, and she seemed to take it as a compliment.

"What I mean," I continued, "is that our memories orient us just like the furniture in this sunroom."

Olva seemed to think about this. "And the view sure is different depending on where you're sitting."

Now, that was not at all what I'd meant. She'd taken my comment a tad literally. A rare slip for Olva, who knows my mind better than anyone. We grew up together, after all. Then it occurred to me that we have never moved any of the furniture in this house. Each piece sits where it did when we were children. It suits me, I suppose, when everything is kept in its proper place.

While I grew attached to the furniture, my brother had his own special relationship with things. Quincy's commodities, you understand, weren't the kind you could touch or lift. They were vaporous, coming to him through hushed voices over fences or eavesdropped conversations, and although they might have remained as innocent as air if left undisturbed, he was a great conjuror, capable of transforming whispers into millstones. Because of this, people pussyfooted around him as if they might bring down the sun if they sneezed.

No one was immune to Quincy's snooping, not even our own mother. We were teenagers when he discovered Mama helping Olva and the other colored folk pick cotton. Quincy promptly alerted the field foreman, a hulking, glandular fellow whose skin, the color of ham, wept sweat even when he wasn't out in the sun.

"Olva," I said, glancing over at her. She had moved on from studying her ants and was sitting there with a gentle gaze. "What was that field foreman's name? The one Quincy sent to reprimand Mama."

Olva's body jerked as if the chair had abruptly withdrawn its comfort. "I can't say I recall," she said.

In fact, I knew his name (Amos something-or-other), but the piece of information was less important to me. I had gotten caught up in the memory. "Quincy was hoping Mama would be punished," I went on. "But when that foreman realized who Mama was and that Daddy Kratt might become embroiled in the conflict, he merely congratulated Mama on how clean her cotton was, which was a polite way of saying she hadn't picked very much for a full day's work. Poor Quincy. He was always trying to claim Daddy Kratt's attention."

I turned to Olva, in search of a shared laugh, but she was staring out the window.

"I'm planning on doing some spring cleaning," she said.

"It's springtime, so your timing is germane."

Her gaze floated back into the room. "Sometimes, all the

things must be taken from their boxes before they can be put back again."

"Don't you go moving around things so I can't locate them," I replied. "I've got my inventory to think of."

My eyes sifted through the contents of the sunroom—the silver-plated butler's tray, the Amsterdam School copper mantel clock, the Hamilton drafting table. My younger sister, Rosemarie, is still living, but no one should be fooled into thinking she might be another source of information about our family's heirlooms. She hasn't set foot in Bound for ages. A month ago, we received another blank postcard from her, postmarked from Huntsville, Alabama. Over the years, Rosemarie's blank postcards have turned up, all addressed to Olva and hailing from different cities along the East Coast: Lowell, Baltimore, Englewood, and more. "All mill towns," Olva once remarked. "Or once were." I asked Olva if she didn't think the one from Alabama was insultingly close, but she merely gave a half smile and resumed her dusting.

Leaving those postcards blank was a melodramatic gesture, but that is Rosemarie for you. One spring during our grammar school years, she adopted a family of slugs that had taken residence on the retaining wall of our front porch. I found her early on a Sunday morning lying belly down, her head telescoped out over the edge of the porch, watching the slugs squander their riches in long glistening trails. So lost was she in this diversion, it escaped her notice that her new companions had also feasted on Mama's petunias.

Rosemarie was wearing a white cotton frock, one of the pieces of Easter clothing that Aunt Dee had sewn for us. I had watched her cavort around in it with Easter service still a week away. The frock had already scaled the tallest water oak in our front yard and scuttled beneath the canopy of our crepe myrtle, flush with buds.

"You'll ruin your frock," I said, my arms folded, standing behind her outstretched body. I studied the hem of her dress, fringed with dirt.

"No," Rosemarie replied, watching her slugs. Her head lifted only once to follow a group of colored boys making their way along the road toward the fields. This was another indication it was Easter time, the beginning of cotton season.

"You'll ruin your frock," I repeated, louder this time, tightening my arms across my chest, as if making my body more compact would distill my message.

Her head swiveled toward me. As she propped herself on her forearm, I saw how the brick floor of the porch had pricked up the white material on her chest.

Her mouth snapped open. "I will not ruin my frock," she said. "This is your frock."

Then her face almost broke in two with that smile of hers. We dissolved into giggles right there on the spot, and I squatted down next to her, mussing my own gingham skirt in the process. I sometimes lost track of myself when spending time with Rosemarie.

But I always managed to find myself again.

The morning after Easter service, when our preacher had made note of my sullied dress, his lips puckered in disappointment, I took matters into my own hands. I salted her slugs and, for good measure, also daubed them with a slurry of molasses and arsenic, which we used on the boll weevils that sometimes plagued our cotton. A whole year slid by before Rosemarie forgave me. And how could I have known that her gray-marled cat, a grizzled thing and already far too old at the time, had a taste for molasses?

"Olva," I said, breaking from my contemplation. "I would enjoy some coffee at the moment."

"Would you like to give me a hand?"

I didn't answer quickly enough, because she lifted herself from the chair and disappeared into the kitchen.

I heard the honk of a drawer opening in the kitchen. I braced. Olva moved back through the doorway and stood in front of me, clutching a squall of junk mail—coupons and flyers and whatnot. A single postcard sat on top.

"Ah, Olva! I knew I'd put this week's mail someplace but couldn't recall where. I haven't sorted through it yet. Thank you for finding it."

Olva stepped forward and handed me the stack of mail.

I examined the postcard. Perhaps I thought slipping it in the drawer would forestall its news. Or prevent Olva from seeing the connection between it and my new need for an inventory. More than anyone, she should understand the necessity of chronicling our family's history. It is prudent, after all, to keep a record of how one sees things, especially when others perceive matters so differently. On the desk is a letter opener made of cut glass that we played with as children; we marveled at how, held to the window, it produced a different color for each of us. And isn't that how memory works, too?

I studied the postcard again. Addressed to me, it pictured a majestic building. The architecture looked Greek Revival. The caption across the top of the postcard read *Montgomery, Alabama* and across the bottom *The First Capital of the Confederate United States, 1861*. The whole bottom line had been crossed through with a red ballpoint, as though history could be changed with the stroke of a pen.

"Olva—"

But she was gone. I flipped over the postcard, which was unsigned. But I had known from the moment I saw it. It was unmistakably my sister's hand, a muddle of agitated letters. The message had been scrawled off, with the last word sitting a bit apart from the others, as if she had been in the process of getting up from her chair as she wrote it.

Sister, I am coming home.

I stood with the postcard held aloft in my hand, as if aiming it at something. Or someone. It is important to know that Rosemarie has never been bound by any sense of responsibility to our family. You see, Quincy gathered secrets, but Rosemarie's impulse was to scatter them to the wind. And my sister believes I killed Quincy.

Well now. It was time to get my inventory underway.

Windsor chair
Wooden spinning wheel
Mahogany secretary
R. S. Prussia vase
Pie safe—Grandmother DeLour's
Butler's tray (silver plated)
Amsterdam School copper
mantel clock
Hamilton drafting table
Letter opener (cut glass)

TWO

Our family's misfortune began on a day meant for celebration. The date was Saturday, June 1, 1929, and Bound was slated to receive an electric current, an achievement for which Daddy Kratt considered himself responsible. The gentlemen at the Southern Public Utilities Company tasked with handling his aggressive and persistent requests were no doubt relieved that their business dealings with him were coming to an end.

To herald the electric current, Daddy Kratt had arranged for an open house at our store, which was the grandest structure in Bound in those days—ever since then, too. My father had given Bound its first department store. The store's stature alone was impressive: twenty-six thousand square feet, four grand floors, built in 1913 from brick Daddy Kratt had commissioned at a cut rate from a local mason. There was Wanamaker's in Philadelphia, Jordan Marsh in Boston, and Macy's in New York. And alongside those, the Kratt Mercantile Company in Bound, South Carolina.

As luck would have it, selling unrelated goods under one roof was Daddy Kratt's particular talent, honed from his days dealing bric-a-brac when Bound was just a trading post. He could sell a man a shoehorn and a chicken as though they were a matching set. Running a department store also required an understanding of how to manage large numbers of people in one space. There again, Daddy Kratt's early experiences—this time with livestock—came in handy.

The Kratt Mercantile Company spanned two generations and was the lifeblood of Bound for nearly twenty years, selling provisions for families (furniture, groceries, clothing, and shoes) and local businesses (farm implements, cottonseed, buggies, mules, and cattle). At its height, our store housed the town's only bank, the Kratt Bramlett Bank of Bound, and its lone car dealership (Chevrolets at first, then Fords). Not to mention that my father's Cadillac had served as the local ambulance because it was the only car in town for many years.

The morning of the open house, I walked to the store, the day full of promise. The sky, honey-colored, was lifting the sun into view, and I paused to consider the light as it stretched in every direction, the red-breasted nuthatches dipping in and out of sight as they gleaned insects from the smooth bark of white pines. Despite a fine sun-soaked day, I would be obliged to remain inside the store. I didn't mind. It was the first time my father had allowed me to manage the store's inventory—I was just fifteen years old. That morning, I would check the new merchandise on the floor against our inventory ledger. Afterward, when customers arrived for the open house, I would take them on tours, every hour on the hour, which would culminate that evening in the first display of the electric current.

When I arrived at the store, Olva was helping our cook, Ima, set brass trays of strawberry shortcakes on an entrance table. Ima was in her forties, around Mama's age, although she looked a good deal older than my mother. Ima had four children, if I recalled correctly, or perhaps five, and they lived somewhere on the expansive acreage of our family's land that abutted our house. As Ima surveyed the shortcakes, her face shone with satisfaction, even a cautious kind of pride. She had been required to show up when darkness still hung over the store to bake over a hundred strawberry shortcakes in the workers' kitchen. I knew her shortcakes personally, each one a precise union of sweet berries and snowslides of whipped cream, all heaped on the bottom half of a buttermilk biscuit, the biscuit's lid a golden crown. We stood admiring Ima's creations.

But then the store's double doors flew open. It was Daddy Kratt. He stood backlit for a moment, as if his dark figure had burned a hole straight through the weak morning light, until the doors smacked shut behind him and he strode forward. Luckily, Ima had set down the final tray of shortcakes—there were ten in all—or surely she would have dropped it. My father said nothing as he advanced on us, although he paused for a beat, long enough for one of his horned eyebrows to twitch when he saw Olva.

He stopped in front of the shortcakes. They sat quietly in their rows. With a steady and quick hand, Daddy Kratt sent three trays, one by one, sailing down. The trays flipped as they landed, the metal clattering and the shortcakes detonating as they hit the floor. Ima let out a cry, and Daddy Kratt merely looked down at his work boots, which were covered in a massacre of berries. His face held no note of emotion as he walked on, flattening a shortcake under his boot as he passed.

It was like that with Daddy Kratt. Even when you got

everything right, you never knew which of his reactions might decide to open the door and greet you.

Ima's expression was assembling and disassembling itself, and before her face could settle on any one feeling, she dropped to her knees and began scooping the mess with her hands onto one of the trays. Olva reached down and touched Ima on the arm, but Ima jerked away. Olva retracted her hand and studied the wrecked shortcakes with a blank stare, as if her thoughts had dropped there, too. I knew what she was thinking. Ima's rejection of Olva was not surprising to either of us, but she seemed no less hurt by it. Ima—not only Ima, our maids, too—regarded Olva with some aloofness, I'm afraid. Olva once told me they kept their distance because of her closeness with our family. "Maybe they're envious," I had said, and Olva had responded with a tired smile.

I looked again at Ima kneeling, Olva standing next to her, and the shortcakes in ruins on the floor. With a sense of determination, I turned around and steered myself toward the middle of the store. Retrieving the daily ledger, I set to work on the store's inventory, knowing I was capable of completing my duties. I was still worried my father would show up and punish me for some small mistake—or some accomplishment—but I didn't see him all morning. Going about my tasks, I accounted for a shipment of finely made Junghans mantel clocks we had received last week. I moved from floor to floor, making notations in the ledger, and then I checked the numbers on the new high-arm Singer sewing machines. These were a sight to behold: each measuring 17 by 8 by 13 inches, made of black cast iron with swirls of gold and red on their bodies and large hand-crank wheels on the ends. With their needled noses pointing down, the machines resembled a row of people bending over, doing some kind of work. I thought of Ima hunched over, cleaning up the floor where I had left her and Olva. I considered whether I should have stayed to help.

But the noise of customers interrupted my thoughts. It was time for the tours. I smoothed my dress and moved toward the entrance. Seven trays of shortcakes sat on the table, the floor below them spotless, no evidence of the earlier scene. No evidence of Olva or Ima either.

All that morning, the tours ran easily. Daddy Kratt had insisted Quincy join me in leading the tours, but Rosemarie—who was thirteen years old, just a year younger than Quincy and not a child any longer—had been permitted to forgo the task altogether. Rosemarie had been let off the hook, as always, but perhaps it was for the best. Quincy and I were working well as a team, and customers seemed lighthearted and willing to listen to my details about the history of the store and its merchandise.

But then Byrd Parker showed up, and the atmosphere sobered.

Byrd Parker had the long face and hushed manner of a funeral home director, and he possessed such a profound capacity for stillness that I never once saw him draw or release a breath. Byrd was the owner of the only cotton gin in town our father had not managed to acquire, though he had tried several times. Looking back, Byrd was not responsible for our family's troubles, but we should have seen it coming when we saw what happened to him.

Dreadful circumstances had recently befallen Byrd, and wherever he went, a gloom followed. Three Sundays earlier,

Byrd's wife had left their church service, complaining of a headache. Rather than go home, she had crept out to the unnamed lake, into which she had swum two pew lengths and drowned herself. No one offered any reason for her suicide, and Byrd, already the melancholy sort, seemed to regard the tragedy as another in a long line of scourges that defined his life. In this way, Byrd was Daddy Kratt's most stubborn business rival; his despondency made him impervious to our father's threats. According to Byrd, something worse was always around the corner.

There he stood among the other customers, his face drained of expression and sorrow lifting off him like an odor, medicinal in quality, a bracing mixture of camphor and pickling lime. People edged away from him, as if the smell—and his suffering—might leach into their clothing. But Quincy leaned in. He leaned in with the look of someone who wanted to learn.

"Sir!" Quincy crossed over to where Byrd was standing. "Would you like to see something very special?"

Byrd's lips parted queasily. He glanced around at the rest of the tour group as if someone might answer for him.

I knew what special thing Quincy meant.

"Quincy, I hardly think—"

"Now, Sister, here's a man who deserves to see something special."

A few murmurs arose from the crowd—Quincy was bringing them around—but I knew that my brother's interest in Byrd was not rooted in sympathy.

"Let's take this man to see the Tiffany lamp!"

There was no stopping my brother. This, I knew. He

launched up the grand mahogany stairs, leading the group toward a roped-off section on the wide landing between the two main staircases of the store. I followed. I knew we weren't supposed to take people to the lamp yet, but all I could do was keep an eye out for Daddy Kratt.

Quincy had thrown his arm around Byrd. My brother wore a broad-shouldered dress suit, or rather it was wearing him, because he had bought a larger size than needed to mask his featherweight body. It was no use: the acute angles of his body jutted like icebergs through a sea of material when he moved. The fabric was the same tan color as the freckles crowding his nose, and he had custom-ordered the suit to match one of Daddy Kratt's. When our tailor, Mr. Redmond, had finished the suit, he was surprised to find he would be earning no money on it; my brother had laughed when he told me how he had paid Mr. Redmond with a promise. The promise was that Quincy would not divulge to Mrs. Redmond her husband's weakness for gambling.

Quincy had information like that tucked away about everyone in Bound. He knew, for instance, that Clay Babbitt juggled four mistresses and that Randall Clark, the car mechanic, took long walks to avoid his own home. He knew that Prudence Dean drank more corn liquor than all the men in Bound combined; that William Greeley, our butcher, had a taste for prurient literature; and that Priscilla Brown, age seventy-five, had poisoned her own dog, a terrier mix.

Quincy was not careless with these secrets, nor did they possess him in any lurid way. He was dispassionate, and apart from the rare times he used this backdoor information to his own advantage, he disclosed nothing unless Daddy Kratt made a request. But when this happened, Quincy acted swiftly and without mercy. No sooner had Priscilla Brown back-talked Daddy Kratt at a county council meeting than she found the ugly truth about her dog spread all over town. She lived by herself, and afterward, no one would visit her, not even her own grandchildren. She died quite alone. My brother said I had a sensible enough head than to go repeating the secrets he shared with me. I listened quietly and carefully to everything. He seemed to enjoy simply having someone to talk with.

Climbing the staircase with Byrd, my brother looked ridiculous to me, all dressed up in his suit as if conducting some crucial piece of business. But then again, Quincy was always in the thick of some kind of operation, making a dozen transactions a minute in his mind about how Daddy Kratt might ruin a person's life. The tours meant something different to me: they were meant to honor our family and all the things we had brought to this town. I had opted to wear a cotton dress in a subdued floral pattern so that I wouldn't detract from the merchandise in the store.

Quincy was awfully good at making people feel comfortable or at least distracted—a gift of manipulation rather than compassion—and he got Byrd talking. Heads tilted in confidence, the two became absorbed in conversation. No one seemed to notice except me, because in embracing Byrd, Quincy had put everyone else at ease, and their minds were free to wander away from his despair and back to their own. By the time we reached the landing, the group was fizzing with everyday complaints.

I was not surprised that my brother had transfixed Byrd. To Quincy, it came easily. When he studied a group of people, he saw a more complex design than the rest of us. If he looked long enough, gestures passed unobserved by the average person—the ghostly caress of a wrist, an imperceptible nod, or a breath held in a heartbeat longer than usual—drifted into his view and took on startling shapes, like clouds twisting and untwisting in the sky. Quincy was a reader of the air, a diviner of the ordinary.

Byrd was talking in Quincy's ear, but for a moment, my brother's attention fell away from their conversation. Dovey Aiken had joined our tour. Dovey was the daughter of our town's pharmacist, and she was beautiful in a classic, wholesome way, though her large eyes were set a little wider on her face than was perhaps necessary. It gave her a look of persistent wonderment. She was always fussing her hands with something—tugging at the hem of her sleeve or pressing her palm lightly against her hair. I am a person who can recognize beauty but is rarely sent into a swoon by it. Dovey, though, seemed a rare sort of loveliness, the kind unaffected by the power it might afford her, and that, I appreciated. When she looked at Quincy, it was with an open and earnest face. My brother, noticing Dovey's eyes were on him, went a degree paler, like a leaf flipped to its underside, and he appeared a bit confused or like a spell of indigestion had taken hold. I wondered if he had eaten too many of Ima's shortcakes. Or was it something about Mr. Aiken? Had he discovered some secret about Dovey's father? Yet Mr. Aiken was bland as they came.

By now, the entire group had made it to the landing. The Tiffany lamp claimed our attention, finally Quincy's, too, but he was still sneaking glances back at Dovey, as if she were a thing that could be misplaced. The lamp was a magnificent specimen. Nothing like it existed in Bound. A yellow-and-brown acorn motif adorned its shade (diameter 16 inches), and the base, in the shape of a Greek urn, had an exquisite moss-colored patina that managed to be both earthy and refined. It stood at 21¾ inches and was designed by Louis Comfort Tiffany, the son of Charles Lewis Tiffany. The lamp was not for sale—it was our personal property—but part of the thrill Daddy Kratt offered his customers was showing them things they couldn't possess. What's more, that evening, the lamp would take on even greater significance: the first electric current in Bound would spring forth from it.

I stood staring at the lamp. It had enthralled me all over again, and for a moment, I forgot how or why we had gotten there. Until Quincy lifted the rope so that Byrd could get a closer look.

"Quincy!" I cried, but he waved off my alarm. His spirits seemed high, as if Byrd had said something that pleased him.

"You see, sir"—he was instructing Byrd to peer underneath the shade—"there are three separate key switches for each of the lamp's three light bulbs. Now that's fine craftsmanship."

Before Byrd could respond, Quincy impulsively stuck his fingers underneath the shade and gave one of the switches a vicious crank. The light bulb didn't turn on, but the switch made the sound—unmistakably—of something breaking. A few feet away, Dovey's hands were fluttering at her neck, as if checking for a necklace that had vanished.

Quincy retracted his hand, his breath quickening. "It's fine. It's fine."

The tour disbanded on the spot. People hurried away from the mere thought of Daddy Kratt's wrath. Byrd just shook his head glumly, as if to say he could have expected it, how living skewed toward misery and how the occasional rattle of joy, when it did occur, was far-off and muted and happening to someone else.

After breaking the key switch on the Tiffany lamp, Quincy disappeared. As he left, his face was tense with worry. This frightened me, and I felt a surge of concern for my brother. I was left to execute the remainder of the tours with a knot in my stomach. On my way to the midday tour (I wolfed a piece of cornbread Ima had packed for me), I rounded one of the aisles and stifled a surprised cry. Daddy Kratt and Quincy stood with their heads drawn together in confidence. I retreated behind a display shelf, hoping to hear some of their conversation.

"Byrd Parker said what?" Daddy Kratt cried, a kind of frenzied pleasure in his voice. "Tell me more!" He eased in toward Quincy with a chumminess that irked me. My brother had obviously not told him about the broken switch. My concern for Quincy drained away; if my brother didn't admit to breaking the lamp, he would have to blame someone else. I leaned forward to listen.

Quincy's voice was faint. I heard it crack—his bravado could not stifle his fourteen-year-old hormones. I edged my head around the corner for a chance to read his lips.

"How about that!" Daddy Kratt boomed with such abruptness, I thought I'd been spotted. I hadn't. The two were carrying on like old pals.

As my brother continued to talk, in tones too low for me to

understand, my father's head nodded in affirmation. Quincy's eyes, for a split second, slid past Daddy Kratt's and locked onto mine. With a startled gasp, I recoiled, knocking back into the shelf and upsetting its contents (cans of motor oil, sent tottering, and odd-looking mechanical instruments, fussing and clacking into one another). I pressed my hands over my face.

Silence whirred in my ears, but after a few beats, their muffled conversation resumed. Quincy had not given me away, and Daddy Kratt, pleasantly distracted by whatever he had learned, did not inquire about the racket I had made. The two continued talking, but I heard none of it. Afterward, they parted ways, my father heading deeper into the store and Quincy the opposite direction. Quincy had told Daddy Kratt something about the tour with Byrd Parker, but I didn't know what.

I scrambled after my brother. "What did you tell Daddy Kratt?"

Quincy turned around. With a friendly shrug, he said, "Don't worry. I didn't give you up, Sister."

"Didn't give me up?" My throat was constricting. "I didn't do anything! *You are the one who broke the lamp.*" I could barely get the words out, my heart thudded so recklessly in my chest.

Quincy nodded his head in consideration, as if things that happened were always up for interpretation and another version of events, light and intangible, were as possible as the present moment.

"I wasn't talking to him about the lamp," he said. "Something much more important came up."

"Regarding Byrd?"

Quincy smiled. "Yes!" He drew his head close to mine. "I

knew there was more to the story than Byrd's wife cheating on him."

"Oh!" I said, startled. "Cheating? Who was the other man?"

Quincy's forehead widened. "A colored boy, that's who. At least his wife was dutiful enough to punish herself."

I stiffened at the word. *Punish*, as if she were a child.

"Where is he now?" I asked.

"Who?"

"That colored boy."

"I don't have a clue," he said. "But he ought to stay hidden, if he knows what's good for him." Quincy shrugged. "For our purposes, we don't need him. What we've got is enough."

"Enough for what?"

Quincy drew back a bit, studying me for a moment. "Enough to put the screws to Byrd, that's what."

I marveled at my brother. Quincy had used Byrd's own nature, his state of perpetual gloom, to draw the very information from Byrd that would be used against him. Byrd was always expecting the worst, which made him careless with disclosing his sorrows.

"There's more," Quincy said. "Byrd's wife was *pregnant*."

"With Byrd's child?" I whispered.

"Not Byrd's child," he sang, pleased by the scandal of it all. With a broad smile, Quincy took off through the store.

"Quincy!" I called after him. "Our next tour starts in a few moments!" But he had disappeared behind a rack of women's fancy drop-waist dresses, disturbing them as he slid out of sight, and they swooshed into one another in a slaphappy way, like boozy women at a party, giddy he had brushed up against them.

I thought about our unnamed lake, which sat to the north of town. I could not stave off an image of Byrd Parker's wife. There she was, belly thriving, standing barefoot, two feet at the edge of the lake like two smooth white stones ready to sink.

It would take me years to connect the events. To realize that Byrd's sudden change of heart—selling his cotton gin to Daddy Kratt a few weeks later, after years of refusal—was the outcome of our father blackmailing him. It was one thing for Daddy Kratt and Quincy to know about Byrd's wife and an entirely different thing for the rest of town to find out; Byrd might be loose-lipped about his troubles, but he was also no fool. Had I thought on it harder at the time, the blackmailing would have been plain. But the way luck always seemed weighted toward Daddy Kratt was a nonchalant truth, almost genealogical in its depth and sureness, like the way my eyetooth, its particular curve, had been shaped by generations before. I was untroubled by the way business transactions inevitably fell in his favor, and it never occurred to me to question it.

With Byrd's fall, Daddy Kratt's cotton fortune was solidified. He and his business partner, Shep Bramlett, now owned all three cotton gins in town. This was a huge step for Daddy Kratt. Byrd Parker came from plantation money in Charleston, but my father started with nothing. Bound was merely a crossroads junction when he showed up with his horse and wagon, establishing a trading post to buy and sell goods. He waited as a settlement lurched into existence, the crossroads junction graduating to a chartered town with the coming of the Charleston, Cincinnati & Chicago Railroad in the late 1880s. Just as the town was transforming itself, our father seized the chance to remake himself. He had no lineage to speak of and was nineteen years older than Mama, whose father was a lucrative cotton wholesaler, but Daddy Kratt was as persuasive as they came, and in the end, he got Mama plus her generous dowry. Daddy Kratt was living in high cotton, as the saying goes.

The final tour of the day was miserable for me. Quincy was nowhere to be found. I kept straining for a sight of him, a distraction that rendered me useless for answering questions. After forgetting some details about our supply of cottonseed, which I knew by heart, and flubbing an answer about our millinery shop, people in my group took to talking among themselves, and I lost authority, my voice flattened by the steady roar of their conversations. I was sinking into exhaustion, too, having been on my feet all day, but despite my ineptitude, more people joined the tour group. We were nearing the important moment.

Dusk was falling, and light dwindled in the store. People's voices, rowdy the moment before, collapsed into whispers. There was already a tingle of electricity in the air, a pulse of expectation and unease, as though the lights had fallen in a theater for a new and strange performance. Mothers huddled with their children. Men, on break from farming duties, shifted restlessly in their spots. I saw the five Sullivan girls holding hands in a neat row, tangled hair rising from their heads; they came from one of the poorest families in town, but my father possessed the charisma to draw together unlike elements. Daddy Kratt had shut off the store's Delco generator, which charged rows of battery jars so that he could conduct business after nightfall. As the store fell further into darkness, people's whispers dissipated, and a silence swept in that bristled with anxiety and left the hairs on my arms whiskered out.

Clop clop clop. The footfalls of some distant horse.

It took me a few moments to realize it was my father. He was, I could tell from the sound, wearing his church shoes, a detail that struck me as poignant, because he rarely wore his church shoes to church even. He came into view, rounding the corner and starting up the stairs. The shoes, buffed to a high gloss, seemed to extract the remaining light in the room, and they glinted and winked with each footstep.

"Folks, it's time!" he roared.

He strode to the lamp. Mama was already there. I could tell someone else had positioned her, her hands clasped and elbows bent in a staid and uncomfortable manner. Her body was present, but her gaze flickered like a candle. They were a comical pair. Next to Mama, who possessed a porcelain beauty, our father appeared especially coarse, as though he had been blasted from a quarry, clothes and all, and had simply dusted himself off and fixed his hat on his head before carrying on down the road.

As the twilight matured into deeper shades of blues and purples, I placed myself behind a farmer who had forgotten to remove his large straw hat. He smelled of sweat and stinkbugs, which lately had been swarming our juvenile cotton plants. I breathed through my mouth and sifted through faces in the crowd. I was looking for my brother.

Daddy Kratt stole my attention. He swept open his arms, and everyone hovered in stillness, as though he were a conductor on the verge of storming into his first movement. The gesture erased all my anxiety. Arms raised, my father had set the evening into motion, ordaining a sequence of events I was powerless to alter.

He didn't seem to notice Mama, stationed right next to him. His eyes flew in my direction. "Now, my eldest child is here. Come join me, Judith."

My lungs tightened. Light-headed, I emerged from behind the farmer, my body floating along, and as I stood on the other side of the lamp, the crowd acknowledged me with a patch of feeble applause. Daddy Kratt nodded gruffly at me and then reached underneath the shade.

Prepared for the worst, I stood, my breath trapped in my lungs, when, with a flick of my father's wrist, light cracked open from the first bulb. Radiant! The color of the first healing rays of dawn in my room each morning, lapping onto the pine planks, sparking the dust in the air. My father, crouching now, his face pressed into the light, refulgent in its glow, the tips of his beard sizzling in its brilliance. All at once, breath rushed out of my lungs. The crowd roared, and Daddy Kratt gave an impish little grin. He flipped the second key switch. Light again! I was flush with joy. I saw the faces of those around me, mirroring my wonder. My father was a hero.

Daddy Kratt clicked the third switch. The bulb sat dumbly. He tried it again, and again and again. Terror seized my throat, but Shep Bramlett's voice bellowed through the tense silence.

"Here! Here!" he cried. "Mr. Brayburn Kratt has brought electricity to Bound!" The audience erupted into anxious applause.

Mr. Bramlett strode a few feet forward to congratulate

my father with a slap to his back, pushing the failure of the third light bulb into the past. Until that moment, I had never had much use for Mr. Bramlett. He was a boorish man whose two-storied face had extra square footage on his forehead—square footage that, based on his ruthlessness in all business matters, he would probably be willing to sell off in hard times. Despite my distaste for him, he had turned a dire moment around, and for that, I was grateful.

The crowd disbanded, and Daddy Kratt motioned for Mama to leave. I watched her walk down the stairs and, without saying a word to anyone, glide through the crowd and approach the front door. When she got to the door, she didn't exit but rather melted off toward a set of side stairs that led straight to the fourth floor. On the fourth floor was the milliner's office, and above that, the store's attic, where Charlie Watson lived. Charlie was a Negro who worked as our mechanic. Daddy Kratt's eyes followed Mama. She climbed the stairs all the way to the fourth floor, where she slipped out of sight.

Mr. Bramlett, who was admiring the lamp, elbowed Daddy Kratt in the side. "Too bad you didn't have Rosemarie with you," Mr. Bramlett said. "She's a pearl to look at."

Daddy Kratt drew his eyes from the staircase and gestured toward me. "This one's got a sturdy mind. She's the smartest of the three."

Mr. Bramlett turned his giant face toward me and drew a look as if taking a pull on a cigar.

"Don't forget, Shep. She solved our boll weevil problem," my father said.

During the outbreak, I had been the one to suggest paying

workers a penny for each of those nasty critters, which were devastating our cotton crops, and my plan had helped Daddy Kratt and Mr. Bramlett salvage more product than their competitors. A bud of pride stirred in my chest.

The satisfaction was short-lived. My father was no longer looking at me. He was staring again in the direction Mama had gone. He said something I couldn't hear, and Mr. Bramlett motioned to Quincy, who had materialized from the crowd. My brother made his way over, and Daddy Kratt said something in his ear.

Quincy's face remained passive. Then I heard his question, clear as anything, as if he were holding it up under the light for illumination.

"You want me to spy on Mama?"

I couldn't believe what my brother had said. But Daddy Kratt nodded, confirming it. After a moment, my father glanced at the lamp with a scowl. The memory of the broken key switch had returned; it hadn't taken long. He turned to Quincy. "Was it Olva?" Daddy Kratt asked.

Quincy paused, studying our father. "No. It wasn't her."

"Mmm," Daddy Kratt grunted, as if he hadn't believed it would be Olva, but she was on his mind. I remembered how he had taken particular notice of her before he sent the shortcakes flying. It made me nervous. To be in our father's thoughts was to be a target of them.

"Who broke the goddamned lamp?" Daddy Kratt said.

My brother's eyes cut toward me. As he turned to our father, I knew what was coming. Before I ran, I saw Quincy's mouth form the word *Judith*. I dashed down the stairs, managing to escape the store. As I raced home, I saw Rosemarie up in a tree, one bare foot dangling. She watched me go. My sister had always lived a nymph's life, far from the concerns of the everyday world, climbing trees while the rest of us toiled on the ground.

Windsor chair
Wooden spinning wheel
Mahogany secretary
R. S. Prussia vase
Pie safe —Grandmother DeLour's
Butler's tray (silver plated)
Amsterdam School copper
mantel clock
Hamilton drafting table
Letter opener (cut glass)

Tiffany lamp (diameter 16";
21¾" height)—broken

THREE

The next morning, I found Olva in the kitchen, her back to me. On the counter, biscuits bloomed their aroma, broad and consoling, which put to mind the warm smell of the seaside. When I was a child, we vacationed on the Carolina coast only once, because Daddy Kratt thought we should, and despite our accommodations, the finest hotel cotton money could buy, my sister chose to sleep on the balcony every night. I shook my head to try to release the memory. My sister was always creeping into my mind without invitation, outstaying her visit like a guest with poor manners.

"Would you like to know my progress on the inventory?"

Olva upset the saucepan from which she poured our instant coffee. I hadn't meant to startle her. "Miss Judith, you need more sleep, I do believe," she said, mopping the spilled coffee with a rag.

It was true that I had worked into the late hours. As a result, I felt sluggish, and a pinprick of pain had lodged itself between my eyes.

"Would you like to know my progress on the inventory?"

Olva dropped a metal measuring cup, which sang a plaintive note as it hit the floor.

"Are you quite all right?" Then I realized what might be

bothering her. "Don't you worry about Rosemarie's postcard," I said. "She never was the type to make good on her word."

Olva bent down to retrieve the measuring cup. "Miss Judith, since spring's days are numbered, we should enjoy our breakfast on the front porch."

"I couldn't agree more." I saw that Olva was preoccupied with her duties. We could discuss the inventory later.

When Olva righted herself, she reached for the two coffee cups with their twin exhalations of steam. She set them on the old wooden tray and loaded the rest of the contents of our breakfast onto it. I studied the tray for a moment, dismissing it. The tray had been in our family for generations—I knew that—but nothing distinguished it. It was not valuable enough for the inventory.

As I headed toward the front porch, I marveled at my new lens. I cast my eyes about the room, and the objects there—Victorian chaise longue, octagonal Jacobean parlor table, and mahogany sewing cabinet—sat up on their haunches expectantly. With a mild nod or shake of my head, I told them their fates regarding whether they would be remembered in my inventory. What hopes they had!

I reached the front door and turned my head back. "Bring out the doilies," I said, but Olva was already moving through the door, doilies in hand. She set up our folding table, tucked a flowering branch of honeysuckle in a vase, and spooned little banks of orange marmalade alongside our biscuits. The doilies rose to the occasion, too, fulfilling their obligations by guiding our coffee cups back to their spots.

We sat drinking our coffee, and I shielded my eyes from

the sun. How bright the world was! Our street was as sleepy as usual, even though it was one of the main arteries through Bound. It was possible to sit on our porch and not lay your eyes on another house; a few were there, of course, about an acre away to the east and south, but hedges or rows of mature red cedars hid them. Our neighbors did not want to see us as much as we did not want to see them.

My gaze returned to what was in front of me. An earthworm, waterlogged from an early morning rain, lay marooned on the brick lip of the porch. Bird songs filled the air, and I considered how their calls would change as the day lengthened, how their light and constant morning chatter would cede to an afternoon of sporadic, urgent cries, and how at nightfall, their conversations would be drowned out by the shattering trills of crickets and frogs. When I looked down again, the earthworm was gone.

A burgundy Pontiac Grand Am crept into view on the street. It was Marcus, our paperboy. Paper*man*. Olva has reminded me of this distinction, even though from our vantage point, a man in his thirties counts as a boy. From the driver's side window, his thin black hand extended.

I turned to Olva. "I wonder how long he will retain *this* job."

Marcus could not seem to settle on any one way of earning a living. Olva didn't say anything, so I went on. "It's a shame he doesn't earn enough money fixing things." Despite his lack of ambition, Marcus possessed considerable skills as a repairman. He had once ably restored my Westclox alarm clock (Big Ben model), and I even talked him down to a lower price for his work.

"I'd say his difficulty keeping a job is not entirely his fault," Olva said, and her face went a little slack, the caramel skin around her eyes sagging, as if what I had said about Marcus had pushed her deep into thought.

"What do you mean by that?"

"Bound is not always the most welcoming place."

"Welcoming? Marcus's family has lived in and around Bound for generations. Everyone remembers that."

"A long memory is sometimes the problem," Olva responded.

"Good grief, Olva, all I'm saying is that Marcus's family has a history here."

She exhaled. "Memory and history are bound up with one another. Where does one end and the other begin?"

She didn't pause for an answer, because just like that, her expression snapped back to what was in front of her, and she called out "Marcus!" as she lifted herself from her chair. Before launching down the steps, she shifted her body back toward the table to grab one of the unopened jars of marmalade.

"Is that necessary?" I asked. "We already pay for the newspaper."

She dismissed me with a wave of her hand and made her way toward the car. Marcus met her halfway. The two smiled at one another, and Olva traded the jar of marmalade for the *York Herald*. She said something to him and leaned back to give him a view of the porch.

Because it was required, I offered a little wave. He squinted at me, not waving back, and the two kept talking.

As I watched them, my attention was stolen by a burst of finches from a nearby bush. One hopped on the porch, angling its thimble head at me. It was clear in that gesture, splendid in its precision, that he wanted some portion of my toast. I didn't give him any but marveled at our communication, at my ability to know his meaning without a word exchanged. How different it was with people, who always seemed to take offense, no matter how thorough my explanations.

Suddenly, the Pontiac's back door flew open. Marcus's six-year-old daughter jumped out, clutching the stuffed brown bunny I had never seen her without. A white blanket and several toys fell out of the car as well, and she hastily gathered the items up and stuffed them where she had been sitting.

"Good morning, Ms. Kratt," Marcus said as the three of them approached me.

"Hello, Marcus."

Marcus always struck me as taller up close than my usual view of him from the porch. He stretched so high, in fact, that his slender body assumed a slight sway, not unlike the fir trees out behind the henhouse that always seemed to be looking down on me as a child and judging my juvenile decisions. He would have benefitted from a sturdier build, for he appeared beset by a fatigue that whittled down his already gaunt frame. A boy wearing the exhaustion of old age.

I nodded at his daughter. "And hello to you, too, Amaryllis."

The child wore a thin yellow sundress but no shoes of any kind. Her poor bunny was naked, its fur frayed. I had known Amaryllis since she was a baby. Olva would bring her to the house when she was too young to accompany her father to whatever job he held at the moment, whether that was house painting or working as a dishwasher at the Bound Grill. The poor thing was motherless. A car accident as her mother returned home alone with bread and milk from the market. In what casual corners tragedy lurked! After the death, Olva told me Amaryllis would survive because Marcus had a maternal way about him. The next day, Olva asked me if I wouldn't mind not mentioning that to him. Marcus and Amaryllis were the only black folk Olva spent any time with. Olva once told me this was because she and Marcus were both outsiders in their own ways. At the time, I had thought I might respond, but not knowing which words were suitable, I settled on none.

The child's eyes met mine. "Why are your earlobes so big?"

"Now, Amaryllis," Marcus said. She ran around to cling to the backs of his legs.

Children can be cruel, and I don't know why that isn't a more frequent topic of conversation.

"Is your bunny named Peter Rabbit? Are you familiar with that book? It is a classic."

She shrugged and moved around to hang on her father's arm. The child was always draped on him in some fashion or another, but it didn't seem to bother him. In fact, he seemed to enjoy it, though it could not have been comfortable in the least.

"If your bunny is indeed Peter Rabbit," I said to Amaryllis, "then he should be wearing a smart blue jacket with brass buttons. Did you lose his clothes?"

"Now, Miss Judith," Olva said.

Marcus appeared to be studying me. I coughed. "I will get her the book," I said. "I seem to remember we have an old edition in the house somewhere."

Amaryllis swung the bunny in circles by one of its legs.

It was a wonder the thing had managed to retain its limbs. "He lost his jacket in the garden," she said. Then she stopped twirling the bunny and planted a look on me. "You are old like Mr. McGregor."

"I will take that as a compliment. It was Mr. McGregor's property, after all." Amaryllis dashed toward the side yard, but I called after her. "And Peter Rabbit was the trespasser! One can hardly impugn Mr. McGregor for his actions!"

I looked over at Olva and Marcus, who were both stifling smiles, which they thought they could put past me. I pressed my lips together to let them know they could not.

Olva had something else on her mind. "Did you hear about the car manufacturer?"

"I did, Olva. As I've always said, Bound will survive." A foreign car manufacturer had chosen Spartanburg, fifty miles to our west, for its North American headquarters. Its proximity would benefit Bound: our people could find work there, and if Spartanburg proved hospitable, other companies might follow. And then perhaps one of those companies would someday choose Bound.

Olva sniffed. I knew what she was going to say.

"Like a nickel in a fifty-gallon barrel," she said. "How will those jobs make up for so many textile factories closing in South Carolina?"

Bound was once a classic cotton gin town. Nowadays, people don't know what that means. Since the late nineteenth century, the Piedmont of South Carolina, where Bound is located, was a magnet for the textile business, partly because the fleet-footed rivers hugging our hilly terrain made for good waterpower but also in no small part because of the sure-mindedness of residents like my father. It was true that the cotton industry had been on the decline in our area since the 1960s. Lately, so much cloth was imported from the far reaches of the globe. But I, for one, had faith that we would pull through. Towns like Bound built the South, after all.

"Don't be so pessimistic," I told Olva. "You need to leave off watching the nightly news."

"I agree with you," Marcus said. "I'm always telling Olva to look forward rather than backward." With this last word, his hand cartwheeled to indicate our surroundings. I wasn't sure if his gesture meant the South, our town, or my house in particular.

I wasn't sure if Marcus had understood me completely. Of course Bound needed to look forward, but there was still value in looking back.

"You know, Marcus, you inherited your skills as a repairman from your great-grandfather Charlie. There was nothing he couldn't fix in our store."

Rather than let Marcus respond, Olva promptly gestured to something out in the yard, guiding him toward whatever it was, and they continued to talk with one another, their voices fading into the background. My eyelids settled over my eyes. Visitors were exhausting.

"Are you sleeping?"

"No, Amaryllis, I am not sleeping." I opened one eye, then the other. The child had crept beside me without a sound.

"Do you sleepwalk like Miss Olva?"

"Olva does not sleepwalk," I corrected.

The child shook her head doggedly. "She told Daddy she has been sleepwalking through life. She said that was about to change."

I opened my mouth to question Amaryllis, but a riot of birdcalls filled the air, luring her attention. She wheeled off toward one of the large oaks in the yard. As she did, a blue jay dropped fluidly from the same oak and made off with another earthworm. He bolted upward into the lean clouds before sinking back toward the roof of the house. Just when it seemed he might land there on the red clay tiles, he pitched right, heading south toward our town's main street. I saw him disappear down York Street.

I imagined that blue jay crossing the railroad tracks before he soared over the post office and the site of our old family store, which now sits abandoned. If he continued flying south, that jay would pass over the old Kratt residence, a squalid shotgun house that Daddy Kratt bought before he made his cotton fortune. He was sentimental about it, the first house he bought with his own money, where he went from being a nobody to a somebody. He built this impressive house, but I don't think he ever loved it as much as that first one. If Daddy Kratt were alive, I wondered, what would he think of my inventory? He was certainly not shy of price tags, but value ran deeper for him.

It was a curious trait of my father. For all his hardness, wistfulness could visibly transport him. (We grew skilled at using those moments to dash out of rooms, away from him.) It might be an old horseshoe from his favorite mare. Or just as likely a bird's nest saved from his childhood. I once did find a nest hidden away at the back of his cedar closet. It was perfectly thatched, which made me realize that every bird's nest I've ever found—tucked underneath eaves of roofs or abandoned in old oaks—was whole and complete. Never in my life have I come upon a partial or damaged nest. You have to admire a house built so doggedly by a creature whose prevailing instinct is to fly.

That blue jay. I imagined him swerving over the abandoned train depot, gliding further west above the site of the old schoolhouse on which nothing else was ever built, then shooting straight up to take an even wider view of Bound: fields clotted with kudzu, creeks inlaid with blinding mica, and our unnamed lake to the north, where Byrd Parker's wife drowned herself and her unborn child. The lake was now so overrun with bluegill that it had assumed a moldering, feculent smell. On the other end of town, along the southern boundary, that jay would spy a row of houses—shacks really—that were old sharecroppers' lodgings. The Bramlett sisters now owned them.

"Miss Judith," Olva was saying. "Marcus and Amaryllis are leaving."

They were already walking toward the car.

"Marcus," I called after him. "Do you still live in one of those rentals owned by the Bramlett sisters?"

He stopped in his tracks. There was a long band of silence.

"Do you still live there?"

Marcus moved his chin so that I saw his profile. "Yes, we do."

My mind drifted back to the blue jay. Up he flew, taking that towering view again, looking down on where Marcus and Amaryllis lived. The Bramlett sisters, Jolly and Vi, were the daughters of my father's most trusted business partner, Shep Bramlett.

"Have they come here? Looking for me?"

"What?" I said to Marcus. "No. Why would they?"

Silence settled between us again. I tried to think of something pleasant to say about Jolly and Vi, but a wind seemed to rattle around in my mind. I was therefore grateful when Marcus said he needed to get back to his route and gave Olva a polite salute before joining Amaryllis at the Pontiac. He hurried the child into the car.

As the Pontiac headed off, Olva returned to her seat beside me on the porch. We watched as earthworms continued to be picked off. I had never seen so many blue jays in our yard. Small blue bodies everywhere, as if the sky were relinquishing bits of itself.

"Life is bound by certain rules," I said to Olva, "and I guess we've got to play along." She didn't say anything, so I kept talking. "It puts your mind at ease when you think of things that way, wouldn't you say? Survival of the fittest, I suppose."

After a few moments, she spoke. "Just like old man Darwin taught."

She said it like she had seen him last Wednesday at the Piggly Wiggly. I do enjoy Olva's company. Her response sent us both into a little eddy of laughter, the gay sound rising into the morning air and carrying to the tops of the trees, where I wondered if the birds might be appreciating it in the same way we found enchantment in their songs. We sat in each other's company in silence, watching the birds and lizards and earthworms and butterflies and every other cog in this brilliant mechanism churn on and on.

After a while, Olva began to stir.

I was still thinking of Darwin. "At the end of *Origin of Species*," I mused, "Darwin talks about the *most exalted object*. Doesn't that remind you of my inventory?"

"Mmm," Olva said.

"What I mean—"

"I don't think he's talking about an actual object, Miss Judith."

"Of course not."

"If I remember correctly, that most exalted object is the evolution of a human being." Olva paused. "A person."

I sometimes forgot that growing up, Olva and I shared all the same books. And whenever tutors were thrust upon the three Kratt children, our Aunt Dee saw that Olva was there alongside us.

"Well, it's possible you are right, Olva. Details sometimes escape me. At any rate, the phrase is beautifully put. *Most exalted object*. Darwin was a scientist but a poet at heart. I've always appreciated how he had the courage to write the way he wanted."

Olva seemed to consider this. "It's a luxury to be able to write or speak in the way you want." She didn't appear to invite a response to this, and she began clearing the plates.

I didn't mind, because there was something else I wanted to know.

"Olva, I have a question for you. Amaryllis mentioned something about your sleepwalking."

Olva paused suddenly, a plate in each hand. Her face dialed

in on something out in the yard. When I followed her eyes, I heard her breath catch. She had keener eyesight than mine, for all I saw was a smudge of motion in the place she was looking. It resembled a gray blemish of grease, like the residue of a nose pressed to a window, which I wanted to clean off with the cuff of my blouse.

"Is that Miss Rosemarie?" Olva said. Her voice seemed to carry less surprise than elation.

I stood up, but an acute rush to my head forced me back into my chair.

Olva didn't notice. She squinted at the sidewalk, her face crimped in pleasure. "Oh, it is! Miss Rosemarie!" she cried.

Olva lifted her right hand and waved even though she still had hold of a plate. She snorted, put the plate down, then picked it up again. She was in such a state, I'm afraid she didn't quite know what she was doing.

Rosemarie waved hysterically, prompting Olva to run out to meet her. Reaching one another, they embraced for so long, I had to turn my head.

My blue jay, from his grand height, had not seen everything. Here was my sister, after sixty years.

Olva accompanied Rosemarie all the way back to the porch. When they managed to get there, Rosemarie hauled one muddy boot on the first step and exhaled as if she had walked clear from the edge of the world without stopping until that very moment. I saw she had no plans to remove those boots before entering my home.

"You'll have to do something about those boots." It was an inadequate thing to say, these first words uttered to my sister in more than half a century, but Rosemarie would have to earn my graciousness.

My sister bent down and unlaced her boots, leaning one arm at a time against Olva to remove them. When she lined them on a step, I noticed that her socks were even dirtier than the boots that had sheltered them. She leveled her chin and looked in my general direction.

"Sister."

The word came out like she had poured it into an empty container and it had not quite reached the mark.

I was not prepared for my sister to be an old woman, and—with a distressing jolt—I wondered if she was having the same thought about me. She had been the town beauty. Both golden-haired and golden-eyed, she had learned early on what extraordinary beauty reaped: people tended to indulge her every whim just to see her face dance with pleasure, but accompanying that privilege was the constant scrutiny of older men, especially Shep Bramlett, whose gaze dispersed strangely when he stared at her.

Her faced had thinned considerably. I could see the muscles working under her cheeks as if they had been removed and rethreaded closer to the surface. Down her back hung a tassel of thick silver hair, tied off in the middle with a length of butcher's string, and she wore a gray dress that held the sad promise of once being black.

"Do you have any other clothes in that bag?" I motioned at the small camel-colored duffel she had set down on the step. "You look like one of the Sullivan girls."

"I'll be staying here, Judith. In the house."

I coughed. It was ridiculous for her to think she could waltz back into our lives. I wasn't about to acknowledge the idea of her staying with us. Instead, I said, "Do you remember the Sullivans?"

My sister's gaze settled somewhere above my head.

"It's apparent you have forgotten a great deal, Rosemarie." To supplement her memory, I reminded her of the time I invited the Sullivan girls, all five of them, into our house.

The arrangement was that those girls would pay me two marbles each to wash off in our parents' shower. It was one of those summers when humidity curdled the air and dark clouds buzzed like hives over the hills. We had grown accustomed to ferocious afternoon storms, which churned up the Carolina clay and dressed in a punitive shade of terra-cotta those wilder children who could not be coaxed indoors. I considered it a civic duty to clean up those girls, whose house did not have running water. Once a week, they were permitted a hasty scrubbing in the aluminum washtub that sat in their backyard. The Sullivans agreed to my arrangement when they realized the experience would involve going *inside*, the whole concept of bathing indoors being new to them. It wasn't lost on me that it would be a real treat for them to step into our house, what with the reputation our family had for collecting fine things.

At that time, a walk-in shower was one of a kind. Ours was especially magnificent, with thin rectangular tiles stained a rich caramel and a rainfall showerhead made of pure copper that dangled from the ceiling like the face of a giant sunflower. Those five Sullivan girls stripped down to their undergarments and ushered themselves into the shower. Too petrified to move or make eye contact with one another, ever so faintly turtling their heads into their shoulders, they seemed relieved when nothing more than water rained down on them.

Once clean, their gratitude was less forthcoming than I expected. In fact, the whole occasion was cast with a somberness that I couldn't quite seem to wash away, no matter how strenuous my reassurances. On their way out, the eldest sister, Lindy, paused to look at the wooden spinning wheel that towered in a grand and frightening way on the landing of our staircase. I told her it was not part of the tour, thank you kindly, and pried an extra marble from her clean little fist.

When I had concluded my story about the Sullivans, I folded my hands in my lap. But it was like my sister had not absorbed a word.

"I plan to stay here, Judith. In the house."

I looked to Olva, whose mouth was set in a way I understood to mean she was not going to object to Rosemarie's proposal.

"Stay?" I said to my sister. "Here?" In my voice rose an old fury newly minted. "And how long do you intend to visit?"

Olva tilted her head in the way she did when calculating sums or noticing a grasshopper's shed skin, the brittle rind of a prior life. "Technically, isn't this house half Rosemarie's?"

I was stunned into silence. "Olva, really," I finally said. I didn't want to call attention to her ignorance, but we all knew Rosemarie had relinquished her part of our family's estate when she ran off from Bound.

So it was a shock to me what came out of my sister's mouth.

"Yes, it is," she said, climbing the steps and striding toward the front door with renewed strength. In one swift, deliberate movement, she opened it. As she started across the threshold, she paused. Something new came into her face, and she leaned one arm against the doorjamb and plucked off her socks before continuing into the house.

Looking at that dirty little twist of socks in the doorway, I found myself wishing she had left them on.

Olva and I followed Rosemarie into the house as though she were giving us a tour and not the other way around. My sister never did understand how to make a proper arrival, in which she might bring a loaf of currant bread to show some courtesy to her hostess. When we were children, her version of a gift was an outstretched fist with a spring-loaded grasshopper hidden inside. It never ceased to astonish me that we Kratt children grew up in the same hot cocoon of childhood yet emerged as such singular organisms, barely even the same species.

Rosemarie swiveled her head around the living room, taking stock of its contents. "You haven't moved anything. All this clutter." She clucked—in judgment of my housekeeping!

I followed her eyes and studied the room myself. The large bookcase that stretched up the far wall was crowded messily with books, their covers in muted shades of brown and green. Books filled every vertical slot, and other books were stacked, balanced on lips of shelves, giving the bookcase the appearance of a majestic oak plagued with a bad case of bracket fungi. On the floor surrounding the bookcase sat more books, stacks upon stacks, as if waiting their turn for a proper spot. From the look of things—a frosting of dust on the shelves—their wait would be indefinite. How long had it been like this?

My eyes trailed across the rest of the room. An empty picture frame, all scroll and gilt, propped against the wall. A tangle of clothes—whose, I wasn't sure—on the sofa. Various drawers sat ajar (the Hepplewhite side table, the old watchmaker's workbench) as though someone hadn't bothered to push them back fully, and this gave the sense of the room having been tipped on its side and shaken by a curious child. I suddenly felt very warm. When I rubbed my hands together, they were covered in a film of moisture.

"Olva," I said sternly, but she was already trotting over to Rosemarie.

"Tell us everything!" Olva said, grabbing my sister's hand.

"Everything?" Rosemarie was enjoying the attention.

"Don't dare leave out a thing!"

"I hardly know where to begin," Rosemarie said and then fell silent, as if her experiences were threads too fine and numerous to catch hold of. An idea brought her around. "What is that dead traffic light in town?"

"Bound got its own traffic light!" Olva cried. "Can you believe that?"

Rosemarie laughed—uncharitably, I thought.

"It used to be a true traffic light," Olva went on, "and then a few years back, they replaced it with a single blinking yellow light. Then they turned off the blinking light. But they didn't even have the consideration to remove it."

"Is that right?" Rosemarie said, a perk in her voice. She no doubt found great satisfaction in the way Bound had gone down since she had left. I didn't think it was an exaggeration to say she probably saw her absence as contributing to its decline.

People can be wrongheaded in their assumptions about why somebody would stay in a small town. They imagine there must be a meekness in you for choosing to remain in a place where your possibilities are laid out in front of you so far in advance. I was not bothered, for instance, that my neighbor Ruth, who was a member of the Associate Reformed Presbyterian church, was buried in the same cream calico suit she was married in fifty years earlier.

I gave a little cough, but no one noticed. "Is anyone going to bring the breakfast plates in?"

Olva looked at me crossly, and neither one of them did anything, so I suppose I got my answer. I marched outside and cleared the table. When I returned inside and made a direct course for the kitchen, I heard Olva padding behind me.

"Go talk to your sister!" she said in a hard whisper. "You haven't seen her in half a lifetime."

I wheeled around. "Aren't you the least bit irritated she hasn't shown her face in sixty years?"

"Start small," she said gently. "Ask her about her trip home. How hard is that?"

I thought it over. "Not hard at all," I said, surprised by my answer. I was buzzing a little with the possibility as we made our way back to the living room.

When I saw Rosemarie, all possibility evaporated. I felt something hard crest inside me. She was tipping back and forth in the burgundy rocking chair, and I found merely the way she was sitting infuriating. She had an elbow planted in the upholstery, and her finger was pointing up at the floor lamp that flanked the chair. It looked as if she'd been waiting like that, frozen in that position, while we were in the kitchen. My sister always made the assumption that someone would arrive to take notice of her.

"We need a new light here," she said. Then looking around, she shook her head critically. "It's so dark in this house."

"Taking up your landlord duties so soon?"

For the first time, Rosemarie looked directly at me, squinting a little as if she would have to get used to the practice by degrees. "Is there a general store in town?" she asked, turning to Olva. "I can pick up some light bulbs."

What little knowledge my sister possessed! She would not even know where to go in Bound for light bulbs. Our family store was no longer an option. Shep Bramlett bought it from Daddy Kratt in 1930 but shut it down shortly afterward. Mr. Bramlett lacked the business acumen of my father, and it was alarming to see how quickly the store went downhill. While I didn't like to see it go, I felt its closing was a testament to Daddy Kratt's abilities.

Shep Bramlett's grandson now owns the only store in town—a scrawny convenience store—and his mother, Jolly, has shared with me, on too many occasions to count, how he can barely make a living selling those low-quality, disposable goods, which are delivered in filthy trucks that grind and belch down the road. Olva once witnessed a delivery in progress. It gave me great pause to hear how the cellophane-wrapped merchandise crashed to the ground, flung there without the least bit of consideration by a pimply-faced boy who hardly looked old enough to drive the delivery truck. When I was in charge of the inventory at our store, I held some reverence for my duties. Our customers often had very little, and the items we sold helped them live their lives the best they could.

My sister was still sitting there in the burgundy rocker, glaring at me. I was so perturbed by her company, I had to leave the room. Olva and I had a laugh about it later, my storming out of the room on account of light bulbs. It just goes to show that conversations with siblings cannot be separated from all the conversations that came before. That is just the way of it.

The day after her arrival, Rosemarie and I sat on the porch in silence. The cicadas let off their metallic drone as twilight approached. Earlier, Olva had said I was risking the mosquitoes by going outside, but I told her my old blood no longer interested them. She replied that my old blood was doing me just fine. I laughed and remarked that maybe it was the other way around: my blood had turned up its nose at those pests. Natural selection at work, I said to her.

For the past two days, Olva had been helping Rosemarie settle into the house, which generated more commotion than I judged necessary. I had heard Olva making a grand fuss over locating the linens for my sister, who could have found them herself within two minutes of searching. Rosemarie had taken it upon herself to move some items in the house—including a pair of Edwardian neoclassical brass candleholders (10 inches tall)—and while I moved them back promptly, I was immune to her provocations, because I had more important matters to attend to. I had shut myself in the study all day to work on my inventory.

As we sat on the porch, I turned to my sister, but her chin was locked forward. She seemed keen on not missing a moment of the fading light.

Into the driveway swooped a white Taurus sedan. Two figures emerged.

"Should you be driving at this hour?" I called out.

"Who is that?" Rosemarie asked.

"You don't recognize the Bramlett sisters? I sometimes forget how long you have been away."

Rosemarie escaped into the house.

Walking along the path toward me were Jolly and Vi Bramlett. I had known the Bramlett sisters my entire life. As children, we spent a good deal of time together, on account of our fathers' business partnership. Although that hadn't drawn us together, as it might have, we still shared the acrimony of being something like kin. From an early age, I had determined that Jolly was doomed to live up to the expectations of her unfortunate name. She had always been ebullient to a fault—a forced cheerfulness, the kind that blunts a terrible temper—and over the years, she had gained considerable weight, which had taken up residence exclusively in her cheeks and belly, making her appear, impossibly, even jollier.

Vi cut a different figure. She was alarmingly thin, and her mouth hung open. Her eyes had a soft, pleading quality, as if soliciting help for her mouth problem. Vi's name was not short for Violet or Viola, and early on in life, she seemed to accept this as a mandate that she was to occupy only about a third of the space of a regular person. Next to one another, Jolly and Vi paired like a set of souvenir salt and pepper shakers.

Well now, I wondered what they were thinking about me.

"We were coming back from checking in on our rental properties, and we saw you sitting on your porch," Jolly said.

"Do you always check on your properties so late?"

Jolly's mouth flattened. "Dealing with tenants is like having children all over again." Suddenly, her right hand reared up and smacked her arm. "Aren't you getting eaten up by mosquitoes?"

I supposed it was going to be a war of questions, and fatigued by the idea, I pretended not to hear her. Undeterred, Jolly helped herself to a chair on the porch beside me. Vi remained at the bottom of the steps, rocking on her feet to the rhythm of some sad song in her mind.

Jolly was incapable of a quiet moment, so she said, "Do you remember when we used to put straight pins on the railroad tracks, and the trains would fuse them into Xs?"

"We used to play on the crossties, too," I replied. "The ones stacked up next to the depot." Here we were, having some memories.

"There was that young black fellow who got caught stealing from the depot office," Vi said.

Jolly and I stared at her, and our shock at her unsolicited words momentarily dulled our reaction to what she was saying.

"What a sad thing," Vi finished, shaking her head.

Jolly snapped to her senses. She waved her hand. "Oh, it wasn't as sad as you remember, Vi. I think he just got in trouble because he was on the whites-only side of the platform."

"No," said Vi, and she was uncharacteristically firm. "He got caught stealing—it wasn't very much, a few dollars from the till—but some of the boys from our high school caught him and cut off the tip of one of his fingers. I think they used a cotton hoe. It was wrong of them."

"Good Lord, Vi," I said. "What in the world are you talking about?" Yet I remembered the boy, too, and what had happened to him.

Jolly set a stern look on her sister. But Vi had already retreated, settling into a doleful contemplation of the yard. "Saturdays were my favorite," Jolly said, pressing on as if Vi's comments had been an unpleasant detour. "The baseball games in the summer! And the laying-by time when all the cotton had been planted."

Jolly turned to me, as if it were my turn to supply a good memory. I did not recall going to any baseball games—I hadn't been invited to any—so I said, "Did you know that the site of the baseball field is of some historical interest?" Vi actually turned her head toward me, which for some reason gave my heart a jolt of stage fright. I coughed and went on. "It is my understanding that during the War of Independence, a patriot colonel and his troops made camp there after the battle at Kings Mountain. In his custody were several captured Tories, who were hanged and then buried at the site."

Jolly murmured, "Very interesting."

"Is it not funny," I continued, "that when kids play baseball there now, they are running over Tory graves?"

Vi's forehead wrinkled.

Jolly looked equally puzzled. "Kids do play there, Judith, but it's not a baseball field any longer," Jolly said. "It's a playground now."

"Of course it is," I said quickly.

Jolly threw her hands on her knees and said, "Let's go down to the playground right now." Her eyes widened. "Or the depot. Let's go down to the old depot!"

I shot out of my seat. "No!"

"Is everything all right?"

It was Olva, peeping her head out the front door. When she saw Jolly, her face tensed. I had returned to my seat, the sudden movement making me woozy.

"Everything is fine," I said. "Jolly and Vi were just paying a visit." I turned to Jolly. "Was there something you wanted?" I was tired of being hospitable. It was wearing me out.

Jolly pressed her lips together. "I suppose you've already received your newspaper?"

"Of course we have. What kind of question is that?" I said. "Do you want to borrow it?"

Vi shook her head gently, as if to dissuade her sister, but Jolly went on. "What time would you say that black boy delivers your paper every day?"

Not missing a beat, Olva said, "It changes every day."

Jolly tilted her head in disapproval that Olva had replied to a question directed at me.

Olva saw this but pressed on. "Today was midafternoon, but there is no set schedule." She turned to me. "Your bath water's getting cold, Miss Judith."

Jolly moved her eyes from Olva to me.

What Olva had said was not the truth, but I was ready for this conversation to be over. "Jolly, let's chat another time," I said. "My bedtime approaches."

Olva walked inside, and when I approached the door to

follow her, Jolly stepped in front of me. She placed her wide hand on my shoulder. I could feel the warmth of it through my blouse. Inside her mouth, a piece of white gum flipped from one side to the other.

"Call me the next time you see your paperboy."

"Good grief, Jolly, can you not find him yourself?" I moved out from under her hand. "Bound does not stretch very far in any one direction. He may be my paperboy, but he's your tenant."

"I'm shocked you would take a paper from him in the first place, Judith," Jolly snapped. "Seeing that he's related to that Negro who shot your brother."

"Jolly!" Vi cried.

"Charlie was his name, wasn't it?"

"Jolly!" Vi cried again. "Hush!"

To my surprise, Jolly closed her mouth.

I cleared my throat. "And how is your son, Jolly?" I struck off in a new direction, like swerving a car off the road, eager to find distance from her words.

Jolly's face drew together as she weighed whether my question was genuine. She could not help herself when the topic was her son, Rick. He was always in a sorry state, which was never his fault. Jolly's face released. "Oh, that poor thing!" she said, flapping her hands in the air. "He's just *awful* these days. But he's hardly to blame. He can't earn a living running that store of his, and he's a hardworking boy. It's always the hardworking ones who get punished, isn't it?" Jolly's voice was getting louder, and I was satisfied with my distraction. "And those welfare blacks don't lift a finger!"

"Ah!" I said. I had not distracted her but sharpened her purpose. "I have my bath running. You will have to excuse me, ladies."

"It was such a pleasure to see you, Judith," Jolly said, her voice high and tight. "I will be expecting a call from you." The two sisters returned to their car, and it sailed away, the darkening sky taking the car and the road with it.

When I stepped inside, my sister was standing at the window, peering around the curtains. Olva stood a few feet from the door.

"You'll run into Jolly at some point," I said to Rosemarie. "If you intend on staying in Bound for any length of time, that is. We all know that is not your habit."

Rosemarie turned to Olva. "What did Jolly want with Marcus?"

Olva looked at me. She hesitated. "He owes them money."

"What kind of money?" Rosemarie asked.

"Rent money."

"Then they are justified in looking for him," I said.

"I doubt that!" Rosemarie countered.

"Who are you to know anything about it?"

"I know that the Bramletts are callous," my sister told me. "*That* is what I know. And if Olva vouches for Marcus, then he is beyond reproach." She turned to Olva. "I want to help Marcus. We'll figure this out."

"Into old age, you have carried your penchant for melodrama, Rosemarie," I said. "What a heavy and florid load."

My sister could not help herself. She huffed out of the room, just like old times. My satisfaction at having successfully goaded her was cut short when I noticed Olva staring into the living room with a distracted look, as if tallying the chores she had to accomplish before bedtime. I did not envy her the task, the house being exceptionally large and freighted with so many objects.

Olva's eyes seemed to land on the rolltop desk. Perhaps she was thinking of my inventory, because I had opened the desk earlier to work on it.

"Did you know, Olva, that this rolltop desk is an Abner Cutler original?" She didn't respond, so I said, "Do you think it would remember Mama?"

Olva paused, letting out a deep, slow breath. I could tell I had hooked her, because she replied, with true pleasure, "Desks *can* have memories, can't they?" As if I had gotten to the real point, the one that confirmed the strange wonders threaded through everyday life. "Of course the desk remembers her. She was a sweet old thing."

"Old thing?" I said.

A laugh galloped out of Olva. It was a familiar joke of ours, the one in which Olva forgets she is the old thing now. I am fond of reminding her that she is a year older than I am. She calls it being chronologically gifted.

"She was a gentle soul," Olva said.

"That's what I'm getting at. You remember how we used to say that when Mama sat on the sofa cushions, she left no indentation, no impression at all that she had been sitting there?"

Olva chuckled, and a silence settled on us, the kind in which the conversation keeps going. Then she crossed to the window, and I felt a sudden heaviness in the room, like a new piece of furniture pushed between us, blocking my way to her.

"I hope Jolly doesn't get her son involved," Olva said, the dark window framing her. "A nasty fellow, that one."

I stood behind her. Night had fallen, and the cold trill of a cricket rose from some unknown place in the house. "I'm sure Marcus will sort it out on his own," I said. "Is it really any of our business?"

Olva reared around. "*It certainly is.*" Her voice flared at the tips.

She walked past me and through the living room, and I watched her climb the stairs a little more quickly than usual. When I turned back to the window, its wide, dark eye was staring at me, and I stepped forward to draw the curtains. But closing them seemed to drive the darkness to the next window, like a creature skittering from one opening to another, angling to see me, its breath hot against the glass. I hurried to sweep the curtains closed on that window, but as I did, the darkness ran to the next window, and when I secured those curtains, it sprang to the next, always a step ahead of me. The cricket cried sharply at my foot. When I snatched the final drapes closed, I had to lower myself into the Windsor chair to rest.

Sitting there, I thought of Jolly's son. I hoped he would stay far away from us, too.

Windsor chair
Wooden spinning wheel
Mahogany secretary
R. S. Prussia vase
Pie safe—Grandmother DeLour's
Butler's tray (silver plated)
Amsterdam School copper
mantel clock
Hamilton drafting table
Letter opener (cut glass)

Tiffany lamp (diameter 16";
21¾" height)—broken

Victorian chaise longue
Octagonal Jacobean parlor table
Mahogany sewing cabinet
Westclox alarm clock
(Big Ben model)
Hepplewhite side table
Watchmaker's workbench
Edwardian neoclassical brass
column candleholders (10" tall)
Abner Cutler rolltop desk

FOUR

It had been a week since the inauguration of the electric current in Bound. Most homes had not, like ours, been wired for electricity, so while life probably went on about the same for the greater part of Bound, we Kratts felt on top of the world. During the day, our yellow house was the sun, and now, at night, it glowed from the inside like the moon. We could be everything to this town. Yet I wondered about my place in it all. The subject of the Tiffany lamp—its damage—had not been revisited, and I prayed every evening I would escape punishment from Daddy Kratt.

"Go get your brother and sister," Daddy Kratt said, not turning around.

He was doing some ledger work at the rolltop desk in the living room. I had wandered into the room, not aware of his presence. I stood, stunned, and when I didn't move, he cocked his head as if detecting a faint noise, the filament of some conversation in another room. I heard only cold silence between us, and then I realized he was waiting on me. I ran toward the door. I knew better than to make him speak again.

I went to find Quincy first. Wherever he was, I knew he would be there alone.

At the end of our driveway, I took a right, heading south

toward town. On my way to find my brother, I passed the milliner, Mr. Burns, whose office occupied the fourth floor of our family's store. He was walking—and this was curious—with Mrs. Greeley, the wife of our butcher, and when he saw me, his face expanded in alarm before it shrunk to a tight smile. I crossed from the street to the sidewalk, and there I saw Mr. Clark, the car mechanic, walking in the opposite direction. He sped up when he noticed me and tucked his head, creating an egg of flesh between his chin and neck. Moments like these were not uncommon, and they gave me no offense. I knew I carried with me a reminder of Daddy Kratt. It was like living in a town full of siblings, each with his own anguished tale connected to our father.

After Mr. Clark, I passed Dovey Aiken, who was walking from the direction of our filling station. Unlike the others, she stopped in her tracks.

"Judith!"

She was wearing a cornflower-blue dress, which matched her eyes perfectly, and her blond hair hung in one long plait against her right collarbone. A blue ribbon had been woven into the braid, and while I thought she was too old for adornments like that, she had said my name with such warmth, it was hard for me to fault her.

"Dovey."

I didn't quite know what to say next.

Her large eyes blinked. Maybe she didn't know what to say next either. She then touched the fabric of my dress and said softly, "How lovely."

My gaze followed her hand to my simple cotton dress with

gray flowers so tiny, they were almost illegible. I squinted at the design, trying to find loveliness in it.

"Well, you have a nice day, Judith," Dovey said with a gentle smile, and she continued down the street.

I turned to watch her leave, and I couldn't even bring myself to criticize the way she was walking, which was rather like a half skip, a bit childish, but there was something appealing about it all the same.

After my encounter with Dovey, I found Quincy at the filling station, which Daddy Kratt owned and ran. He was throwing rocks at a line of tin cans while listening to the drunken boys playing poker inside.

They worked for our father, these boys, a grim coterie of unwashed and mannerless fellows from the poorest families in town. They were intensely loyal to him. I suspected they reminded Daddy Kratt of himself at that age. I remembered one night being torn from my sleep by loud raps on a lower window of our house. When we had opened our bedroom windows to peer down, one of those boys had hollered up at us.

"Mr. Kratt!" he had bellowed. "Mr. Kratt, I come to tell you I got home all right!" He had then stumbled a few feet before collapsing to the ground. The next morning, we had found out that after a particularly wild night of drinking at the station, Daddy Kratt had arranged for someone to escort that boy home, and the poor thing was a tad premature in his gratitude, having gotten all the way home only to turn around and walk back to our house to offer his thanks. Daddy Kratt had driven him back home. That the boy had passed out was a shame, because not many people got to ride in our father's Cadillac.

Quincy angled his head toward the open window of the filling station. One of the boys had said something, told some joke perhaps, because riotous laughter tumbled through the window. Quincy laughed, too, and then he said a few words I didn't hear, some response that they couldn't hear either. They were too drunk to know Quincy was spying on them, keeping tabs as he did on everyone. Quincy mumbled a few more words, shaking his head in amusement, and it occurred to me that my brother had no friends of his own.

I thought he didn't know I was standing there, watching his pretend banter with those boys. But then he said "Daddy Kratt wants me, I take it?" as he nipped a can with a rock.

"No," I said, startled. "He wants all of us. Up at the house."

Quincy's hand, which had been lifted midair to sling another rock, fell slowly. I was pleased to deflate him a little. With his town secrets, Quincy had become indispensable to Daddy Kratt. It must have come as a surprise to my brother that the talents he already possessed would be the very ones to make his father proud. Quincy's curiosity, left unchecked, could fray into recklessness, but now, he had been given focus. The whole town feared Quincy, but respect from Daddy Kratt was new to my brother, and he took to it as if he'd been breathing the wrong kind of air up until that point.

"He wants all of us up at the house," I repeated. "Don't you dawdle." Before turning to leave, I said offhandedly, "I passed Dovey on my way here."

Quincy reared around, and I flinched, because the rock he had lifted to fling at another can was now aimed at me. "What's it to you?" he snapped.

All at once, I knew there was something between them. "Nothing!" I replied. "Put your arm down!" I remembered how he had looked at her during the tour a week earlier. "It's merely that I like her," I continued, trying to calm him. "She doesn't bother me in the least." I laughed a little. "And most people bother me."

Quincy chuckled. "She's innocent, isn't she?" He smiled, a little bashfully, and I marveled at that.

"Yes, she is. It's nice."

We stood there together, smiling. I could tell his head was still full of Dovey when he turned to throw his rock at the final can. It missed by a wide margin, and he stood there with his arms hanging by his sides as I hurried away.

It didn't surprise me that it took the longest to locate my sister, that distractible child, who would follow a butterfly on its jagged flight clear to the next town if you didn't keep an eye on her. She had climbed up the water oak in our front yard and *fallen asleep*. How she managed such things, I would never know.

When we arrived home, Daddy Kratt lined up the three of us in front of the staircase. His eyes were the color of brass. He pulled at his beard, a grizzled thicket that extended well below his chin. For a few moments, we watched him prepare to speak, which was a chilling demonstration, because he was a man of few words, making potent the ones that did manage to escape his mouth. Breaths labored, he stood there coercing an utterance from deep inside as if trying to wrest a boot from the mud. Without warning, a ragged and bottomless "Whooo?" released with such force as to knock him slightly off balance.

He knew who had damaged the Tiffany lamp. Or he thought he did. The way he kept peering over at the front door gave me the sense we were lined up for something other than an ordinary punishment, but I didn't know what. No one spoke. This piqued his anger. He walked slowly down the line, pausing in front of each of us. After examining Quincy, he took a step that placed him squarely in front of me. The moments clicked by. It was the longest my father had ever looked at me.

Suddenly, he squeezed one eye shut, as though examining me through a jeweler's loupe.

"Joo-dith," he taunted.

I felt guilty even though I had no reason. There, in front of Daddy Kratt, I stood like some wretched, shamefaced thing, and out of nervousness or stupidity, I don't know which, I zeroed in on Daddy Kratt's one open eye. I could not stop looking at it. It was transfixing, and it seemed to hold me aloft there in front of it. I was nearly to tears and ready to confess to spoiling the Tiffany lamp, the combination of fear, apprehension, and pleasure proving too much for me to master, when I saw a flash of light through the window.

Daddy Kratt saw it, too. He seemed to be expecting it. Someone was on the porch.

He strode over and swung the door open with such force that the doorknob punched the wall behind it. Little wonder people never visited on their own terms. Our terror was blunted momentarily by our confusion. In crept Olva, who looked on the verge of passing out. In her hand was our father's old riding whip, which he always kept in the passenger seat of his Cadillac.

"Ah, there it is."

Olva passed the whip to Daddy Kratt, and her whole body seemed to lighten for releasing it. Her feet shifted weight, toward the porch.

"Stay," Daddy Kratt said.

Olva sank into herself, but she complied. When she stepped across the threshold of the door, our father motioned for her to join us in the line.

Daddy Kratt looked at his riding whip with almost loving consideration. I was fairly certain he had never looked at any of us that way. We were familiar with the whip, and it gave us some puzzlement, because we associated it with the unkempt boys he employed, the ones Quincy had been spying on. Daddy Kratt would take his riding whip, a relic from his horse and buggy days, and pretend to giddyap his Cadillac, his arm loping up and down against the black wheel well. Those boys would fold down on themselves in laughter. It was the happiest I ever saw my father, clowning around with them.

It wasn't as if I couldn't anticipate what a fearsome tool for punishment the whip might be. But it didn't stop me from feeling betrayed by the thing, perhaps even more so than by Daddy Kratt, because it was the whip, not my father, that was acting so unlike itself.

I looked at Quincy and Rosemarie. Their eyes were trained

on the whip. Possibilities filled our heads, each one more horrifying than the last. Our imaginations were another form of violence, which we were willing to inflict on ourselves, with unblinking devotion. I never considered us particularly obedient children, but we were loyal to our father's vision of the world.

Daddy Kratt approached us again, but this time, he stopped in front of Olva.

"Do you know why you're here?"

She stared at him.

He leaned in toward her. Their faces almost touched. "The answer to that question—the answer to *every* question—is *yessir.*"

"Yessir," she whispered.

He backed up. "How did you come to us, Olva?"

She could barely breathe, it seemed to me, let alone answer another question. When our father opened his mouth again, she said quickly, "By way of Tucker's farm." She caught herself. "Yessir. Tucker's farm."

I knew exactly which route she meant, up the east side of the farm and along the dried-up creek.

Daddy Kratt laughed. "That's not what I meant, is it? Not how you got to us today. How you got to us in the beginning. But you were just a baby then."

It was true. Olva was abandoned on our Aunt Dee's doorstep in a breadbasket lined with a canary-yellow tea towel in 1913. I hadn't made my earthly arrival yet, but Aunt Dee could be forthcoming when she wanted, and I had cobbled together the information over the years. Dee always did things differently. She had caused quite a stir by giving Olva the DeLour name, which Mama had given up to become a Kratt. And by her own choice, Dee remained unmarried. "I never found reason to take a husband," she had once told me, as if a husband were something to take or leave, and preferably leave.

Daddy Kratt changed tack with Olva. "What's Dee been busying herself with lately?" He paused. "And my wife?" When Mama wasn't in her room, where she mostly stared out the window, she was at Aunt Dee's.

My father was waiting for Olva to answer him. "I don't know, sir," she managed to say.

Daddy Kratt considered this, and the conclusion to his thoughts was not in Olva's favor. Looking at her, he jabbed the riding whip toward the fireplace and cleared a bit of phlegm from his throat. Olva obeyed, and before she reached the fireplace, Daddy Kratt began striding at her.

"Stop!" Quincy cried.

I had never been more surprised in my life. Here Quincy was, showing some mercy. More surprising was that our father did as he was told. He stopped and turned to hear what my brother had to say.

"I said she didn't break the Tiffany lamp. I already told you who did."

Daddy Kratt looked at me with the steadiness of someone who pours liquid metal into a mold.

My heart sank. I returned his gaze and swallowed hard.

"I did it," I said.

I could tell by a change in the air beside me—it lightened a molecule or two—that Quincy was impressed by my boldness.

If I could have blamed him, I would have, but his word was too strong with Daddy Kratt, and there was no sense getting Olva involved in our family affairs.

Daddy Kratt stood still for a heartbeat. Then he walked toward Olva. With one strong lash, he thrust the whip down against the back of her right knee. Her body buckled to the ground, but she made no sound.

Beside me, Quincy took a discreet step in front of Rosemarie, a movement of protection, so that his body stood between her and Daddy Kratt. Slipping one hand behind his back, Quincy motioned to her, and when Rosemarie saw this signal, she emitted a thin whimper and took off up the stairs. This was an angle familiar to me, the back of my sister's head, her ivory hair fluttering as she ran away from whatever the rest of us were forced to endure.

Daddy Kratt twisted his head and watched Rosemarie flee. He paused, considering things, and then gave Quincy and me a *stay put* look before returning to his business. It was the first time I realized—it came as a single, serrated thought—that my sister would one day leave Bound.

Daddy Kratt turned at Olva again, and we cringed. But he merely asked a question.

"Has my wife been spending time with anyone in particular lately?"

Daddy Kratt seemed more agitated than usual. I didn't know if it was the stress of taking on Byrd Parker's cotton gin. Or maybe it was the transgression of Byrd's wife—Daddy Kratt had said it was a stain on our town, even though he had benefited from it. Something was amiss in my father's world, even though he now laid claim to more wealth than ever before. He did not usually suffer from lack of answers.

Olva remained silent. This, I realized, took a staggering amount of resolve.

Something new came into Daddy Kratt's face. He lifted the whip and thrust it against the back of Olva's other knee. Then he began hitting her torso. She curled into a ball on the floor, absorbing the blows. She began to cry, a low moan that did not keep rhythm with the pace of my father's arm.

I squeezed my eyes shut as the beating continued. Olva was sixteen, too old to be disciplined in this way, but what did Daddy Kratt care about the etiquette of punishment? We felt powerless to stop it. The whip whistling through the air had unpinned every thought in my mind. Eyes closed, the sound of the whip magnified, and I imagined it was coming down on me, too. The whip had transformed itself yet again, from something solid to a liquid sensation, hot and terrible, clinging to me like boiling sugar syrup as it lashed the back of my bare thigh.

The next thing I heard was a slam. I opened my eyes to find Daddy Kratt standing, whip in hand, staring out the window. Olva had made her escape through the kitchen and out the back door. What I had heard was the screen door beating itself against the frame as she fled.

Quincy and I backed out of the room wordlessly. Afterward, we stood on the rear porch steps.

Questions collided in my mind. I turned to my brother. "Why did you blame me?"

He shrugged. "I knew you could handle it."

Anger and pride rose within me in equal measure. It was a heady mixture, but I steadied my thinking. I had another question for him.

"Why did you try to protect Olva?"

"I thought I would spare her." He had that distant look in his eyes, the one that kept him from holding allegiance to any one outcome. He was squarely on his own side, which left him to pick up and put down people's causes at will, based on whatever whim guided him that day. If I were Olva, I wouldn't hold out for Quincy's continued loyalty.

I didn't like my brother's changeability. It left me wondering who I was, what exactly I was working against. This was the way of siblings, how my existence, my very selfhood, grew partly from what Quincy was not. And from what Rosemarie was not. It was like that for them, too. It seemed as close to natural law as anything else, but Quincy was flouting it, as he did whatever laws didn't suit him.

As I thought this, my eyes landed on the expanse of grass between the porch and the woods, where the shadow of a bird of prey looped in a wide circle, its dark wingspan impressive, its body inscrutable. A chipmunk darted away. When I looked back at my brother, he was studying me. I wanted to push his eyes away, get his lens off me.

"I can tell you one thing, Sister," he said, done for the moment with his scrutiny. "Olva's problems are only going to get worse."

"What are you talking about?" I was still stung he would spare Olva but not me. "Why did Daddy Kratt beat her? Why was he asking after Mama?"

Quincy sighed, bored by my ignorance. "He has some suspicions about Mama. And about Olva."

"And who gave him those suspicions?"

He snorted. "If they're true, the messenger doesn't matter."

"Are they true?"

Quincy looked up at the sky, as if the truth might drop from there.

"Yes."

After Daddy Kratt whipped Olva, autumn arrived. The angle of light in the sky shallowed, and the sugar maple outside my bedroom window turned vermillion. There had been another turn in the air. When I admitted to breaking the Tiffany lamp, I had earned Daddy Kratt's approval. To my delight, he seemed to admire the bravery of my confession. Not only had he allowed me to continue managing merchandise at the store, but he had also entrusted me with seeking out the necessary repairs for the lamp.

"See Charlie about the repairs," Daddy Kratt said after summoning me to his office on the first floor.

I stood close to the door, my hands laced behind my back. My father's beard rustled under his chin.

"Yessir."

To find Charlie, I set out from Daddy Kratt's office toward the attic, the lamp my companion. The venture required weaving through the milliner's office on the fourth floor—chock full of mannequins, but absent that day of Wade Burns, the milliner—and up a wrought iron ladder. I set the Tiffany lamp at the foot of the ladder. Placing my shoe on the first rung, my mind landed on Mama and how she had slipped up toward the fourth floor on the day of the electric current.

"Charlie," I called out as I began climbing, "can you invent no better access to your shop? You are the mechanic, after all."

Along with fixing broken merchandise, Charlie ran and repaired the store's freight elevator. It was currently in disrepair, and earlier in the week, I had witnessed how Charlie had spent an entire day examining every nut and bolt of the thing before putting it back together again. He was waiting for a part, no bigger than a bottle cap, which would arrive by mail. Only the department stores in the big cities had similar elevators. Charlie had explained to me that ours was the traction variety, with wire cables and a pulley system, all of which was not unlike the traction of a train's wheels on the tracks. When you thought about it, we had a train shooting vertically through the heart of our store every day. And like the train, it brought us things. What marvels Daddy Kratt supplied!

I called Charlie's name again, but he wasn't listening. The whir of an electric tool played in the air. Goggles covered his eyes, and cotton stuffed his ears. He seemed to be about Mama's age, and his hair, black with traces of gray, stood off from his head.

"Charlie!"

His head popped up—he was grinding down a fragment of metal with a motorized gadget—and I laughed, because he looked like an adventurer-scientist working on a time machine, surrounded by the indecipherable tools of his trade. Equipment concealed the floor around his workstation, and everything was steeped in oil, even the air that met my nostrils.

Charlie put down his equipment and replaced his goggles with tiny round spectacles. He was a lithe and easygoing fellow, well-liked by everyone at the store, and the other Negroes who did manual labor, unloading boxes or hauling equipment, appeared to consult him for advice.

Charlie was the one person I had met in my life, other than Olva, with whom my tongue did not continually trip on itself. I usually ran into him on the first floor while he did his regular maintenance work on the elevator, and sometimes, I would sit with him for a long spell, watching him tinker with the cables, after I had completed my own inventory duties. Sitting with him was almost like being alone, as though he weren't there at all, so complete was my comfort in his presence. When he did speak, which was rarely, he seemed incapable of small talk and got to the heart of things immediately, sharing parts of his past that were sometimes startling to me. I already knew, for instance, that he had been married once and that his wife was no longer alive, but one day, he let slip that she had died in childbirth. "Charlie! You have a child?" I had cried. He had nodded calmly. "A son. Lives over in Tirzah. I don't see him much. He's a grown man now, isn't he?" And he had resumed his work without another word.

My attention returned to the space of the attic. I looked at Charlie in front of me, and a thought cut across my mind: What else didn't I know about him?

"What can I do for you, Miss Judith?"

His voice broke the spell of my contemplation. I remembered

Daddy Kratt had entrusted me with a task. "Charlie, I have a job for you."

He stood up, and I cringed when his head nearly hit one of the attic beams. I motioned for him to look through the ladder opening. He walked over to assess what I had brought him, the corners of his eyes lifting with curiosity.

"Ah! The lamp," he said. "I can fix it."

"Would you like to know which part is broken?"

He looked at me in a gentle way.

"I suppose everyone knows," I said.

"Not to worry. I will bring it up now," he said. As he climbed down the ladder, he called, "Company!"

He returned, carrying the lamp. His height made it possible for him to climb only a few rungs before depositing the lamp on the attic floor. Following him through the opening were Mama and Olva. They both looked surprised to see me, but neither commented other than to offer a quick hello. Surrounded by the three of them, I felt out of place, an intruder.

"We bring news," Olva said, brandishing the *New York Times*. I wondered if she had nipped it from Daddy Kratt's desk. He was a small-town man who read big-city newspapers. If Olva had taken it from him—and he was the only person in town I knew who subscribed to that newspaper—it was both a gutsy and foolish move.

"You sound serious," Charlie said. He gestured for them to find a seat, immediately falling into contemplation about where that might be among the mechanical detritus around his desk.

Olva didn't wait for Charlie. She cleared a spot on the floor and found Mama a low stool by first removing from it a hand-crank adding machine that was missing several keys. When Olva sat cross-legged, her pleated wool skirt lifted to reveal the skin between her skirt and one of her knee-high socks. Across the buttery brown of her knee was a raised scar, a souvenir of Daddy Kratt's beating. We all saw it. Charlie took a step toward Olva, his face grave, and Mama pressed her lips together and turned away.

Noticing our attention, Olva stood up immediately and walked toward me, shaking the newspaper at eye level.

"Did you read the papers this morning, Judith?" She gave the main headline a hard tap with her forefinger. STOCKS COLLAPSE IN 16,410,030 SHARE DAY. It was Wednesday, October 30, 1929.

"No, I did not. I was too busy with the store's inventory." That morning, I had been in awe of our stock of shoes, worth well over eleven thousand dollars. Then I had put in a purchase order for car tires and cash registers. I had concluded, with satisfaction, that if our store didn't sell it, the people of Bound didn't need it.

I surveyed the rest of the newspaper's headline. "It says the bankers are still optimistic," I offered.

"The stock market has *collapsed*," she said.

"Really, Olva," I said. "You make it sound as if it's a body taken ill." I considered the matter for a moment. "Now that I think on it, I suppose we do talk about our nation as if it's a body. *Head* of government. The *long arm* of the law." It was not the cleverest thing I had ever said, but it would do.

"If the nation is a body," Olva replied sharply, "whose body is it?"

Well, there was no arguing with her. Olva had a keener interest in world politics, so I waved her off. The store's inventory, my local share of history, was what mattered to me.

"Now, girls," Mama said, a beat too late. We all looked at her, because she rarely intervened. She didn't finish her thought, retreating at the sudden attention, but it seemed to pain her whenever Olva and I argued.

"I wonder how it will affect the trains," Olva considered. "If the trains don't run, there's no shipping the cotton, is there? We've got no convenient river transport."

Olva had a point. A worry about Daddy Kratt crawled into my head. He had been ginning cotton at an increased pace lately, so confident was he about its demand. He was always chasing his personal best, when he had ginned over a thousand bales of cotton in 1919, selling it at over thirty-five cents per pound. On that return, Daddy Kratt built his fortune.

"I'm sure everything will be fine," I said, pushing away my concern. "We've always survived, haven't we?"

"On my way here, I overheard Mr. Clark saying his brother in Charlotte already had financial struggles with his farm," Olva said. "What will this do to him?" She shook her head. "People will lose their farms. Their businesses."

"Nonsense, Olva. Anyway, he could always train-hop." I was trying to lighten the mood, but my comment was met with silence. I pressed on. "If he did, what a twist that would be. One member of the Clark family escaping while the other won't leave her house."

Olva gave me an admonishing look. I couldn't help bringing up Mrs. Clark, the wife of our car mechanic. She fascinated me.

Don't all small towns have their curious cases? Some years ago, she had stopped leaving her house, for what reasons we could only speculate. The Clarks had no children, and for a spell, Mrs. Clark had worked as a hairdresser's assistant, tasked only with sweeping up the orphaned hair, but she abandoned that job as quickly as she had taken it. The Clarks were not poor, and Mr. Clark was a kind enough man. When we were younger, we would ring her doorbell and run away. Once, Quincy dared me to peek into the east-facing window, its curtains hanging open in a desperate sort of way, as if the house itself had flung them open. What I saw both awed and frightened me. The furniture was pressed together in an odd sort of way, as if huddling for warmth, and knickknacks occupied every surface, mostly figurines of a gnomish sort, grimacing at the papers that littered the floor. When I dashed back to Quincy and Rosemarie, I did not tell them what I had seen. Perhaps Mrs. Clark never left her house simply because she could not navigate through all the things in between her and the front door.

Olva had taken her newspaper to the far corner of the attic. It was possible, due to the attic's expanse, that she could claim something like solitude to read. Charlie had deposited the Tiffany lamp on his main workstation and was already absorbed in the task of repairing it. As he removed the lampshade gingerly, he glanced up for a few moments to gaze at Olva in the corner, a look of concern on his face. Then he returned to his work. This left me with Mama.

"Do you see Charlie often?" I asked her, breaking the silence between us.

She laughed—nervously, I thought, but it was hard to

attribute emotions to Mama, because sensations seemed to pass through her like mist.

As she was searching her mind, I had the sense of something happening below us. There was no noise to alert me, just a feeling of space taken up in a way it hadn't been the moment before. Leaving Mama to her thoughts, I stepped toward the opening to the millinery shop and looked down.

The constellation of hats I saw below was impressive. Every shape and size of hat imaginable was represented. Hats molded snugly to mannequin heads, and others perched lightly as if anticipating the cranial sensitivities of their future owners. Hats the color of soot and others canary yellow. Hats that expressed themselves horizontally and equally as many that sprouted vertically. The milliner, Mr. Burns, was a precise man, and he lent that precision to his hats. Times were hard, apparently, but the hats argued otherwise.

I squatted to see more of the shop, and along with mannequin heads, their bodies cut off below their shoulders, Mr. Burns had a row of life-size mannequins because he liked to coordinate his hats with items of clothing for sale in the store. He had received permission from Daddy Kratt to buy these full-size mannequins, and while Mr. Burns boasted that they came from Siegel & Stockman in Paris, I knew they had not, my inventory duties making me privy to the expenditures of the store. Regardless, the new mannequins were impressive. Made from papier-mâché instead of wax, they were sleeker and more sophisticated than their Victorian predecessors. Mr. Burns dressed them with care and upbraided anyone who dared touch them. I once heard him tell Mrs. Greeley, the butcher's wife, that she was as lovely as a mannequin. I hoped she knew that was high praise.

Nothing appeared out of the ordinary in Mr. Burns's shop. Suddenly, I noticed—with no small amount of shock—that one of the full-length mannequins against the wall wasn't a mannequin at all.

There Quincy stood, smiling at me.

I stood upright and walloped my head against a low attic beam. The others rushed to me, and I cradled my head while peering back into the shop below. I scanned the mannequins and landed on the space, empty now, where my brother had been.

The next week, I was on my way again to Charlie's attic. A sharp November wind was whipping around the store's brick exterior, and I heard a branch lashing against a far window. Grateful to be inside, I rounded the corner to pass through Mr. Burns's office, and I found Jolly Bramlett there with him. He was leaning over her head.

"Oh, pardon me!" I said, and Jolly let out a little yelp.

Mr. Burns rotated his face toward me, his expression serene. "No need to apologize, Miss Kratt," he said. "I am merely measuring Miss Bramlett's head for a hat." Mr. Burns was a boyish man, his chest slender and the voice that rose from it tidy and colorless. He spoke as impeccably as he dressed, and his unwavering air suggested that no stitch out of place would be tolerated, not in his work and certainly not in life.

Jolly's surprise fell into a smile. She seemed to measure my envy with that smile, which burned brighter as she watched me considering the news that she would have a new hat. Mr. Burns went about his business with the tape measure, and Jolly sat properly, her hands clutched in her lap. What an extraordinary moment for her. Not many fathers would commission a hat for their daughters. I thought about the expense, too. Olva's voice echoed in my mind. Two mornings ago, she had said that President Hoover lacked clear-sightedness. I doubted it was appropriate to criticize the president, but she was adamant that his optimism about the recent economic troubles was dangerously misplaced. I wondered if there might be a time when a fancy hat would be considered absurd in its indulgence. For some, it already was. A laborer in one of our cotton gins would sacrifice an entire day's income to buy his wife a hat.

Mr. Burns was now taking notations on Jolly's hat. A week ago, I had found him alone in the study of our house. Daddy Kratt sent people to the study when he wanted to question them about some matter or another. Judging from the grave faces of visitors who emerged from the closed doors, I gathered the topics were sensitive ones.

The day I had found Mr. Burns there, the double doors to the study had been ajar, and Daddy Kratt had not yet arrived. Mr. Burns was waiting in the window nook, reading an edition of John Henry Newman's prose, and he was seated in such a way, his back pressed against the glass, so that when he glanced up from the pages, he looked into the room rather than outside. He was missing a fine view. Of the lily pond, laden with curds of algae, and of the clovered field that broadened away from the house before erupting into a belt of woodland. I had been in those woods many times with Rosemarie. They were full of mystery, dark and moss-slicked and gauzy with gnats. But Mr. Burns seemed content with his perspective, the giant chandelier that commanded the ceiling and the globe on the desk that no one ever turned. He waited with his lips pressed into a tight smile, an indication of his self-possession even while he waited for my father's appearance.

When I heard my father arriving, I ducked into the hallway. Entering the study, he left one of the double doors cracked. I sidled up and listened, finding that Charlie was the subject of Daddy Kratt's questions. He wanted to know if Charlie had frequent visitors to the attic. My ears strained, but I couldn't hear Mr. Burns's response. I leaned in closer and closer, and suddenly, the door at my nose flew open, Mr. Burns stepping out in front of me. He regarded me with no change in his expression, that same composed smile hovering on his face. Mr. Burns had fared better than most visitors to the study. The only time I had seen any change in Mr. Burns's composure was some months back, when I had found him in the post office with Mrs. Greeley, the wife of our butcher. As he stood cozily next to her, I had glimpsed a look of unguarded joy on his face before he noticed me and swiftly parted ways with her.

I continued to watch Mr. Burns as he deliberated over Jolly's hat. As if reading my thoughts, he looked at me with a strict gaze.

"What kind of hat will it be?" I asked.

"Peacock," Jolly announced proudly, and Mr. Burns nodded in accord.

"My sister loves peacocks," I replied carelessly. "They are as absurdly beautiful as she is."

"I'm done with the measurements, Miss Bramlett," Mr. Burns said in a clipped way.

Jolly thanked him and offered me a smug look before she walked out the door.

Later, I would wonder at what moment Jolly had figured out the hat was for my sister and not her.

Two weeks after I had watched Mr. Burns measure Jolly's head, I was standing on the front porch of our house, my sister and Mr. Bramlett on the lawn below. It was early, and he had come to retrieve my father for that day's work, and he clutched a Kratt Mercantile Company shopping bag in one of his hands, his fingers short and blunt and squared off at the ends. The way he was looking at my sister made me think he had come looking for her, too.

Rosemarie, thirteen years old at the time, obeyed no circadian standards, so she was waltzing around as if it were midday. I had lifted my pointer finger, about to chastise her for wearing a sleeveless dress on a winter morning, but before I had the chance, Mr. Bramlett was approaching her.

"It's cold, little bird," he said, taking her hands. He placed them in a prayer position and pressed his two palms around them. Then he bent over and blew into them, his lips grazing her fingers. "We'll warm you right up."

In front of Mr. Bramlett, Rosemarie stood immobile, although her eyes curled up ever so slightly toward a dawn that had not quite prevailed over the darkness. She seemed to have fallen into a slumber of compliance, so stationary was she, but Mr. Bramlett happened to loosen the pressure on her hands momentarily, and she dashed away with unexpected speed, her hair flapping behind her. Running away was always Rosemarie's first reaction to difficult matters. In that moment, I could begin to understand why.

Shep Bramlett's face—that giant, two-storied countenance—set itself toward the direction Rosemarie had flown. He spat hard on the ground and whipped his eyes at me. Jabbing his hand into the shopping bag, he pulled out a hatbox. Letting the bag fall to the ground, he rifled through the box and lifted the hat for me to view. The hat, made of peacock feathers, was stunning. Purple and blue, its iridescent plumes shimmered skyward. Despite Mr. Bramlett's vulgarity, he had chosen well for Rosemarie.

Mr. Bramlett strode toward me, and as I backed away, he thrust the hat into my hands. "You can give this to your goddamned sister." His roughness could not mask his embarrassment.

After watching him storm off, I lifted the empty bag off the cold ground, returned the hat to its box, and buried it among the random effects in our cellar.

When my mind returned to the present moment in the millinery office, I found Mr. Burns staring at me.

"Oh, I really must be getting up to Charlie in the attic," I said, gesturing toward the far end of the room at the ladder. "I have some business to attend to with him."

Hearing Charlie's name, Mr. Burns's unflappable face twitched momentarily, and he looked at me with a kind of gaudy interest. His expression quickly resumed its usual restraint. I hurried toward the ladder and through the opening into the attic. There was Charlie. He stood triumphantly next to the restored Tiffany lamp, his elation erasing Mr. Burns's odd behavior below.

"Charlie!" I cried. "Well done! How did you get the parts so quickly?"

"Improvisation," he said, winking.

"You are quite marvelous."

He busied himself with a soft towel, wiping the base of the lamp. I had embarrassed him with my praise. He moved on to cleaning the light switches, his fingers easing across their contours.

"You find it beautiful, don't you, Charlie?"

"I do, Miss Kratt."

"Why don't you keep it a bit longer? No one expected you to fix it in a flash."

As Charlie smiled at me, Olva's head popped through the opening in the floor, and she crawled into the attic, followed by Mama. They regarded me pleasantly enough, perhaps with a measure of surprise to see me there again. How often had they excluded me from these secret meetings? The scent of rose water flooded the room. Mama had taught me how to make the perfume, heady yet delicate, same as she wore, but I had given mine to Olva after one of my schoolmates suggested that a sweet fragrance on me was as good as wasted. Now, Mama and Olva smelled the same.

"Was Mr. Burns still there?" I asked, pointing below us. Because the entrance to the attic could only be accessed through Mr. Burns's millinery shop, he would be privy to anyone's comings and goings from the attic. I remembered the strange weight of Mr. Burns's gaze when he saw I was paying Charlie a visit.

Mama and Olva exchanged a look. No, Mr. Burns was not there any longer. I wondered if they always chose moments when he stepped out of his shop to sneak into the attic.

"The lamp!" Olva cried.

Charlie's smile brightened. He patted Olva on the arm, a soft and familiar gesture, and he bowed his head slightly at my mother. "Rosemarie, a pleasure to see you, as always."

I thought it was very familiar of Charlie to use my mother's first name. It made me think of my sister, who was named after Mama. Shep Bramlett was fond of saying that the name was fitting for my sister because it took two women's names put together to convey the scale of her beauty.

Charlie set the lamp on one of his worktables and plugged it in.

"Drum roll!" Olva announced before fulfilling the request herself.

Charlie turned the first key switch, and the fanfare from Olva was so boisterous that out of bashfulness, he quickly turned the other two switches. The lamp illuminated was no less resplendent in the humble setting of the attic. The gadgets and tools strewn across the floor caught the light at various angles and seemed to crackle to life.

Light brought new clarity to the setting. "I had no idea you three gathered regularly here," I said. "Have my invitations been misplaced?"

Olva managed a small laugh, but Mama appeared more alarmed than anything. Charlie switched off the lamp.

"At least Olva knows I'm joking," I said. We stood in the awkward silence I hadn't intended to bring on. Rather than make my exit, I remained. My curiosity outweighed my chagrin. I wanted to see what they did here in the attic.

It turned out they talked and laughed. When they grew

comfortable with my presence, I was surprised to hear how many names of people in Bound came up and how freely they spoke of them. I heard Mama's voice more than I had in the past five years. Maybe in my whole life. Olva made some comment about Mr. Burns, and everyone laughed, me included, even though I hadn't heard what was said. Then Charlie jabbed his index finger toward Mr. Burns's shop below, and we all fell silent before Olva erupted into laughter again, unable to bridle her mischievous joy.

"Mr. Burns and his mannequins," Olva tittered. "If one of them came to life, he'd leave town with it."

"Who's to say Mr. Burns is not himself a mannequin come to life?" I said, getting in on the joke. "He wears his head on his shoulders as stiffly as if he remembers a time when he wasn't real."

Laughter rose from the group once again, and their shining eyes, the merriment there, grew partly from their surprise at my naughtiness. My face warmed, and the attic, despite its expansiveness, felt cozy, and I was suddenly as fond of it as I had been of any place in my life.

Mama and Olva began trading jewelry back and forth, as if Mama were a teenager. Then Mama reached around Olva's neck and said, "Now try this one."

I knew it was her cameo. It had been my grandmother's, a rare double-sided Edwardian coral cameo (1½ by 1 inches) set in gold. One side displayed the face of the goddess Athena and the other the god Ares. I had never before seen it depart my mother's neckline. I felt tightness in my throat as Mama placed the cameo around Olva's neck. It was not that I objected to

Mama letting Olva wear the necklace, but it was more that they had not thought to include me in this ritual.

For distraction, I turned my attention to Charlie's shop. Some objects were from the store—a cash register sat mutely on the floor in disrepair—but other items I recognized from some of the affluent families in town. In one corner towered a grandfather clock I had seen in Shep Bramlett's house, a Samuel Thompson from the early 1800s, which stretched its head through the rafters with the imperturbable air of a monarch.

"Charlie," I said, "you are surrounded by things that would ordinarily be unknown to a man like you."

The silence was leaden. Mama and Olva turned their faces toward me. I opened my mouth to try to cover up my old words with new words, but Charlie spoke before I could make my shabby attempt.

"You are right about one thing, Miss Judith." This drew a raised eyebrow from Olva. "I do come to know the things as I work with them. And they, in a way, come to know me, as the oils of my fingers remain on them." Charlie's voice was smooth and worn. "It has always seemed to me that the more we touch something, the more we draw it up into ourselves, so that when that thing goes away, it is still within reach, its traces lingering on our fingertips." He then looked at Mama, whose eyes darted downward.

"Beautifully put, Charlie," Olva said with a touch of uncertainty, as if she wasn't entirely sure what he had meant.

I decided to leave. I said my goodbyes, not swiftly enough, because Charlie insisted on walking me out through the milliner's shop. He checked first to see that Mr. Burns was still away, which he was. Mama and Olva came, too—it seemed the three of them could not be separated—and as Mama made her way down the ladder, Charlie approached to help. That was when I saw it. Charlie's and Mama's hands met on one of the ladder rungs, and as her hand slid into his, he squeezed it.

I turned on my heels to exit the milliner's shop. Head throbbing, I began my unsteady descent to the third floor. What I saw below made me take in a sharp whit of air. Farther down on the same staircase ran Quincy. I watched as he scrambled hastily, leaping onto the landing of the stairs and taking a route through a back door that led down to Daddy Kratt's office.

Before ducking out of sight, my brother paused to look back. Catching my eyes, he flashed me a dark wheel of a smile.

Windsor chair
Wooden spinning wheel
Mahogany secretary
R. S. Prussia vase
Pie safe—Grandmother DeLour's
Butler's tray (silver plated)
Amsterdam School copper mantel clock
Hamilton drafting table
Letter opener (cut glass)

Tiffany lamp (diameter 16″; 21¾″ height)—~~broken~~ fixed

Victorian chaise longue
Octagonal Jacobean parlor table
Mahogany sewing cabinet
Westclox alarm clock (Big Ben model)
Hepplewhite side table
Watchmaker's workbench
Edwardian neoclassical brass column candleholders (10″ tall)
Abner Cutler rolltop desk

Riding whip—Daddy Kratt's
New York Times (Wednesday, October 30, 1929)
Peacock hat
Edwardian coral cameo (1½″ × 1″)

FIVE

It was early in the morning, and the summer sun had already begun its staring contest with my eastern-facing house. I sat behind the slim shadow of one of the porch columns, and I peered around it to see an old Ford truck, rust eating at its edges, parked but running its engine at the edge of my lawn.

I had seen the truck before. Two men were sitting in the cabin, but my eyes couldn't discern exactly who they were. Cigarette smoke rolled in waves from the open windows. What nasty habits people indulged. I didn't like them sitting out in front of my house like that. Just as my mind was sifting through where I had seen the truck before, the stink of gasoline and cigarettes met my nose, and a pulse of fury flew through me. I was not about to have my home invaded like that! I stood from my seat, but the truck gunned its engine and shot down the road.

I lowered back into my seat, temples throbbing, but the sudden movement had knocked a memory loose in my mind. I had seen Jolly drive that truck on occasion. One of the men in that truck was her son.

Suddenly, Marcus's Pontiac pulled up and parked in the same spot the truck had occupied moments before. Marcus had arrived from the opposite direction, not crossing paths with the truck as it sped away. Amaryllis burst from the Pontiac's back seat with our *York Herald* in one hand and Peter Rabbit in the other. As Marcus sometimes did, he was going to let the child bring us our paper.

Amaryllis struggled to shut the back door of the Pontiac as several of her blankets and stuffed animals tumbled out. A pillow had dropped out, too. She gathered the things in her already-full arms and pressed her small body against the load. Marcus had to get out of the driver's seat to assist her. He was back in front of the steering wheel before I could acknowledge him.

"You certainly have a lot of things in your car," I called out to Amaryllis.

I wondered if Marcus had the Bramlett sisters on his mind. I certainly had them on mine. Amaryllis skittered up the porch stairs, depositing my newspaper on the porch floor as she coasted past me and into the house.

"What are you doing?" I managed to ask as she flew by. "Is your father leaving you here?"

"Miss Rosemarie!" was all she said before the house swallowed her.

I looked back out. There was no trace of the Pontiac, not even on the road ahead.

"Amaryllis, should you not be in school?" I called out as I entered the house.

I moved toward voices in the dining room but stopped just short of entering. I lingered outside the doorway. The child and Rosemarie were sitting on the floor in front of the highboy chest. The highboy's top drawer had been upended and its contents spread over the rug: hollow matchboxes, pieces of grosgrain ribbon too short to be useful, a rusted miniature screwdriver, chipped marbles, jacks and a pair of dice, a small wooden shoe on which I had never before laid my eyes, and nameless bits of metal and plastic. Not to mention the keys. The number of keys was astonishing. Scattered everywhere, muted silver and bronze, resting like dumb coins at the bottom of a fountain.

I looked from the items to my sister. I wondered how my seventy-three-year-old sister had gotten down on the floor with all those things. My next thought was that she would surely need someone to help her up when she was done, and I was not going to be that person.

Rosemarie had been with us for several weeks, and during that time, she and Olva had taken my car whenever they felt like it. Rosemarie did whatever she wanted, of course, never asking for permission, but I was alarmed by how her behavior had temporarily corrupted Olva, who as a rule would ask at least a day in advance when she wanted to use my car.

Whenever Rosemarie and Olva went on these excursions, they always returned singing little snatches of songs in unison and laughing the way children do, with a kind of reckless, unspooled delight, as if merriment were in unlimited supply. It was the same with my sister and Amaryllis. From the moment they were introduced, the two had hit it off like old friends, as if making up for a long and unfortunate separation. Their heads were always tipped together, their conversations speckled with laughter.

Amaryllis looked with awe at the flotsam and jetsam on the

floor. She plucked from the debris a short segment of silk ribbon in deep mauve. The child lifted the ribbon toward my sister.

"Thank you, Amaryllis," Rosemarie said, making too much fuss over the offering. "What a fine gift indeed."

My sister could add it to her collection. Since her arrival, Rosemarie had been on the receiving end of a startling number of gifts. Last week, I opened the front door to find a loaf of pumpkin bread sitting on my porch chair. It was not yet the season for pumpkin anything, but I suppose people now used that canned nonsense. I knew who had brought the bread (Trudy Lipscomb from our own Hillwood Presbyterian), because it was covered in red-tinted plastic wrap.

In the intervening days, other gifts had arrived on our doorstep, all with notes bearing Rosemarie's name. There was a clay pot of black-eyed Susan one morning. The following afternoon, I found a blue tea towel wrapped around some quince muffins. Even Wray Little's wild strawberry jam showed up, which not many people were fortunate enough to taste. The offerings were small and sometimes not at all things you'd count as gifts: a paper bag full of river rocks, two jars of store-bought pickled beets, and the caboose of a toy train, broken in the spot where it would connect to the penultimate car.

Judging from these gifts, Rosemarie had made use of her time so far in Bound, reconnecting with old acquaintances and making new ones. They probably got an earful about what my sister had been up to over the years. I had heard nothing from her. It was true I had not asked her, but why was I responsible for extracting the mystery of her life from her closed mouth? My life was on display, piece by piece, right here in the house. At the very least, she owed me some small parcel of knowledge about what kind of life she had been leading. Instead, she left me to glean what I could from the gifts people left her.

Just this morning, I found a tiny cairn of acorns on the top porch step, and I was at a loss whether it was another gift for Rosemarie or if it was the work of an industrious squirrel. With a kick of my broom, I swept the acorns off the step, and they scattered like gravel sprayed from a tire.

I was still standing at the doorway. Rosemarie's back was to me.

"Your hair looks lovely, Amaryllis," my sister was saying.

The child brought her small hand to the rows of neat braids lining her head. "My daddy did it," she said proudly.

"He's very skilled," Rosemarie said.

"Where are you from?" Amaryllis suddenly asked my sister. "Where is your home?"

Rosemarie didn't speak right away, but the child didn't hurry her for an answer.

"I don't have a home," Rosemarie finally replied. Then she laughed right away as if to cover up what she had said. "What I mean is that I've moved around so much, it's hard to say which place exactly is my home. That's what I mean."

Amaryllis nodded. "My home moves around, too."

"Miss Judith."

It was Olva's voice, and I jumped. She had entered the dining room from the opposite entrance.

"Miss Judith, would you like to join us?"

"Oh," I said, walking in. "I just came in from outside." I turned to Amaryllis. "Should you not be in school?"

She peered at me and squeezed her bunny. "You already asked that. *It's summer!*" she said with no small amount of fury, the kind children seem to generate upon the slightest provocation.

"So it is."

"We are helping Marcus," Olva explained. "He delivers the newspaper more efficiently when alone. And he has been doing a little repair work on the side, which he needs time to attend to." She looked at Amaryllis. "Your father is a very accomplished mechanic, even though he wouldn't describe himself that way."

The child sheepishly buried her face in Peter Rabbit's belly. Without warning, she jumped up and ran past me to the back of the sofa in the adjacent room. On the sofa table, she spied the butterfly tray, an antique from the DeLour side, which was inlaid with actual butterfly wings. Her eyes widened.

"Don't touch that," I said, moving toward her. "It is fragile."

"I wasn't touching it," Amaryllis said.

"You were thinking about it."

"I was not." The child spun away from the tray and ran back to my sister.

"Judith, you couldn't be less hospitable if you tried," Rosemarie said, her back still to me.

"You have found the junk drawer," I said. "Its contents are suitable for your attitude."

"Now, ladies," Olva said.

When we were children, Rosemarie spent all day outside. She would be dispatched to some far corner of our family's land, sampling the honeysuckle, lying in stretches of wild violets, or imprinting her palms with bark patterns from the time she spent hanging from limbs. But since her return, she's been wandering the house as though discovering it for the first time. I find her peeping in bureaus and investigating the contents of cupboards.

Rosemarie leaned forward and ran her fingers through the contents on the floor as if caressing the skin of a pond. She picked up a random key and inspected it.

"What does this unlock?" she asked Amaryllis.

"The gate to Mr. McGregor's garden!" Amaryllis laughed. She glanced over at me.

"It unlocks nothing," I said.

"It must unlock *something*," Rosemarie insisted.

I shrugged. "Maybe, maybe not. The locked drawers around the house are so numerous that they long ago ceased to be mysterious to me."

Rosemarie handed the key to Amaryllis, who circled it through the air while making engine noises.

Next, Rosemarie picked up a silver comb, no longer than a pinky finger.

"Do you not recognize that, Rosemarie?" said Olva. "It is the comb for the doll you called Penny."

"Penny!"

"The one with the cloth body and the porcelain face," Olva continued, standing up and turning toward me. "Miss Judith, can I get you some coffee?"

"No, Olva, you don't have to do that," Rosemarie interrupted.

I looked straight at Olva. "I don't care for any right now. Thank you anyway."

"Olva, you don't have to wait on my sister," Rosemarie said.

Olva said nothing, and I cleared my throat. "If we could find that doll," I pressed on, "I suspect she'd be worth something. We had such well-crafted dolls. Nothing like the cheap ones kids carry around nowadays. So many of the things from our youth would be valuable today. Olva, I was just thinking of that edition of the *New York Times* you had, the one the day after Black Tuesday. It would be considered a treasure now. I think I saw it last in a box in the cellar."

"Only you, Judith, would find a way to extract value from people's suffering." Rosemarie shook her head. "And my doll Penny would be worth something to me, but not in the way you mean. She was the first doll of mine that wasn't passed down from you!" She tilted her head. "How do you know what kind of dolls children have? Other than Amaryllis, when are you spending time with any children?"

"I see them running down the street occasionally, when I'm having my coffee on the porch."

"You certainly spend a lot of time on the porch."

"I can see everything I need to see from there!"

"Lord, Judith, calm down. Don't work yourself up," Rosemarie replied.

With as much commotion as she could muster, Olva reached into the pocket of her apron and retrieved her pair of round-rimmed glasses. She brought them to her face. "Now, let's take a look!" she said loudly. She peered down to get a better view of the items on the floor.

I pressed my hand to my chest, containing a chuckle, for Olva looked like an old lady when she wore those glasses.

Rosemarie placed the doll's comb gingerly on the floor, as if it belonged in that sacred spot, next to an empty bobbin and a queen of diamonds playing card.

"My, my," Olva said, her head stooping over the sea of items. "I suppose there is always a drawer full of things that have no use, but for some reason, you cannot bear to part with them."

"Should we clean it out?" I suggested. "Olva, you said you were up for a spring cleaning. I suppose we're officially into summer now."

"Maybe that's not the kind of spring cleaning she meant," Rosemarie said. "Why must you be so practical?"

"Someone's got to be! Isn't it unfortunate it always has to be me?" My legs tiring, I walked to the sofa and lowered myself onto it.

"Now, ladies," cautioned Olva again. She had crossed over toward the window, away from both of us.

But Rosemarie would not let up. "Just because these things are odds and ends does not mean they are worthless. They have found a home together right here in this drawer."

"*My* drawer," I reminded her. "And what's in *my* drawer are *my* bits of rubbish."

Rosemarie leaned her body over the things like a mother bird, as if protecting them from my beakish words. "Is that why you're writing that ridiculous inventory?" she asked. "You've always been possessive, Judith. It's a poisonous trait."

I shot a look at Olva. Her back straightened, but she did not turn around. "I might have mentioned the inventory to your sister, Miss Judith."

"Olva, really," Rosemarie said, making a face. "You needn't say *Miss*."

We stood silent for a moment, Rosemarie and I looking at one another, Olva looking elsewhere.

Rosemarie broke the silence. "Why would you want to write about the Tiffany lamp?" Her eyes swept the room. "Where is it, anyway? I haven't seen it." She shook her head. "What an awful history it has."

"You know nothing of its history!" I said, pointing my finger at her. "Even if you did, you can't change the history of an object because you don't fancy the story it tells. Then again, escaping history seems to have been your life's work."

Rosemarie laughed bitterly. "Isn't it convenient for you that you're the one writing—"

"Furthermore," I went on, "just because I don't find myself fawning over a bunch of debris in a drawer does not mean I lack feeling." How the junk drawer had become a measure of my compassion was beyond me.

I had more to say, but Amaryllis was raising her hand.

"Are you waiting to be called upon?" I asked her. Children were peculiar creatures. "You needn't raise your hand."

She lowered her arm and turned to Olva. "Are you the maid?"

Such a question!

"Oh, Amaryllis," Rosemarie cried, her voice full. "Olva is not our maid."

The child shrugged. "My mama was a maid before she died. She worked over in York."

We fell into chastened silence.

"Where is your family?" Amaryllis asked Olva.

Rosemarie leaned over and placed her hand on Amaryllis's arm. "Sweet child, that is why Olva wrote me. That is why she asked me to come home. To help her figure that out."

My breath hovered in my throat, and I heard my heartbeat in my ears. I looked at Olva, who still faced the window. I could hardly believe it. She had summoned my sister here. For the early years of my life, aided by Quincy's insights, I had known all there was to know about the people of Bound. How my knowledge had narrowed! Now, I was ignorant of what was happening right under my own roof. My head began to buzz, a headache coming on. Rosemarie and Amaryllis returned to sifting through the items from the highboy drawer. I lifted myself from the sofa and climbed the stairs.

There was a phone call I needed to make.

About an hour later, I made my way downstairs again, but the sound of voices made me pause in the hallway. Olva, Rosemarie, and Amaryllis had moved to the living room. The reflection from the Cheval mirror in the corner showed me that they were all three nestled together on the sofa. Olva held a thin red book in her hands. When she opened it, a piece of a page flew into the air as if the book had been withholding a sneeze for a decade. The paper flew so suddenly away that Olva and Rosemarie began laughing, Rosemarie with her big gulping laughter and Olva with her compressed hiccups.

"You two are crazy," Amaryllis said, and she sounded so

nearly like an adult that this made Olva and Rosemarie fall into another fit of laughter.

Rosemarie, scooping a tear away from her cheek, said, "You do the honors, Olva."

Olva pressed her large round glasses to her nose, turned a page, and read, "'This is a watchbird watching a picky eater.'"

Now, I knew which book Olva was holding. It was a picture book called *The Watchbirds*. It's not as old as some of our other first editions of children's classics—along with Potter's *The Tale of Peter Rabbit*, we have Defoe's *Robinson Crusoe*, Kipling's *Just So Stories*, and Kingsley's *The Water Babies*—yet *The Watchbirds* is notable for its instructional value, as it tells the story of crow-like creatures that spy on children engaged in naughty behavior.

"'This is a watchbird watching a sneaky,'" Olva read.

Amaryllis giggled. "Who's sneaky?"

"My brother was sneaky," Rosemarie said. "But he watched out for me."

Olva was quiet.

"I suppose the watchbird would have a hard time watching me," my sister continued, "seeing as I've been gone for so long. This is a watchbird watching a ghost."

"You had your reasons for leaving," Olva responded.

"I suppose I did."

Everyone was always letting Rosemarie off the hook.

"But who's the watchbird?" Amaryllis whispered, her eyes wide. "The one collecting all the secrets."

"Now *that's* a good question, child," Olva said, chuckling. "Who is the watchbird itself?" Suddenly, Olva craned her head to peer in the hallway.

I staggered back and fled to the kitchen, where I slipped in through its rear entrance.

Midday, I noticed my car was gone. Olva, Rosemarie, and Amaryllis had taken it. The house bore no trace of them. I happened to glance out one of the large front windows, and when I did, a shadowed figure on the porch peered inside. My shock was so great, I had to rest against the arm of the sofa until my woozy head settled. Regaining my composure, I stormed over to the front door. I did not open it but reached for one of my sturdy canes sitting within the entryway. I rapped it vigorously on the inside of the door.

"Go away!" I yelled, still rapping. "No one is home!"

I gave the door a final crack with my cane to make my point.

My heart sped up from the exertion, and I had to sit down a few moments, because my vision began to swim. Finding my equanimity again, I slowly approached the window.

When I looked out, I saw no one at all. A chuckle over my misplaced alarm was brewing in my chest until I peered farther out into the yard. A man!

It took me a moment to recognize the man as Jolly Bramlett's son. I had forgotten his first name but not his temperament. A genealogical rung down, Jolly's spiteful buoyancy had degraded into a blunter kind of malice in her offspring. I unlatched the door and stepped onto the porch. Sunlight flooded my eyes, and I squeezed them shut. Opening them again, I found the Bramlett boy glancing up at me from the yard, an unlit cigarette dangling from his parted lips. Long graying hair clumped onto his shoulders, and an old brown belt held his black shirt and pants together.

"Ms. Kratt," he said wearily. When his lips moved, his cigarette popped up and down. He said no more but crossed his arms over his chest and took his tired gaze away from me.

"What is your name?" I asked. Age gives one the occasion to be blunt.

Jolly typically referred to him as *my poor son*. Her *poor son* this, and her *poor son* that. She once told me that despite his woes, having a child was all she ever wanted. Then I remembered she flashed me a look of pity, as if I hadn't been so lucky. What a shot of fury that sent through me. As if she had a clue what I wanted!

Jolly's son fished in his pocket for a lighter. He flipped it open and shut, open and shut. He cupped his hand over the cigarette and lit it. It all took a very long time in my estimation, during which I was standing there like a fool, my question dangling in the air.

"Rick," he said finally, not looking at me.

He was spared the threat of more communication with me when his mother's Taurus pulled into the driveway. Jolly hoisted herself from the driver's seat, and Vi floated from the passenger side a few moments later. Seeing her son, Jolly threw her arms wide, beckoning him for a hug. He didn't protest, and they embraced.

Jolly released her son. "Why didn't you eat the pimento cheese?" she asked. He shrugged, and she brushed something off the front of his shirt. All at once, it was clear to me: he lived with her! I took stock of his sad, dirty clothes and understood that his life had been less prosperous than his mother's.

I took my time to step down from the porch. As I approached Jolly and her son—Vi stood to the side—I saw in my peripheral vision my Oldsmobile Cutlass moving down the road. Finding another car in the driveway, it slowed to a stop in front of the house. It looked as if it might keep going, but Amaryllis shot out of the back seat, dangling her bunny by its ears.

Olva got out of the car, calling after Amaryllis, but the child was already running headlong toward us. Rosemarie, who had been driving, cut off the engine. Amaryllis was already standing beside me when my sister began walking toward us.

Jolly stood, hands on hips. "I heard you were back in town," she said to Rosemarie, her usual strained mirth giving way to complete acrimony.

Rosemarie said nothing.

"How long have you been away?" Jolly continued, seeming to enjoy her own question, as if she had been in a state of celebration since my sister's departure.

I thought her attitude toward Rosemarie was in poor taste, and I almost said something.

But Jolly was still going. "Daddy always thought you were pretty," she said flatly. "Couldn't tear his eyes away from you."

My sister did not respond to any of it. Her face was cautiously still, as if she had arranged her expression and was holding it in place.

Jolly leaned her body toward Rosemarie, angling for another line of attack, but Rick had lost his patience. He seemed to be in no mood for bygone rivalries between old biddies. The folds of flesh around his mouth quivered a moment, which was a preamble to a nasty smile, and his lips then parted so widely, I thought I might be able to count each and every one of his teeth.

"We're here for that black boy," Rick said. "He owes us rent money."

I felt a twist of nausea in my stomach. I looked at Rick, then Jolly, half expecting one of them to say something to me, but they had turned their attention toward Olva, who had tucked Amaryllis behind her skirt. Jolly stepped toward them.

"Where have you been, child?" Jolly's voice was like lemon in milk.

"Hickory Grove," Amaryllis said, eyeing Jolly. I thought it was brave of the child to answer.

"And why did you go there?"

Rosemarie opened her mouth to speak, but Olva gently touched her arm as if absorbing a charge. My sister's face quieted.

"Miss Olva and Miss Rosemarie talked to a preacher, but he had a dog," Amaryllis said, loosening up as she remembered the animal. She stepped out from behind Olva's skirt. "I got to play with the dog! His name is Henry. Then Miss Rosemarie and I got to play with Henry while Miss Olva talked to the preacher some more."

From Jolly's expression, I could tell she did not know what information could be located in Hickory Grove, our neighboring town. But I did. The black church there, Walnut Grove Baptist, possessed an uncensored history of the births and deaths of colored folk in upstate South Carolina.

"That's nice," Jolly said blandly. She lifted her brows. "I understand your daddy will be picking you up soon. Is that right?"

"You don't have to answer," Olva told Amaryllis.

Jolly laughed. "I do believe your maid has airs."

Rosemarie's breath escaped her loudly, but otherwise, she remained silent.

Rick took a hard pull on his cigarette, worn out by having to condescend to sort out his mother's problems. Faster than he looked, he stepped between Olva and Amaryllis. "Tell us where your daddy is!" he said, towering over the child.

His bluntness was miscalculated. Uncowed, Amaryllis narrowed her eyes at him and dashed back to Olva, who swept her up the porch stairs and into the house. The door closed behind them. Rick watched them depart with hooded eyelids. He seemed to skip from apathy to rage and back again, with no notes in between.

"White trash," Rosemarie whispered, finding her voice but just barely.

"Shut up, bitch," Rick said languidly, not looking at my sister.

"That's enough, son," Jolly said. "It's time to go."

Rick wheeled around and took off toward the road. "Don't you want a ride home?" Jolly called after him. But he had already crossed the road and was heading toward town. She hurried to her car, beckoning Vi to follow. She would attempt, I could see, to pick him up down the road.

Before opening the car door, Jolly paused and looked at me. "Anyway, Judith, even if we didn't find that black boy here, thank you for giving us a call. I knew we could count on you. We're old friends, aren't we?" She seemed to consider this. "Well anyway," she sniffed. "We stand on the same side of things at least."

The door slammed, and the car backed out of the driveway with force.

Rosemarie stood wordlessly. I could hear her breath, a pant.

"I see now that I made a mistake in calling Jolly."

Rosemarie didn't speak.

"I made a mistake," I said. "I can admit it." I was hardly going to beg.

My sister stepped toward the front door. I intercepted her, but she didn't say a word. Her eyes met mine with conviction, greater than before, as if she'd found something, proof of my offense, on which to hang her lifelong suspicions about my character.

"Please don't tell Olva," I said.

Rosemarie moved me aside. When she entered the house, I followed, but there was Olva, and I could entreat my sister no more.

"Amaryllis is safely upstairs," Olva said.

A knock at the door punctuated her comment. We all stiffened, but when Rosemarie peered out the window, she glided toward the door and opened it. Marcus stepped in, a smile on his face until he noticed our expressions.

"What happened?" he asked. "Where is Amaryllis?"

"Did you run into the Bramletts?" Olva asked.

"No. They were here?" His face went slack.

"Amaryllis is fine," Olva said, gesturing for Marcus to join her. The low murmurs of their conversation carried them up the stairs.

I tried to give Rosemarie a meaningful look, but she was already following the two of them. I retreated to the sunroom, moving to the far corner, where I sat on the uncushioned wicker seat as a form of penance. The sun shone coldly through the windows. I closed my eyes, falling into a willed slumber, and I was not sure how much time had passed or if I had truly been sleeping when my ears detected a conversation in the living room. I lifted myself from the seat and crept closer to the sunroom door to listen.

"You haven't been back to your home," Rosemarie was saying. "Where have you been living?"

"Our car." It was Marcus.

I heard the fatigue in his voice. I thought about the repair work he did around town—clocks and generator engines and whatnot—and I wondered if a consequence of his work was that he transferred whatever sputter of life he possessed to those failing things.

"You will come live with us," Rosemarie said. "Just for a time. Until you figure out your next step."

"I'll think about it. It's a generous offer."

"How can you think about it? You have a child to consider."

"I can make my own decisions about my child."

"How can you say that?" Rosemarie pressed.

"Because she's mine."

Rosemarie did not respond at first. I thought they had abandoned the room, but then her voice broke the silence.

"I want to tell you, Marcus, about a hat that was once made for me. I was thirteen years old, and Jolly's father commissioned the hat for me. It was a fine hat indeed, made of peacock feathers. I have never seen this hat myself, but Mr. Bramlett told me about it one evening, when he happened to catch me alone in the store after the doors had been locked. I was on the third floor, getting ready to climb out a window, which was my preferred state of entry and exit, when I heard him call my name. He liked to say my name in two parts. *Rose. Marie.* As if he were getting two girls for the price of one. I froze. He had cornered me.

"'I bought you a hat, girl, but you ran off,' he said, approaching me. He began describing the hat, holding out his hands, as if he wanted to measure my head. 'I think it would have fit you, but I want to check,' he said. Then he moved his body against mine, pinning me against the windowsill, and he placed his hands around my neck. He pressed my head into the glass. I thought it would shatter. Out of the corner of my eye, I could see snow begin to fall, the kind that danced through the air, and I imagined myself dancing right along with it, held aloft by a current of air. He kept one hand on my throat and moved his other hand to my torso. I was a sprite back then, wearing clothing too light for the season. It required very little of his effort, then, to thrust his hand inside my underwear. I closed my eyes, and against the backs of my eyelids, my snowflakes continued their frantic dance. I imagined the cold numbing my body. All at once, he stopped. I didn't open my eyes but felt the presence of someone else in the room. He released me. I fell to the floor, my hip hitting the edge of the windowsill. The pain made my eyes fly open, and I saw my brother, Quincy. He was standing across from Mr. Bramlett.

"Quincy and Mr. Bramlett stood in silence. Suddenly, I felt as if the air were filled with lead, and the weight of the room tipped toward my brother. There was Quincy, the secret gatherer, my father's eyes and ears, and Mr. Bramlett was no fool. He had just as much reason to fear my father's wrath as anybody. After a few excruciating moments, Quincy brushed his hand to the side, an invitation for Mr. Bramlett to leave the room. Quincy nodded, letting Mr. Bramlett know what he had done to me would remain a secret. I closed my eyes and let my head fall to the floor. Quincy's betrayal was worse than my violation. But as I lay there, I felt Quincy's breath above my head. 'If he touches you again, I will kill him,' my brother said, helping me up, and in his eyes, I could tell it was the truth. He would be my protector. He draped his coat around me, and he retrieved some suitable clothing for me from the women's clothing department. I changed in the third-floor bathroom while Quincy guarded the door. He eventually took me to Aunt Dee's, where Olva took care of me for the rest of the night."

I stood out of sight in the sunroom, listening to my sister's story. I had never before heard it. A thought tore through me: after Shep Bramlett had pushed the peacock hat into my hands, I had not told my sister about it, had not prepared her for his fury. Several times I saw her that day, but no word of it crossed my lips. Instead, I had squirreled that hat away as though it had been my own.

From the living room, Rosemarie's voice again. "I'm not telling you this, Marcus, to burden you with some sad tale or to guilt you into moving in with us. I'm telling you so you'll know I have my own ax to grind with the Bramlett family."

There was a spell of silence. An acceptance of Rosemarie's offer.

Marcus's voice. "They raised our rent and raised it again.

And then they locked us out when we fell behind on our payments." He paused. "Rosemarie, I need to tell you that my great-grandfather is the one who murdered your brother."

My sister's voice, softer now. "Don't you worry about that. Olva invited me here to set some matters straight. Now that I'm back in Bound, we can finally tell our family's story. You'll understand soon enough. Now let's get you moved in."

I moved away from their voices. I wanted to hear nothing more.

An hour later, Olva stepped into the sunroom.

"There you are. I've been looking for you." She considered me more closely. "Are you quite all right?"

I nodded, and she took the wicker chair next to me. She paused to notice that the cushion was under her. I searched her face for anger, worried that she knew I had called Jolly about Marcus. I wanted to ask her why she had invited Rosemarie home. But I did not want to stoke anything. I wanted to keep the embers low.

"Marcus and Amaryllis are moving in," I said.

"Yes. They are moving their things in from the car now."

She patted my leg before rising from the chair and leaving the room. I sat unmoored, out of place in my own house.

After a few minutes, I followed her path to the living room, where inside the front door, Marcus and Amaryllis's items had been deposited, mostly electronics Marcus was repairing, along with some paperwork and a few books. Marcus had given

Amaryllis a suitcase to tow her clothing, while he had stuffed his into two pillowcases. The child had so few toys. What little they possessed.

An inventory in one glance.

Windsor chair
Wooden spinning wheel
Mahogany secretary
R. S. Prussia vase
Pie safe—Grandmother DeLour's
Butler's tray (silver plated)
Amsterdam School copper
mantel clock
Hamilton drafting table
Letter opener (cut glass)

Tiffany lamp (diameter 16″;
21¾″ height)—~~broken~~ fixed

Victorian chaise longue
Octagonal Jacobean parlor table
Mahogany sewing cabinet
Westclox alarm clock
(Big Ben model)
Hepplewhite side table
Watchmaker's workbench
Edwardian neoclassical brass
column candleholders (10″ tall)
Abner Cutler rolltop desk

Riding whip—Daddy Kratt's
New York Times (Wednesday,
October 30, 1929)
Peacock hat
Edwardian coral cameo (1½″ × 1″)

Highboy bureau
Butterfly tray
Cheval mirror

SIX

I sat in the passenger seat of Daddy Kratt's Cadillac, black and glistening from a fresh polish, as it glided down the road like an oily crow. Our task was to collect past due rents on our properties. Having a woman accompany him, as he put it, soothed the disobedient tenants. Which was another way of saying that Daddy Kratt remained in the driver's seat, engine still humming, while I knocked on people's doors.

For weeks, I had been nervous, wondering what Quincy had seen when I caught him running ahead of me on the stairs that day in the store. It didn't seem possible to me that he could have seen Charlie squeeze my mother's hand, but when it came to spying, Quincy seemed to have the ability to see through others' eyes. Coasting along the road in the Cadillac, watching the longleaf pines outside my window enduring winter's rawness, I held my breath.

As I went door-to-door collecting money, tenants pleaded with me. They cracked their front doors, not inviting me in, the wind still sweeping inside, leaving their homes colder than before I arrived. Their words were directed at me, but their eyes remained fastened over my shoulder on Daddy Kratt in the driver's seat. They would see him working his gums with a toothpick, and if he sensed defiance, he revved the engine.

Often, I had to repossess belongings, usually the most prized possession in the house, although what counted as prized, I came to learn, was a matter of perspective. Daddy Kratt knew it. He sent me into those homes with lists of the things that mattered most to the tenants. I walked right through their front doors, carrying cursed inventories in my hands. Quincy was the one to collect that information beforehand. What cruel and intimate knowledge my brother gathered! Once, I took a wooden pipe from an old Negro, and to see him let go of it was like watching someone give up the thought of tomorrow. Back on the road, my father had tossed that pipe out the car window.

If Daddy Kratt was hardest on anyone, it was the poor white folks. These were the people he would have felt most comfortable with, owing to his origins, but for them, his kinship and disgust arose in equal measure. In those circumstances, my father was the worst version of himself. From those poor whites, he made me repossess things from their children—a toy train, a worn teddy bear. I wondered whether any of the toys in our house had come from those families. For all I knew, they might still be there, hiding in plain sight among our other toys, even now bewildered by their new surroundings.

That day, as I rode with him, Daddy Kratt was in a particularly foul mood. I wondered if it had to do with his idea to stockpile his cotton. Now, everyone, not just Olva, was worried about the nation's economy, and offended by the slumping price of the crop, my father had devised a plan to hoard his cotton at one of the gins until the prices rose, which he was certain would happen soon. Shep Bramlett was advising against it, and they rarely parted ways on business matters. I opened my mouth to ask my father about it but then thought better of rousing his anger.

On our way to the next tenant, we passed Aunt Dee's house, where Olva also lived. Daddy Kratt slowed the Cadillac to a crawl.

Surrounded by sky-piercing loblolly pines and water oaks outfitted with fat-thumbed leaves, Aunt Dee's house, a simple but sturdy one-room dwelling, sat on a raised callus of earth, a bald spot amid a thicket of trees. When my siblings and I ventured onto her property, she invariably put us to work, snapping beans or digging the stinking guts out of pumpkins. Overrun with all manner of fruit and vegetables, she existed in a continual cycle of stockpiling, pickling, and preserving. You considered yourself lucky when you emerged from her house not brined in a peculiar liquid or stashed in the root cellar. Built with wide hips and solid, ill-proportioned limbs, Dee herself resembled a sturdy tuber, resilient and substantial and guaranteed to be around a long while if stored properly. She often told me that not having a husband was what kept her mind fit and her nerves calm. She said she would outlive all the men of her age in Bound anyhow.

Dee's acreage was full of curiosities: a battered car shrouded in kudzu, some kind of water-measuring device—a giant tub—heaved onto its side, and a teepee that had been built by a real Indian who had lived on her land for a year. Dee had the knack for attracting all manner of wanderers. She was always taking them in and then eventually sending them away with at least a three-month supply of pickled eggs or leathered ropes of dried fruit to tide them over until their next stop.

The vegetation that surrounded Dee's was so various, it seemed suited for a different ecosystem altogether. When we were younger, Quincy and I had played cowboys and Indians there, and we hardly had to stoke our imaginations to pretend we were somewhere savage and inscrutable, where the tendril of some plant might curl around your ankle and pull you down into a barbaric underworld. Dee had cultivated her house, as well as the generous land surrounding it, as a place outside of Bound, even though it was still within the town's limits.

The singularity of Dee's home, I realize now, was what permitted Olva to live there. Otherwise, a colored child living with a white woman from a prominent family would have been forbidden. And the way Dee lived, more like a vagabond than a true DeLour, perplexed people from the start; maybe that's why she took up unconventional habits to begin with, so that anything she did subsequently seemed no stranger than the last. Using this tactic, Dee had educated Olva just as we had been educated, with tutors and a sense of determination about the importance of school.

Aunt Dee's was where Mama lived for an entire year or so before I was born. As Dee told me, Daddy Kratt had barely noticed, because he was so busy with his fledgling cotton business. He had not even noticed when Dee and Mama left town for several months to visit some of Dee's far-flung friends, people who were always eager to return a favor to my aunt because she was so generous with the ones she doled out in the first place. *Cotton fever*, Dee said, describing the way

Daddy Kratt had lost himself in the business, and she shook her head disapprovingly, but she also seemed a little relieved, as if keeping him distracted might not be such a bad thing.

Daddy Kratt stopped the Cadillac outside Dee's house. He gave her front door such a hard look, I thought it might push it down.

"Are we paying Aunt Dee a visit?" I asked quietly. "I don't think Mama is there today."

He ignored me and put his foot on the gas pedal a little more forcefully than was required. The engine roared, and we sailed away from Dee's.

As we did, I remembered a conversation I had overheard a day earlier between Mama and Aunt Dee. Having come upon Mama and Aunt Dee talking in our hallway, I was able to duck out of sight in the anteroom to the kitchen and listen. Aunt Dee's voice guttered with emotion. "You must not give her gifts like that," she said to Mama. "Do you understand the consequences? *Listen to me!* Are you listening?"

Silence.

"*Say something.*"

"I want her to have some of our family's things" was Mama's response, spoken in halting whispers. "Can you understand that?" Her voice thinned out as she spoke, dissipating as she lost her resolve. I heard a small spasm of a sob escape her.

"I know you do," Dee said, her voice softening. "But it puts her in danger walking around wearing Grandmother's cameo on her neck."

My ears pricked at the mention of the cameo.

"Yes," said Mama faintly.

"Oh, Sister," Dee said. "I love Olva as much as you do, and I hardly want to take things away from her—"

"I cannot ask her to return it! Have we not been cruel enough?" Mama began crying again, and I heard Dee's ragged sigh.

I felt impatience twitching in my chest, because even though I didn't know exactly what they were talking about, I was familiar with Mama's listlessness, the way the mere idea of doing something, let alone something difficult, made her fade into shadow.

Looking back, the image of my mother I most remember is her sitting in her bedroom chair, staring absently out the window, unable to do anything but that. Yet she was insisting Olva keep the cameo. Inside my mother's vaporousness, a kernel of strength, and it was the thought of Olva that had shored up that strength.

Aunt Dee's footsteps, hard and mannish, had moved down the hall. Then her steps stopped, lingered for a moment, before she finally sighed, softer this time, and headed toward the living room, leaving me there alone to listen to Mama's contained sobs.

"Judith, I have a task for you."

It was my father's voice, and it jolted me back to the Cadillac. Daddy Kratt's right hand rested lightly on the steering wheel. Not waiting for my reply, he went on. "I need you to assemble a group of men. Loyal ones—you know who they are. Get Byrd Parker involved, too. He won't say no. And, of course, the boys who work for me. They are usually drunk, but under these circumstances, that is fine."

I cleared my throat. "If I may ask, what is the purpose of this group?"

Daddy Kratt had his window down. The air was brisk and rushed into the car, making me pull my sweater closer to my skin. Daddy Kratt stretched his left arm out the window and reached with his fingers, as if trying to take hold of the wind. "That Charlie—"

My hand flew to my mouth. Daddy Kratt looked at me, and I brought my hand down and smoothed my skirt.

"Charlie spoiled something that belongs to me. And here I've given him a job and a place to live." Hoarse laughter seized his midsection, and he labored through it. He turned to face me. "As a matter of fact," Daddy Kratt continued, "Charlie just as good as belongs to me." He seemed to chew on the words. With his eyes on mine, the car eased to the wrong side of the road.

I felt a sick pressure at the back of my throat. My gaze shot toward the windshield to see if a car was approaching from the other direction. If so, we would be in a direct collision course with it.

"Look at me!" my father boomed, and I did as I was told. "Charlie belongs to me," Daddy Kratt said. "And you are in charge of my merchandise, Judith."

He drew his eyes forward, steering the Cadillac back to the right side of the road.

I closed mine, trying to think only of the steady drone of the wheels against asphalt.

After giving dozens of our tenants bad news, I asked Daddy Kratt to drop me off at the train depot. He was pleased to be spared driving me all the way home, and I was relieved to be free of the Cadillac. The smell of its interior—tobacco and sweat—lingered in my nose.

A crowd of people had gathered to watch the arrival of the train, which now sat stiffly on its tracks. When we were very young, Mama and Aunt Dee brought us to the depot frequently. Mama packed egg salad sandwiches and jars of Dee's copper pennies, a pickled concoction of carrots, onions, and green peppers. Quincy, Rosemarie, Olva, and I took turns fishing out the vegetables with our fingers. Our favorite place was perched on the knoll on the other side of the tracks, where we could take in the scene as a whole. When the Negroes loaded the ginned cotton onto the train, we felt a swell of pride, knowing our family was responsible.

Still, for all of Daddy Kratt's accomplishments, he harbored a sour spot for losing the bid for a cotton mill. Cotton gins, like the ones Bound had, separated the seed from the pulled cotton, but the mills, where ginned cotton was made into cloth, held the potential to transform a town into a place that mattered. I remember once seeing a newspaper on my father's desk, the main headline declaring that the "sun of civilization was rising." The money of the mills was bringing luxury to rural folk. But not for our town. In the end, Bound's sun stayed fixed on the horizon. One of the largest mills in the South was already located right next to us in Rock Hill and also in Pelzer, in nearby Greenville County, making a mill in our town a redundancy. For Daddy Kratt, there was always one more thing to want.

I decided I would cross the tracks and sit on the knoll. It would clear my mind so that I could consider what Daddy Kratt had asked me to do about Charlie. Gathering my knees to my chest for warmth, I looked up to see a few of my schoolmates laughing together, children in their winter coats twirling on the platform and collapsing in hysterics, and several men looking expectantly at the train, no doubt waiting for some kind of delivery to be unloaded.

Not one of the people in front of me was free from hardship or secrets. But here they were going on with life, merrily even. Because what was the alternative? Some had come to the train depot for actual deliveries, but most came for the reminder that faraway places existed. Yet when the train left, as it always did, these people would shrug off whatever hopes had been wreathed there and walk away. They would simply return home and face what was waiting for them there.

"Judith," a voice said, and my body jerked.

It was my brother.

"How do you do, Sister?" he asked. He seemed out of sorts.

"Honestly, Quincy, I'm glad you're here. I have awful news."

"Is it about the lynching Daddy Kratt wants for Charlie?"

"Don't call it that!"

Quincy shrugged. "Call it what you like. The result is the same. Ask that colored boy in Smyrna."

Not long after Byrd Parker's pregnant wife had drowned herself, the suspected father of her child was found two towns over, dangling from a tulip poplar tree. Mr. Aiken, our pharmacist, had claimed he'd seen it with his own eyes the day after it happened, and that despite it being a blustery day, the body had hung motionless, as if the wind knew better than to interfere.

After Quincy told me this, he seemed to fall into thought.

"I wonder if Dovey was there with her father," he said. "When he found the body, I mean."

I saw concern on my brother's face. Then, as he sank deeper into reflection, a kind of gentle mischief arose in his eyes. He was taken with her; it was unmistakable. I wondered what that mischievous look meant, and why it made him look older, as if he'd done something of consequence. I thought about Dovey, her openness and innocence, and it occurred to me that she was the best match Quincy could hope for. Perhaps she would serve to redeem him some day in the future.

"Do you see her often?"

Quincy's eyes narrowed. He was in a sour mood, and I had gone too far in asking a question about Dovey.

"Do you think they would harm Charlie?" I asked quickly. "He's so pleasant. People like him."

"I heard something the other day," Quincy said. "*No nigger with a job unless every white man has a job.*" Quincy met my gaze. "And Charlie has a good job, doesn't he? I'm not saying it's fair. But it's the truth. At the moment at least. You see, what I've learned from my, well, line of work, as you might call it, is that the distance from the top of the heap to the bottom is shorter and more precarious than you'd believe, and one idea, if it takes hold of people's minds in the right way, can be the difference between the two. The men in this town have built things they can see, can touch. That great store of Daddy Kratt's. The coarse pluck of cotton. But you see, the world rests on less sturdy stuff. Reputation depends on ideas and impressions, which shift and sort, as a warm breeze might. Or a combustible gas."

As Quincy was philosophizing, and he seemed very pleased with himself for doing so, something else occurred to me. "How did you know what Daddy Kratt asked me to do?"

"He told me he was going to put you in charge of that." The edges of Quincy's voice hardened.

"Hardly a sought-after job!"

"I brought him that information about Mama and Charlie. *I* did that," Quincy said.

"It's merely because I'm the eldest."

"But I'm the eldest *boy*," Quincy said, seeming pained by the admission. In his eyes, he was still not sufficient enough to garner our father's admiration. "He let you handle the repair of the lamp, too."

"You broke it!"

"Still."

Suddenly, I knew why Daddy Kratt had chosen me over Quincy to deal with Charlie. My father had sent me to the attic with the broken lamp in the beginning so that I might earn Charlie's trust, making it easier to trap him later. I felt sick about my part in it. I'd been following Daddy Kratt's orders without even knowing it: managing the inventory at the store, with Charlie as one of the things on my list.

Quincy turned to me. "If you were a boy, I'd probably hate you less."

"You'd hate me more," I said, shrugging.

With a nod of his head, perhaps in agreement, he took off. My brother crossed the field behind the depot, and the dense woods swallowed him.

I looked up. A large cloud pulled apart above me, undoing

itself as the wide sky watched. Then I heard a train whistle to the northeast, its call slicing the air. The sound sent a sharp question through me. What would I do?

SEVEN

It was late morning, the day after Marcus and Amaryllis had moved in. Marcus had already departed for his route. Rosemarie and Olva had left even earlier with my car, before Amaryllis awoke, to make another trip to Hickory Grove. Olva promised it would be their last. They had not asked me to come along, but Olva suggested that Amaryllis would enjoy my company at the house. I told her I strongly doubted that.

"Did you sleep well?" I asked Amaryllis, who had trotted into the living room. Last night, she had shared a bedroom with Olva, while Marcus had occupied the extra guest room upstairs. The child was not listening to me. She was standing beside the rolltop desk and had spied a trinket sitting on one of its shelves.

"You like that?" I asked her, and she nodded with a bit of apprehension. It was a thumb-sized glass rabbit sitting on its hind legs. "You may pick it up," I said, and she reached out with her free hand more carefully than I thought her capable. With her Peter Rabbit dangling, she now had a rabbit in each hand.

Amaryllis's gaze turned back to the desk. She studied its long front drawer, and, not able to master her curiosity, she reached forward, rabbit-handed, and tried to pull it open before I could stop her.

"Don't!" I said, even though I knew it was locked.

The sharpness of my voice surprised her, but she gave the drawer one more light tug. I pointed down at the glass rabbit, and she seemed to forget about the locked drawer.

"You know, Rosemarie once wanted that rabbit very badly," I said.

Amaryllis cocked her head and found a spot on the sofa. She drew her feet up on the upholstery, but I held my tongue. I took the seat next to her.

"You see, Amaryllis," I began, "it was Quincy's idea to raid this rolltop desk in the dead of night. I was eight years old at the time, he was seven, and Rosemarie was six."

"That is my age," she replied, in the spirit of shared accomplishment with my sister.

It was 1922, I told Amaryllis, and the flu was going around town. Mama begged us not to leave the house. We were content to ignore her pleas until, one day, our iceman told us about the Spanish flu, a pandemic that had torn through America only four years earlier. He did not scrimp on details, telling us stories of people turning blue from suffocation and their mouths filling with froth like Coca-Cola bottles set too long in the sun. Confined for weeks, we exhausted every amusement in the house. Before we turned on each other, we turned on the desk, which our savage curiosities had spared until we remembered it was a refuge for Mama, the place where she wrote her letters. She would be devastated if we spoiled it, so our decision came easily. Perhaps our actions would rouse Mama from her dreamy stupor; perhaps they wouldn't. We were just bored enough to want to know.

The desk (54 by 21 by 50 inches) had been part of her

dowry when she married Daddy Kratt. It was—and still is, as far as I'm concerned—a magnificent creature, barrel-chested and solid, with a slatted cover that once ran fluently along its tracks, as if the carpenter's raw material had been water instead of wood. It is an Abner Cutler, and the company's stamp can be located in the bottom right drawer. Abner Cutler was the first person to patent the design for the rolltop desk in 1850, and the appraiser from York says that an Abner Cutler original, which I believe this is, could fetch upwards of five thousand dollars.

The desk's proportions, though, didn't suit Mama. When she guided her finch-like body into its matching oak chair, she resembled a child. Sometimes, Daddy Kratt allowed her to do some of the bookkeeping for the store at the desk, but as the years passed, it was a rare occasion when she helped with matters outside of the home. He was fond of saying that her hands were so small, they were good for little else than scooping up jacks with us. He must not have been paying attention, because we never let Mama play with us.

We all stood on the landing between the stairs, Quincy and I flanking Rosemarie and Olva. Olva had come from Aunt Dee's to do some cleaning at our house, as she often did, but we invited her to join our scheme. It was afternoon, and we were studying the desk from afar.

"Tonight," I commanded. I hadn't come up with the idea, but I was certainly going to be in charge of its execution. Even Quincy gravely nodded his head, the tyranny of birth order still a serious business.

The rest of that afternoon, we took turns keeping vigil, watching the rolltop desk with drawn breaths as if it were a great nocturnal eye, its monstrous lid clamped shut. After bedtime, we crept back down the stairs, and how despairing the house seemed without the sunlight to keep it company. Pieces of furniture closed in on us, edging away from their anchored spots. Shadows loomed over our heads, taking an interest in us as well-meaning adults did, with their sprouted nose hair and glittering eyes and garbled questions. When the upright piano flashed me a stained grin, I ran to the others, who had already gathered beside the desk.

"Rabbit," Rosemarie whispered, knuckling a drowsy eye.

I broke from my story to point to the glass rabbit in Amaryllis's hand. "That one," I said.

Eyes widening, she settled further into the sofa and stroked the figurine with her thumb.

We had seen the inside of the desk every day, I told Amaryllis, but in the dark, it held new promise. It would bestow wishes shaped to the fantasies of whoever opened it. The top was heavier than we'd expected—we held the assumption it would be as compliant as Mama—but as a group, we managed to slide it up.

For a few moments, we surveyed the desk's innards, its endless slots and miniature drawers. It was both majestic and attainable. It was a tiny castle bisected, shelves running through it like little staircases. It was a kingdom shrunk down to make us feel like giants. We stood wordlessly, expelling our heavy breaths, and our restraint showed benevolence.

Quincy was the first to act. He stabbed his hand into a shelf for the glass rabbit, and Rosemarie's mouth wobbled into a smile. As the figurine disappeared into Quincy's hand, the spell was broken. We tore through the desk's contents, leaving no niche unmolested.

Rosemarie whimpered as she hunted for treasures, and Olva was the only one of us to exhibit moderation. She limited herself to the items we knocked to the floor. I saw her reach down to retrieve a rounded mother-of-pearl button, one that Mama had failed to sew back onto a sweater, that we had judged inconsequential. Olva cradled the button in her palm.

When I looked over at Quincy, I was startled by the smile on his face, how his jaw hung open and askew, a drawer off its runner. He had been successful in nabbing a few items I had targeted, following my eyes and anticipating my actions. At the same time, we saw a clay bowl filled with loose change. Both our hands shot for it, upsetting the bowl and sending the coins clattering to the floor.

"*We will wake Daddy Kratt!*" someone whispered.

Our father's name subdued us. We stood blinking at one another, and in settled a silence, like the kind that follows a great catastrophe. His name was a white ash drifting in, shrouding every surface, and giving the room an eerily dimensionless quality. It blurred our confidence, making us feel like children caught in a foolish mistake rather than the grand undertaking we had envisioned.

Our looting was done. Or at least we had lost our appetite for it. We dispersed to different parts of the house. My main spoils were Mama's letters, which she kept hidden in one of the back drawers of the desk. Taking as many as my small hands would accommodate, I darted to my favorite hiding place, a nook behind the standing Cheval mirror in the hallway, and I cupped the letters in my two hands as if I were holding water and did not want to spill a precious bit of it.

At the time, the letters were a disappointment. They were terribly boring, with no treasure maps leading to riches, no mysterious skeleton keys. I couldn't understand half of what they were getting at. They were from Aunt Dee, whom Mama wrote constantly even though they saw each other almost daily. I couldn't be bothered to keep the letters nor return them to the desk, so I intended to feed them, one by one, down the laundry chute.

At the chute, Quincy interrupted me, coming out of nowhere as he always did. He surveyed the letters in my hand. I nodded toward his fist, which held the glass rabbit. He hesitated. I knew he wanted to give the rabbit to Rosemarie—he always had a soft spot for her—but his curiosity was greater. Handing him some of the letters, I claimed the rabbit. Even at a young age, Quincy possessed a keen instinct to collect things that held secrets. Because of his interest, I kept several of the letters. As the years passed, they became more compelling reading material.

When the gentle light of morning seeped into the house, Mama came downstairs, still in her dressing gown. I was lying alone on the living room rug, and my body tensed as I watched her dodge the debris on the floor. She went straight to the desk and began the slow task of restoring what had been expulsed. As she moved through the room to retrieve the items, she did not make eye contact with me. Nor did she acknowledge me in any other way. I suddenly wished for the presence of the others, on whom I could blame the scene, but my silence had already incriminated me, and I remained motionless on the rug, strewn there among the other shunned things.

The restoration of the desk was a gentle, noiseless affair, so it was a long while before I realized Olva had returned to help Mama. As she worked, Olva rolled between her fingers, with the absorptive care of a ritual, the mother-of-pearl button, the one item she had taken from the desk.

"I did not give the rabbit to Rosemarie," I said to Amaryllis. "Perhaps I should have. But then you wouldn't be holding it now."

My eyes moved from the desk to Amaryllis. She had fallen asleep. This struck me as a spectacular feat, seeing as she had just woken up for the day. Then again, I had a vague and dusty memory of what it was like to be a child, the kind of strenuousness involved, what with everyone telling you what to do all the time.

Lifting myself from the sofa, I walked over to the far end of the desk. Our looting that night when we were children had not been the worst moment in the desk's lifetime. I pondered the gashes that riddled the wood on its left side. They had been put there sixty-five years ago. One morning, while the others were away, I had stood, suspended in the doorway, watching Quincy smash a hammer again and again into the desk. He had gripped the tool with two hands, fighting against its weight, and the display was so disorienting that the sound of each blow, it seemed to me, was not the sickening crack of the hammer but rather the desk itself, provoked into utterance, its sharp barks of pain. We had looted the desk two years earlier, but Quincy always had a fresh appetite for damage.

Poor Mama had come downstairs again to find her desk violated. The gashes extended across to the slats of the desk's cover. One slat had been pried off completely, giving the thing a hideous gap-toothed look, as if it had been too dumb to prevent its own mutilation. The missing slat had been secreted away, for it was not visible on the floor or anywhere else in the room, and the area encircling the desk was tidy. No splinters of wood. No sight of the instrument used to wield the damage. The whole scene had an air of disciplined neatness to it, which made the spectacle of ruin all the more plain.

Mama's body seemed to absorb the devastation; she sank into herself. Then she rolled back the desk's top and arranged her pens and papers in front of her as she always did before writing a letter to Aunt Dee. How slight and undemanding was her touch on everything and everyone! When she wrote to Aunt Dee, her pen trembled across the paper, but the curios that lined the top of the desk (a fluted blue vase, ivory figurines of thin-boned animals) remained undisturbed. This time, before she picked up her pen, she drew her hand tenderly across the broken wood.

I looked over at Amaryllis. "It occurs to me as I write my inventory," I told her slumbering ears, "that even though the desk was from Mama's family, it became Daddy Kratt's property when they married."

As a child, this didn't concern me: how Mama tended to things she couldn't call her own. Now, I understand that her light touch on us, the way her fingers whispered a jacket button closed or just barely smoothed down our fine white hair, which stood out from our heads like heat lightning, was her acceptance of these circumstances. In the end, she couldn't claim us either. And even if there were a time when she could, when the crook of her arm was the only thing that held us up, that time was long past, and we didn't remember it anyway. We were bound, finally, to belong to the world and not to her.

I let the child continue to nap on the sofa. I would sit on the porch for a spell. The air held a faint musk. It was too hot to be outside in the middle of summer, but I didn't want to be cooped up in the house, a feeling I had not experienced before. I watched as a small brown lizard, eyes pert and jaw set stoically, clung to a thin branch of one of the bushes fringing the porch.

The lizard's tiny lungs inflated and deflated rapidly, and as I considered the trace of air rushing in and out of its tiny frame, I heard a crunching sound to my left. Footsteps on gravel. The steps came from the carport side of the house. Beyond the carport was the marshy lily pond, and beyond that was a dense stretch of forest.

"No need to get up."

A reedy voice rose from behind me, and I whipped my head around with such alacrity that a bright pain discharged in my neck and my lizard shot away.

"I'm sure your mother didn't teach you to sneak up on people," I said to Rick. "No one else is here. I'm the only one." I glanced back at one of the windows. I hoped Amaryllis would stay inside.

"I didn't ask whether anybody else was home," Rick replied.

I wanted to get up from my chair, but I knew that moving quickly was not one of my strengths. I hardly wanted to risk getting dizzy and requiring his assistance.

"What do you want?"

Rick chuckled and stepped past me to take a seat.

"I want to thank you for calling my mother," he said. "About that black boy."

I wagged my hand at him, indicating I didn't want to rest another moment on the topic.

"You shouldn't bother the child," I said to him.

"I won't do it again, ma'am." He aimed his teeth at me.

"See that you don't."

He looked up, reflecting on something. "I remember the store, you know."

"It was our store first," I said. "My father built it."

"I know that," he said. "I'll give credit where credit is due. I guess it turns out my grandfather couldn't run a business as well as your father."

I turned to look at him. Here he was with some real knowledge all of a sudden.

"I think we got off on the wrong foot," he said.

"How is your store?" I asked. I knew, through his mother, that his store was not all he hoped it would be. I was not yet ready to be on the right foot with him.

"Have you been there?" he asked. Angling his head, he studied me. "No, I haven't ever seen you there."

"Olva does my shopping for me. Not that it is any of your business."

His pale eyes lingered on me. Scratching his jaw, he said, "My store. Well, I'll be honest with you. I can't really make good money there. I sell junk. I'm not afraid to admit that. I sell junk, right? Junk from China. Or wherever the hell it comes from. With all our jobs gone overseas, pretty soon nothing on the shelves will be ours. At least I don't have a family to support."

"A prudent observation."

"I'm not married. No children either."

"You mentioned that."

"Just like you."

The sun flashed in my eyes.

"I doubt you have read much of Edith Wharton," I said, squinting at him. "The short novel *Bunner Sisters*?"

He stared blankly at me, his upper lip twitching a little.

I lifted my hand to block the sun. A bumblebee was zigzagging through our petunias, its flight comically encumbered by its weight. I thought about the heroine Ann Eliza in *Bunner Sisters*, who never marries and is forced to close the shop she owns and pawn all the things inside it. I read Wharton's book as a teenager, and in the years since, I have made it a point to read more books about women like Ann Eliza and me. I suppose we could be called *spinsters*. The term does not rankle me. There is Miss Bates in Austen's *Emma*, Miss Havisham in Dickens's *Great Expectations*, Rhoda Nunn in Gissing's *The Odd Women*, and Miss Birdseye in James's *The Bostonians*, to list only a handful. It is true some of these fictional heroines have challenging personalities, but defects of character are often an outcome of circumstances, are they not? Well now.

"Life is hard," I said to Rick, "and those who can survive alone are flintier than the rest." I hoped he didn't think I was paying him a compliment.

"Doesn't your maid live with you?"

"Olva is not my maid!"

"But she lives with you."

"Yes."

"Then you're not really surviving alone, are you?"

I wondered when he planned to leave.

"You read the paper?" Rick said. He laughed. "Of course you do. That black boy delivers it to you."

Now, he was returning to the purpose of his visit.

"His name is *Marcus*," I said. "Why can't he pay his rent?"

"He can't pay it because we raised it."

"And why did you do that?"

Rick eyed me. "First of all, consider it a favor. I know his relations killed your brother."

"That's in the past," I said. "I'm asking you about what's happening to Marcus right now." I had surprised myself, favoring the present over the past.

He shrugged. "It's still a favor, whether you accept it or not. Besides, that car manufacturer is coming to Spartanburg. And that big tire plant already relocated to Greenville from New York. Bound could soon be a suburb of those two cities."

"And you think people want to live in your little shacks?"

His jaw set. "We'll tear them down. Maybe. I don't know. We'll take full advantage of the new economic circumstances."

"It's a pity our cotton gins closed," I said, mostly to myself.

He spat a laugh. "Isn't that what sank this town in the first place? Nobody would branch out is what my grandfather told me. Dairy, manufacturing—anything else. The people of this town should have *diversified*."

"Cotton built this town!"

"Yeah. Cotton sank it, too."

"Does your mother know about your grand plans for her properties?"

"She's handing down the properties to me," he said. "Pretty soon she will, at any rate."

"Is she not altogether impressed with your abilities?" I asked, not being able to stop myself. His mouth parted slightly. I had embarrassed him.

"This town is pathetic." He was insulting Bound, when he wanted to insult me. How was he to know it was the same?

"We have always found a way to survive," I said. "Bound's population couldn't have been more than two hundred people when I was a girl, and it hasn't exceeded four hundred in the years since. As your mother may have told you, my family helped shape this town. My mama's kinfolk founded one of the first schools in the area in 1818, just down in Blairsville, and they helped establish one in Bullock's Creek, too." Here I paused, deciding if I would choose the wrong or right foot. "Well, the Bramletts were the educated sort, too. Right along with the Kratts."

I had thrown him a bone.

Yet he kept his vision fixed on the yard, as if the trees would up and fly away if he didn't keep an eye on them. He had not gone to college. I had remembered it too late. It was a sore topic for Jolly, one that she didn't often bring up. Two generations of the Bramlett family before Rick had gone to college, but he had not. My attempt to be polite had instead probed a wound. This was why I kept to myself. How did other people manage it?

I glanced at Rick again, and all at once, he reminded me

of the townsfolk who used to come around when I was a child and tuck religious pamphlets under our door. Not because he shared their religious zeal but because of the way they looked when they came to our house. We owned the only car in town for many years, so it was a weekly spectacle when we drove to Hillwood Presbyterian. We were accounted for, then, religiously speaking, but they came still with their pamphlets, tanned men with light eyes and children with moon faces. I used to sit in the Windsor chair and watch them peering into our windows, eyes scanning for something beyond the glass, and how quickly the curiosity was stolen from their faces, with what sad ease disappointment returned, once they recognized their own reflections staring back. I saw this same disappointment in Rick's face now. A hopelessness. Nothing—or very little—to lose. It seemed to me a precarious place to be. If you had nothing to lose, you might be willing to try anything.

"Bound is not much of a place," Rick said. "Never was. Compared to the rest of the world, it's just a backwater plot of nowhere. If you fancy yourself royalty here, you're still a peasant everywhere else."

"My family built this town," I shot back, "and that is more than you can say about yours. As you said yourself, your grandfather could not sustain what my father created." Politeness was now a whisper on the wind.

Rick did not expect my response, and he paused to reconsider me in the way you might regard an upside-down beetle that suddenly righted itself: a flicker of admiration followed by indifference. Then his mouth thinned into a smile, as if something important had been established between us.

"And yet if you ask anyone around town about the Kratt family," he said, "what will they remember? Here's what: a black man murdered your brother, and your father lost all his power. He sold off all his businesses and died penniless. Well, he ran that gas station until he died. In the end, your father was nothing more than a gas station attendant."

My head swam in anger. I took a deep breath and squared my gaze at Rick.

I began telling him about the things in the house, my words pouring out in a torrent, inviolable, a landslide of which there was no way through or around. Rick sat, silenced. I told him of the provenance of the rolltop desk. I told him about the giant drafting table upstairs that tilted on command like a planet turning on its axis. I told him about the Persian Heriz rug in the study that remained unspoiled because no one was allowed to walk on it. I told him about the revolving mahogany bookstand so burdened with books, it could not turn. The Queen Anne chair in dusty rose that Daddy Kratt had looked silly sitting in but about which we had dared not laugh. The rococo cherub figurines with their misleading smiles. The haughty splendor of the Noritake 175 Gold china. The art deco oyster plates. On and on.

Rick sank back into his chair. What he heard was his mother's voice, some old woman droning on. But I kept going with an energy I thought I had lost long ago. I pushed all the objects in the house toward him and, in the process, made a moat of those things around me.

When I was done, I tried to get up, but my balance failed me, and I dropped back into the chair. Rick rocked up and seized my arm. His grip was firm.

"I'll help you up."

"I'm fine on my own!"

"Is any of that old stuff worth anything?" he asked, squeezing my arm.

"Let go of me."

He released my arm. Stepping down the porch stairs, he set off toward the road, the opposite direction from which he had come. He had arrived in stealth but was leaving striding out the front like a peacock. As he did, my Oldsmobile swerved into the driveway. Rosemarie brought the car to a sudden stop, and Olva tore out of the passenger side.

"What are you doing here?" Olva demanded.

Rick stopped, put off by Olva's tone. She looked at me, trying to ascertain where Amaryllis was. I tilted my head discreetly toward the house.

"Get on your way, sir," Olva said, smoothing some of the roughness out of her voice.

Rick stepped toward her. "The best way to find that nigger is by following his child." He looked around. "Where is she?"

"I told you not to bother with her!" My voice rang in my ears.

"She's with her father right now," Olva said in a low and controlled way.

"I'll find her," Rick said. "I'll track her like I track my deer when I go hunting."

Olva's voice was crystalline. "If I see your face around this house again, I will shoot you myself."

From his lips fell one thick curd of laughter. "I doubt you've held a gun before."

He was wrong about that.

Olva stood facing him until he set off toward the road.

"We'll find him," Rick called over his shoulder. "I'll get my money."

When he had gotten far enough down the road, Olva ushered us inside. She locked the door and called for Amaryllis, who came bounding down the stairs. Olva embraced the child tightly. She looked into Amaryllis's eyes. "Tonight, we'll have a big family dinner together," Olva told her. "It will be delicious! Your father will be so delighted when he returns." She clapped her hands. "We have work to do!"

After she clapped, one of her hands trembled slightly. We had no way to warn Marcus. He would have to make it home safely on his own.

Windsor chair
Wooden spinning wheel
Mahogany secretary
R. S. Prussia vase
Pie safe—Grandmother DeLour's
Butler's tray (silver plated)
Amsterdam School copper mantel clock
Hamilton drafting table
Letter opener (cut glass)

Tiffany lamp (diameter 16″; 21¾″ height)—~~broken~~ fixed

Victorian chaise longue
Octagonal Jacobean parlor table
Mahogany sewing cabinet
Westclox alarm clock (Big Ben model)
Hepplewhite side table
Watchmaker's workbench
Edwardian neoclassical brass column candleholders (10″ tall)
Abner Cutler rolltop desk (54″ × 21″ × 50″)—damaged

Riding whip—Daddy Kratt's
New York Times (Wednesday, October 30, 1929)
Peacock hat
Edwardian coral cameo (1½″ × 1″)

Highboy bureau
Butterfly tray
Cheval mirror

Glass rabbit
Persian Heriz rug
Revolving mahogany bookstand
Queen Anne chair (dusty rose)
Rococo cherub figurines
Noritake 175 Gold china
Art deco oyster plates

EIGHT

It was nearing Christmas, and I had arrived at the store earlier than usual that morning. There was none of the vibrancy of a typical holiday season. Fewer carols rang through the air, and the warm smell of Christmas—cinnamon, cloves, baked apples—seemed muted. With customers tentative, sales at the store were falling. Yet I could hardly give those problems any attention, because I had my own turmoil to sort out. I had not followed through on my father's orders to assemble a mob against Charlie. As I stared out the third-floor window, putting off my inventory duties, too, the silence was so profound that I thought I could hear ice crystals squeaking past one another as they overtook the glass. Motion below caught my attention.

A few men had gathered outside the store's front door, which was not yet open. I saw Mr. Clark, who owned the local garage and had the wife who would not leave their home. Beside Mr. Clark was Shep Bramlett. His lips still fell apart whenever someone spoke of my sister, even though she had run away from him the morning he had pushed the peacock hat into my hands. The thought made me shiver, and it had nothing to do with the chill in the air. Mr. Burns walked up to join the two men, followed by Mr. Aiken, our pharmacist, and the butcher, Mr. Greeley. I noticed that Mr. Burns kept his distance from

Mr. Greeley. I heard the bolt of the front door open, and I scrambled from my spot to see who had unlatched it.

Peering from the staircase, I saw it was one of Daddy Kratt's loyal boys. This gave me a jolt, as I thought Charlie, sleeping upstairs in the attic, and I were the only two in the store at this predawn hour. The boy, who had black hair that hung over his eyes and an unlit cigarette pressed between his lips, escorted the gentlemen back to Daddy Kratt's office, and when the door opened, I heard my father's gruff voice, which sent another tremor through me. Over the next few minutes, more of Daddy Kratt's trusted business associates streamed through the door.

I had vacillated, and Daddy Kratt had asked one of his boys to get the job done. The mob had been convened.

I leaped from my spot and scuttled up the flight of stairs that led to the fourth floor. From there, I edged through the milliner's office and up the ladder to the attic. Charlie was already up, arranging his tools.

Calm as ever, he said, "How is the inventory going this morning, Miss Judith?"

"Charlie, I have something awful to tell you."

"Go ahead," he said evenly.

"There is a group of men in Daddy Kratt's office, and they are—" I searched for the words.

"I see."

To avoid his gaze, my eyes roved over the space of the attic until they landed on the Tiffany lamp. I thought about Charlie's face when he had fixed it, his pride and his gentle embarrassment over that pride. I thought about Olva and Mama visiting him. An idea shot through my chest.

"Charlie!" I said. "You must work during the day as if everything is normal."

"I must leave," he said.

"No, that will arouse suspicions."

"They will come for me no matter what!" I had never heard him raise his voice.

"Surely they will not come in broad daylight?" I said, bewildered.

Charlie gave a small smile and shook his head, releasing me of my naïveté.

"Do you have anywhere to go?" I asked.

He made no response. Then he angled his head as if something had come to him. "Dee may be able to help. She has connections everywhere. But you are right. If I fly away right now, they will get me."

"I will find out today when the men are"—I paused, unable to get the words out—"coming for you," I said.

He shook his head in despair.

"I *will*, Charlie."

We talked through my plan. Charlie would treat today as an ordinary one, and when he was done with his work, he would gather a few of his things and hide behind the store in the shed, which housed the large farm implements we sold. If the mob planned to come for Charlie that night, I would turn on the Tiffany lamp in the attic, placing it in the window. If he saw that, he would go straight to Dee's.

Charlie agreed, but he didn't seem convinced. "Nothing says they won't come for me during the day."

"It's all I can think of," I admitted.

"I can't ask for more," Charlie said, his voice sounding flat and faraway.

I left Charlie in the attic, and the men dispersed. The store opened as usual. Fearful I might attract attention if I shirked my duties, I scrambled to get my inventory done in time. As I made my way down the third-floor stairs, Quincy reared up in front of me.

"Sister!" he said, pleased he had startled me.

Quincy smiled, sharp and sudden the way an ax greets wood, and I rocked on my feet, nauseated by whatever thought was entertaining him. "I will tell you one thing," he said, moving toward me. I stepped to pass him, but he swung his body in concert with mine, blocking my way. "You are a lot more clever than you look, Sister!" A convulsion of laughter gripped him. When he had recovered, he asked, "Do you remember how those boys would mock you in the schoolyard about your looks?"

To my surprise, he was waiting for my response. "Yes," I said, still uneasy with his demeanor.

"I defended you," he said, more soberly now.

I thought about that. "I suppose you did, Quincy. But I also recall that your defense was to tell them that my face was substantial, like porridge."

Another laugh ripped through him, as if he were yanking the sound out by its roots. "That may be true, but the point is that I tried, Sister. I have never troubled you"—here his face went slack, sending a flutter of worry through my stomach—"and now you have betrayed me."

"How have I betrayed you?" I cried. Quincy was not prone to exaggeration. He honored words in their rawest meaning.

"Daddy Kratt asked you to gather the trusted men of the town," my brother said. "That should have been *my* job, but I will look past that." His jaw tightened. "But then you didn't have the guts to do it, and you asked those stupid boys to do your dirty work rather than asking me."

"I did *not* ask those boys to do it! Daddy Kratt must have. I was putting off the task—and don't think I won't pay for that later!"

Quincy tipped his head from right to left, as if his mind were a scale, weighing my words against the information stored in his head. His gaze leveled.

"If given more time, would you have done it yourself?" he asked. His voice was cold and serious. This was how he would gauge whether I was telling the truth. He wanted to know if, given more time, I would have convened the lynch mob myself.

"Would you have done it?" he repeated. His voice was free from impatience, because he knew he would get his answer.

"Yes."

Quincy paused before nodding. He believed me. He believed me because it was half true. Sometimes, I felt I was two people in one body, the first reaching out for others, and the second holding back because I was no good at sustaining whatever I managed to establish, all my effort spent trying not to offend with my words, which on their way from my mind to my mouth always became sharper. It was like how the cotton gin worked, refining and refining the cotton, and the same thing was constantly happening with my thoughts, except the end product was something too stripped down, too spare for others' ears, too likely to reveal the brittle and bleached-out feeling that resided in me.

"What did Daddy Kratt tell the men?" I asked Quincy. "What reason did he give for punishing Charlie? He didn't—" I held my tongue, not wanting to mention Mama and Charlie's relationship.

Quincy gave a quick sniff. "He told them Charlie had been looking at Mama and some of the other women in an unwholesome way."

"That was all it took?" I said, more to myself than my brother.

Quincy shrugged. "The mob comes tonight for Charlie," he said.

"I wish those men wouldn't do it."

"Don't worry, Sister. They won't."

"What do you mean? How do you know?"

"Because I intend to get to Charlie first," Quincy said.

His eyes were peeled open wider than usual, and I thought I could see further inside them, back into their depths. They seemed to have more dimension than before. He didn't move a millimeter, and I shuddered. Within his full, dark pupils, I had seen an idea lash, like the whip of a tail escaping around a corner, fleeing as swiftly as it had struck. I turned my head away, but it had left a trail inside me as a finger does through ash.

NINE

Olva began dinner preparations right away. She presided over our duties with a fanaticism that was unlike her, as if she could hold the world together with a proper meal. Our hands moved, chopping and measuring and sautéing, but our minds waited anxiously for Marcus's arrival.

At five o'clock, the table was set. It had been arranged with uncommon care. I was surprised to see the good table linens, because I had not heard the linen closet open, which has a hinge that emits a mournful wail. During the preparation—I had to peel some oranges alongside Amaryllis—my head had started to swim, forcing me to retire to my room for a break.

In my room, I filled the time the others spent laboring by rereading an old favorite, Gissing's *The Odd Women.* Characters in books were often easier for me to understand than individuals in real life. When I returned downstairs to the table, I walked around it once, my hands clasped behind my back, and then I turned around and retraced my steps in the other direction. I heard Rosemarie and Amaryllis laughing in the kitchen.

I admired what I saw in front of me. Each plate had been set at an appropriate angle to its cutlery, and the water goblets were stationed at two o'clock above the place settings. Both pudding spoons and cake forks rested above the plates; Olva had really gone all out, because even when we sat at the dining room table for supper, which seldom occurred, our preference being the smaller table tucked in the corner of the kitchen, we rarely ate a formal dessert afterward. But here was the special dessert cutlery, as well as butter spades placed carefully across the bellies of bread plates.

As I continued to stroll around the table, I couldn't help detecting a sense of martial order. The two butter trays, stationed at either end of the table, seemed aimed at one another like tiny silver tanks. It was the first time, too, in which I noticed the significance of the placement of utensils in a proper place setting.

"Olva," I called into the kitchen. "I have a question for you."

"Yes," she said, emerging with a crystal pitcher in hand. (Waterford, one of our very best in the house, with a striking diamond pattern.)

"Why are the knives tucked in closest to the plates?" I asked her.

"I haven't the—"

"Because *that* is the piece of cutlery you want most handy when sitting around a table in forced conversation with your family!"

I was quite pleased with myself, but Olva rewarded my efforts with a frown.

Amaryllis came bursting in from the kitchen. She began playing with one of the crystal saltcellars, pretending it was a tiny hat for her Peter Rabbit. To my surprise, I didn't reprimand her.

Olva brought the salad plates from the kitchen. They were

delicately arranged with Boston bib lettuce and glistening wedges of mandarin oranges. Next, she ferried out a basket with a cream-colored cloth napkin draped across it, and the smell of freshly baked bread washed across the room. Next was the velvet odor of roasting pork, and I knew exactly which dish it was, one we reserved for holidays, a pork loin glazed with orange marmalade. There would be gravy to go with it, made from the pork juices and the marmalade mixed with Dijon mustard. She brought in a covered vegetable dish, and when she left again for the kitchen, I peeked inside to find the delicate limbs of asparagus, livened with flecks of orange zest.

"I like how you've carried the note of citrus through all the courses."

Olva smiled. "And for dessert, one of your favorites. Orange Supreme!"

She certainly knew how to spoil me. Orange Supreme was a concoction of oranges, crushed pineapple, cottage cheese, and whipped cream, and she had been making it for me since we were children.

Rosemarie emerged from the kitchen, and as she did, we heard the side door in the sunroom opening.

"Daddy!" Amaryllis cried, and she shot out of the room.

Moments later, she rounded the corner with Marcus. His face was grave. He exchanged glances with Olva.

"You all right?" she asked, not wanting to say anything around Amaryllis.

"Amaryllis," Marcus said, leaning down. "Please go wash your hands."

The child, pouting, left the room.

"I parked on the north side of the property and walked through the forest. One of Rick's friends was tailing me on my paper route."

Amaryllis sped back into the dining room. No one had a chance to respond to Marcus. Rosemarie and I seated ourselves across from each other at the heads of the table, and in the middle, Olva sat on one side, with Marcus and Amaryllis on the other. We said our grace.

The music of forks and knives clinking carried through the air, and as we passed dishes to one another, our gestures loosened, the threat of Rick and his friends an impossibility at the table Olva had made for us. Amaryllis was especially enjoying the formality of it all. Olva leveled her chin out over the table, and a slow smile grew on her face. She was preparing to speak. But then my sister's voice rose up from one end of the table, interrupting the air that Olva had momentarily reserved for her words. Rosemarie did not seem to notice.

"Oh!" Rosemarie said. "We should have used the zucchini May Irving gave me a few days ago instead of buying the asparagus. I was helping her harvest some vegetables from her garden. We found one zucchini nearly as long as a baseball bat!" She speared one of the mandarin oranges, which trembled on the tines before she slung it into her mouth. She turned to me. "May Irving is related to Randall Clark."

"I know that," I replied. "You are not the expert on Bound now that you have been home not even two months."

"Randall Clark's wife was the one who never left her house," Rosemarie continued, looking past me. "What a sad case. She must have been very lonely."

"Who are you to know what Mrs. Clark felt?" I said, my voice rising. "Perhaps she was comforted by her home. Perhaps she took pleasure in all the things around her."

Rosemarie raised one eyebrow. Then she kept talking as if the world had started turning again just because she had decided it would. "When I first met my husband," she continued, "we had a giant garden. Our zucchini was so monstrous, and I made such a volume of zucchini bread that neither of us could stomach the idea of that vegetable for years afterward."

I took a giant swig of water, which went down the wrong pipe, causing me to cough loudly.

"Are you all right?" Olva asked.

I turned to Rosemarie, my voice thinned out from the coughing attack. "I have never known you to make any kind of bread, let alone zucchini bread."

What I really wanted to say was: *I had no idea you had a husband, you fool.*

"Where is your husband?" Amaryllis asked. Children were very useful creatures.

"He is dead now. Been dead forty-five years. Half a lifetime." She paused, seeming surprised by the bluntness of her own words. "His name was Carl. He was a cotton mill worker his whole life. He was a card hand." She shook her head. "Hard work. Bone hard. Card hands like Carl worked in the picker room." Rosemarie turned to Amaryllis. "The picker room was the first room where bales of ginned cotton were unloaded. The cotton lappers—that's what they were called—cleaned as many leaves and stalks and seeds as they could from the cotton. Then Carl would feed the fibers into the carding machine, which combed out any other debris and formed the cotton into coils of rope called card sliver. Twelve hours a day he would do that. I worked alongside him a few years. I was a secretary in that same mill. The manager hired me on the spot after looking me up and down. My job was much easier than my husband's." She smiled wanly.

Olva was watching my sister gently. Rosemarie returned her gaze, and here was another moment, all too frequent since her return, in which the two of them communicated in silence in a way that made my presence seem cumbersome and unwelcome.

"I met Carl in Rock Hill, right after I left Bound," Rosemarie went on.

This news surprised me. Rock Hill was nearby, and I had assumed my sister had flown as far away as she could those years ago.

"He worked for a long while in the Rock Hill Cotton Factory. It was the first mill in South Carolina to use steam power—did you all know that? It's on the South Carolina historical registry now. It closed in the sixties." Here was Rosemarie, knowing something about something. I was, despite myself, impressed. "The mill's closing was an end to an era. Carl had an uncle on his mama's side who used to work there when it was called Belvedere Mills. Just like his uncle, Carl called it working on the mill hill. He was very proud of his labor."

Rosemarie's face darkened. She shook her head. "Carl and the other workers weren't compensated what they deserved. The cotton dust? Choking! That's how you got brown lung. Some people tried to do something about it—half the textile workers in South Carolina went on strike in 1944. Carl joined them. I was twenty-eight years old when I went down to Honea Path to watch him marching in the picket lines. The police shot him, along with six other textile workers. They called it one of the most violent suppressions of the labor movement. I ran out to Carl on the street when he went down."

Amaryllis took in a quick breath. Her eyes widened.

Rosemarie, noticing her rapt audience, leaned in toward the child. "I was nearly shot myself!"

Amaryllis's mouth fell open. My sister nodded her head solemnly, and I detected the whiff of self-congratulation, which deflated my sympathies. Here was Rosemarie, like always, planting herself in the center of whatever story she told.

She waved her hand to indicate she was moving on. Facing me, she said, "Judith, do you remember how badly Daddy Kratt wanted a mill? He was disappointed that Bound was merely a gin town. He wanted to govern the whole process, from the picked cotton to the production of cloth. Do you remember when we used to go down to the gin together—Daddy Kratt's biggest one? You used to walk several paces in front of me. You always did have a purposeful way about you. We each had our favorite spots in the gin, too. You on the second floor, among the bales of ginned cotton, where you could claim a vantage of the whole operation. And me down among the workers, angling to get a better look at the way they fed the cotton into the stands and following the fiber as the saw teeth took it up and combed it free of seeds. How hard they worked and for such little compensation! When we walked home, you would rhapsodize on how efficient the process was."

Rosemarie made a face to indicate her disapproval. Then,

as abruptly as she had started talking, she stopped. She had uncorked her memories for a few moments but had shoved the plug back in.

Olva looked at her softly. "Now, Rosemarie, pass me your plate, and I will get you a slice of pork." My sister handed her plate over, and she nodded when Olva suggested a second slice with a tilt of her head. Olva got up and traveled around the table to pick up the gravy boat. She approached Rosemarie deferentially from the side. "Let me put a little gravy on your pork," Olva said.

"Olva, sit down!" Rosemarie cried, snatching the serving boat, causing gravy to capsize onto the white table linen. "You don't have to serve me like that!"

Olva let her eyes rest a few moments on the dollops of gravy that were settling on the tablecloth. "Oh," she said, and I could tell she was embarrassed.

Marcus shifted in his seat, and Amaryllis remained quiet, watching the scene. Olva returned to her seat more quickly than she had left it.

Rosemarie set the gravy boat down without pouring any. "I apologize, Olva," my sister said. "It's just that I don't want you to feel as if you need to serve us."

Olva didn't respond. I felt something needed to be said.

"Wasn't it nice of you, Olva, to get out all of Grandmother DeLour's good china? What I mean is that we rarely get to see her things laid out so finely. Can you imagine that Grandmother used to set the table like this every evening?"

"I'm sure she wasn't the one who set it," Rosemarie interjected. "You are nostalgic for the wrong things, Judith."

I felt the old heat between us. Turning to look at my sister squarely, I said, "You come here with all your high and mighty ideas, Rosemarie, when you have no clue as to the arrangements that have suited us for years."

"Arrangements?" my sister said slowly, as if sorting out the meaning of the word.

I opened my mouth to reply but decided against it when I saw a slight grimace on Olva's face. I have sent Olva on hundreds of errands in our lifetime. But since Rosemarie's return, Olva can merely look like she might *think* about doing something for me, and my sister launches an interrogation. All day long, I hear Rosemarie insisting "I'll get that for you, Olva" or "Oh no, Olva, that's not your job" or "Why don't we clean those dishes together, Olva?" and generally making a great fuss over the simplest of household tasks. To my mind, such scrutiny is more condescending than asking Olva to do a few things here and there.

Rosemarie coughed, indicating she was done with me. She turned to Marcus. "I knew Charlie." Nodding at Amaryllis, she said, "Your great-*great*-grandfather."

"That's a lot of greats," Amaryllis said.

"It certainly is. And here's the thing." Rosemarie leaned in toward the child. "Charlie was as near a perfect gentleman as I ever met." She looked at Olva. "And Olva is just as perfect." My sister winked at Amaryllis.

"Now, Rosemarie," Olva said with a small smile.

"It's true," Rosemarie went on. "I never met anyone like you. Willing to care for another person so completely."

The air seemed to shift at the table, and it seemed to be

shifting in my favor. Olva's face was serene, but I could tell she was displeased by my sister's comments. I brought my napkin to my lips. Suddenly, I thought of our old dead uncle Sally, our great-uncle on the DeLour side, who dined with us on special occasions when we were children.

"I have something to share," I said to the table, aiming to steer the conversation in another direction. No one said anything. As there seemed to be no protest, I went on.

Daddy Kratt was a social man, I explained to them. He was social, not in the merry sense of that term, but he was forthcoming enough to allow others to join our supper table. As a matter of fact, we rubbed elbows with all manner of people—far-flung relatives sat alongside newcomers to town whom our father wanted to size up. Once, he invited one of his store employees, a poor fellow, for Thanksgiving supper, and the boy ate with such ravenous intensity that the rest of us lost our appetites.

Rosemarie let out a heavy breath.

I placed my hands in my lap, closed my eyes, and continued my story.

Most often, I said, it was Great-Uncle Sally, one of Mama's uncles. He could always be counted on to show up unannounced for holiday meals. He was an itinerant Presbyterian preacher, and from the looks of his belly, which rode high and firm on his waist, he got around a fair bit to supper tables. Sally had no facial hair (he would have benefited from some), and the thick white hair on his head was parted right down the center and held in place by some kind of pomade. I had decided, from its smell, that it was probably pork lard.

Uncle Sally made an appearance at Easter; the year was 1926, the one when Rosemarie had worn my white dress and I had salted and poisoned all her precious slugs. Here I heard Rosemarie's breath catch. My eyes were still closed, and I pointed my face at her. "That I killed your cat," I said to her, "was an unfortunate and unintended consequence." Rosemarie's chair scraped along the floor, but she did not get up, at least not that my ears could detect. I continued.

When we gathered for that Easter supper, Rosemarie's slugs had already been salted, and if ever a table was set for battle between my sister and me, this was the one. In addition to Rosemarie's hostility, another current of insurrection coursed through the gathering. Aunt Dee had boycotted the meal for reasons the adults would not tell the children, but I had gleaned, from a few gruff and troubled words that had escaped Dee's lips, that she and Mama were having a disagreement over something of consequence. So there it was: more battle lines, drawn by the grown-ups, which we were not to cross. We bristled under the injunction.

Uncle Sally sat at one end of the table. The other was reserved for Daddy Kratt, who would make a fleeting appearance, as he always did, around the time of the main course to consume the contents of his plate while the rest of us picked at our food until he left. We were fine with this arrangement, because had he remained for the entire meal, the supper table would have been a silent and uncomfortable place for us. Even Mama was more animated during family meals when she was alone with us. But Uncle Sally was playing the role of the adult on this occasion, and we went back to having conversations with our eyes. Rosemarie and I were already locked in silent war. I kept reaching my fingers into my crystal saltcellar and catching her eyes as I sprinkled more and more salt on my thickly cut slices of Easter ham. The ham, as I recall, had already been aggressively seasoned before its arrival at the table.

Uncle Sally turned to me and said, "My, Judith"—I was gulping down water—"you are unusually thirsty this day. But a seed must be watered, and it is a blessing to see you children grow before my eyes." This was the way Uncle Sally spoke. Another water pitcher was brought out, mostly for me, and I managed to sneak a smile at Olva as she placed it on the table and returned to the kitchen. Uncle Sally's eyes lingered on her. I didn't think much of it until he announced, as we were finishing our main courses, that he wanted her to join us for dessert. When Sally said this, Quincy's throat let off a little hoot of interest.

Mama's mouth dropped open. "Now, Uncle Sally," she said, and it was the trace of protest in her voice that got everyone's attention. "Olva is quite busy."

Sally seemed genuinely put off by Mama speaking. I was curious.

But anything further was cut short when Sally ordered Mama to leave the table. She did, as if she were a child, giving Olva a look that I'm sure was intended to comfort, but how could it have meant anything when Mama had diminished what little authority she held by walking away without another word?

Olva stood frozen in the doorway to the kitchen. She was thirteen years old.

Sally said, "Let's see," as he surveyed the seating arrangement. The only available chair was Daddy Kratt's empty one at the other head of the table, and you could tell he had already made up his mind that Olva would not be sitting there. "Quincy," he finally said. "Do your uncle Sally a favor and let the young lady have your seat." He motioned for Quincy to take Daddy Kratt's empty chair, and the elation that shot through my brother's eyes did not go unnoticed by the rest of us.

Olva had edged back toward the kitchen, but Sally noticed and boomed, "Young lady, what did I say now?"

She hurried to Quincy's unoccupied seat, avoiding eye contact with us.

As Olva took her seat, Sally folded his arms over his belly. "I have something bothering me today," he said. "I recently received a letter from a fellow scholar. And this ridiculous gentleman believes that our dear Darwin did not in fact coin the phrase *survival of the fittest.*" Sally's belly moved up and down as he laughed noiselessly. You see, Sally was an ardent admirer of Charles Darwin, and Sally spoke about Darwin's adventures on the HMS *Beagle* with the devotion and giddiness of a young boy.

We settled into our chairs for a lecture from Uncle Sally. But then Quincy piped up. "Who said it, then?" my brother asked. "Who said 'survival of the fittest'?"

Sally cleared his throat and turned away from Quincy as he said, "This fellow scholar of mine—well, I can't stomach calling him a scholar any longer—believes it was Herbert Spencer or some other chap. It hardly matters. Everyone knows it's

Darwin's phrase, and the idea is his crowning glory of scholarship." Here, Sally threw his arms open in an ecstatic gesture and cried, "The survival of the fittest!"

It was a phrase Sally was fond of repeating, always with the same amount of enthusiasm. This time, it proved too much for Quincy, who could not suppress his laughter. I shot my brother a stern look, but it only seemed to encourage him.

Quincy turned to Sally. "You say that so frequently, Uncle Sally, I think you ought to put it on your tombstone!" Another chuckle moved through my brother, which graduated to an onslaught of laughter. He was considering, I suppose, how the power of the phrase might be diminished on a grave marker.

Here, I paused my story, and though my eyes were still closed, I could feel everyone around the table listening. I did not tell them I remembered feeling sorry for Sally. He was a bore, of course, but a loyal bore. For him, Darwin's beliefs structured the world, and I could understand that craving for orderliness. There it was, deep in my bones, too.

Quincy's laughter died down, and Sally's eyes flickered a little, not quite a blink, as if he were resetting the scene in front of him. "Perhaps," Sally said calmly, "we should revisit one of our earlier lessons about Darwin." He then launched into a typical sermon about *the undesirables* and *God's chosen* and *productive attrition*. His voice took on a tone somewhere between scholarly and threatening, which was meant to stifle further interruptions.

But Quincy was not deterred. "Sally," my brother continued, not waiting for a natural pause in our great-uncle's speech. "I still don't understand."

Sally cleared his throat and kept going, ignoring Quincy's intrusion. "You see," Sally said, "the goal of natural selection is that, as a society, we move toward a more perfect version of our species. It is certainly a struggle. But we are up for it, I do believe." Here he leaned in closer to the table, an attempt at intimacy, but his belly stopped him. He leaned back again, his face souring. "As time moves along," he continued, "we begin to learn which traits are preferred for the most perfect form of humankind." This idea put him back in good humor, and he heaved his belly into a great laugh. "We just keep learning! It is a felicitous time to be a scholar!"

Quincy broke in. "I'm not sure you've got your facts straight, Uncle. Have you seen our henhouse?" Sally sighed, but Quincy spoke quickly. "You might recall, Uncle Sally, that the henhouse gate was once constructed from a wood frame and wire mesh. It had a broken latch and a chain holding it shut." Quincy cracked his knuckles and leaned in. My brother always told vivid stories, and with the exception of Uncle Sally, we were already hooked. "Well, one year, we had some thickset foxes mixed in among the lean ones," Quincy said. "Those critters were so hefty, they could just put their weight against the gate and force an opening for themselves each time they wanted to enter the henhouse. As you can imagine, they enjoyed quite a feast that season. And the lean foxes? They didn't have the heft to push the gate open, you see. They got skinnier and skinnier. Now here's the funny thing. The next year, Daddy Kratt fixed the gate. He did a fine job. The latch held firm, and only a narrow gap remained between the gate and its frame. I didn't think much of that gap at the time. Then

I started to see something that made me laugh. All those hefty foxes pushed and pushed against the gate, which didn't budge. They finally gave up and wandered away. But what do you think those skinny foxes did? They squeezed right through that gap!" Quincy reared back and clapped his hands. The sound punctured the air. "And which kind of fox do you think starved *that* year?"

My brother turned to Sally, as if our great-uncle were a child, and said, "Uncle, it was the fat foxes that starved."

Sally readjusted himself awkwardly in his chair, his belly prodding against the edge of the table.

Quincy paused before landing his final blow. "So tell me this, Uncle: Which fox—large or lean—is the perfect one? Seems to me, if you're a fox, it all depends on what kind of gate you find yourself in front of." Quincy leaned back in his seat and, finding a toothpick on the table, began working his gums as he watched Uncle Sally's reaction.

Sally was sweating profusely. But rather than counterattack Quincy, which my brother eagerly awaited, Uncle Sally sharpened his attention on Olva.

"I have a question for you, young lady," Sally said, the varnish of his false politeness wearing off. "Have you heard of Sir Francis Galton?" Olva replied that no, she hadn't, and Sally said, "I didn't expect as much. No matter. There is always time to learn." Sally explained that Galton was Darwin's cousin and that *Origin of Species* was a thunderbolt—*the* thunderbolt—of his life. After reading his cousin's book, Galton became obsessed with variations in human populations.

"I have been reading Galton's lectures," Sally continued,

"beginning with his Huxley lecture at the Royal Anthropological Institute in 1901. You have heard of Aldous Huxley?" Sally shook his head before letting Olva answer. "Of course not, but that's not relevant at the moment. Suffice it to say, Galton gave the second annual Huxley lecture, which was intended to commemorate the scholar. You see, Galton was very interested in talent and character—things a gentleman should be interested in—but what made him a *gentleman scholar*"—here Quincy snorted—"is that he cared that those traits be passed down, and he became very interested in how we might determine a hereditary basis for them. Which amounts to a philanthropic endeavor, if you see it as I do."

As Uncle Sally droned on, he was staring at Olva the whole time. I took a deep breath, and, to distract Sally, I bolted from the table. During my flight, I cast my eyes back (unlike Lot's wife, I was already a pillar of salt) and caught a glimpse of Rosemarie's bewildered face, for she wasn't accustomed to being the one left behind. I can tell you that this pleased me even more than salting her slugs. I didn't dare return to the table, staying in my room until my door cracked open and Olva's head peeped in to thank me. I had sufficiently diverted Sally—his nerves already jangled from Quincy's story—and our great-uncle had to remove himself from the table before finishing his speech.

I was done with my story about Uncle Sally. I opened my eyes at the table. The four of them were staring at me. They did not look as transported as I thought they might be.

"Were you listening?" I asked.

"I almost forgot you were there, Judith," my sister said

tartly. "You blend into that chair. It's as if you're a piece of furniture yourself."

"If you think that is an insult, you are mistaken," I replied.

"I remember the meal with Sally," Olva said.

Amaryllis raised her hand.

"Are you raising your hand because you want to say something?" I asked.

She nodded.

"Well, go ahead."

"I think you left the table because you had to pee," she said. "After drinking all that water because your ham was so salty."

The heat rose to my face. Rosemarie let out a peal of unbridled laughter.

Marcus and Olva were smiling, too. All four of them were baring their bright teeth at me. I pushed my chair back and got up from the table. They could find me in my room if they needed me.

Once I was in my bedroom, having abandoned the supper table, I was struck by another memory of Uncle Sally.

The next Christmas, the year after Quincy embarrassed Sally, Mama mentioned to Daddy Kratt that she thought one of her *other* uncles had been in possession of a first edition of *Origin of Species*. We were rife with great-uncles. Poor Grandfather DeLour had five brothers yet could not sire a son of his own. Most of his brothers had died young—Uncle Sally was the exception—and this was part of the reason many of the family heirlooms had found their way to our house.

Daddy Kratt was not a bookish man, but he sensed when something of value was at hand. "Is it here, in the house?" he asked Mama. The two of them were standing in front of the dining room table. Olva moved silently behind them, clearing the leftovers of our Christmas meal.

"Perhaps," she whispered.

Daddy Kratt's eyes fired, and I had the sense it wasn't the book that interested him. Rather, it was beating Uncle Sally to it. I had seen Sally run his hand across a shelf of books in our study like he was a boy trailing a stick along a fence. Books were a solace to me, too, and part of me felt that if we *did* have the edition, we should give it to Sally. But Daddy Kratt could not pass up a competition.

After our Christmas meal, Daddy Kratt assembled all the children in front of the stairs, and we hoped it was a prelude to something other than a beating. I had recently turned thirteen, and my siblings were on my heels, yet our father could inspire the same fear as when we were children. This time, Mama was there, lined up as if she were one of us.

We were relieved when our father seemed to be thinking not so much about us as the house. He angled his head in mental calculation. I suppose he was trying to assess the locations of all the bookshelves and stacks of books, a task I didn't envy, because in our house, books consumed every shelf, gently edging out other items that might vie for space, such as a vase or bowl. All hand-me-downs from the DeLour library, these books huddled in every nook and cranny, and stacks of them seemed to crop up around every corner, places you swore had been empty the previous day. Most of their covers were brown and worn, soft as fur, and I once saw Olva approach a stack as if careful not to startle them.

When Daddy Kratt was done thinking, he wheeled his head toward us, sending a tremor through the line. He seemed less resolute than normal, and he shook his head as if dissatisfied with the progress of his thoughts. Then his head snapped up. He had decided.

"Bring in Olva."

Mama was standing beside me, and she took in such a swift and tight breath that it seemed to momentarily lift her off the ground. No one moved to take the order. Daddy Kratt coughed, sharp as a gunshot, which roused us from our positions like we were runners at a starting line. Rosemarie dashed upstairs, Quincy melted off to one side of the room, and I rushed into the kitchen to fetch Olva. Daddy Kratt saw us dispersing, and his face weighed the situation and then allowed it.

As I left the room, I heard Mama say to him, "I will help her."

I turned to see Daddy Kratt's face, which had settled into a relaxed expression, heave up again. He boomed, "You will *not*!" and Mama, pushed backward by the force of his words, drifted over by the sofa.

I returned with Olva, who was twisting a dishrag in her hands. Daddy Kratt flicked his finger at Quincy, who had remained in the room, to indicate that he should explain Olva's assignment. Quincy nodded, apparently understanding everything that was about to happen.

Daddy Kratt left the room, and Mama knew she should follow him. I watched Quincy explain to Olva how, at the whim of our father, her plans had changed for the evening. Searching for a book wouldn't have seemed such a terrible task, but as Daddy Kratt's deed, it took on a worrisome heaviness.

Standing there, what most puzzled me was why he hadn't ordered all of us to look for it. Surely five sets of eyes were better than Olva's one?

Yet perhaps he didn't see it as punishment, and he was loath to bring us pleasure. We were all rather bookish, with the exception of Quincy, who favored comics, but even he had taken a shine to the essays of Walter Pater for a period. Rosemarie had the talent for finding the most salacious romances in the house, and *Lady Audley's Secret* seemed to be a perennial favorite. As for me, I read widely and voraciously, and while the essays of Ruskin offered me constancy and the poems of Tennyson succor, at that moment, I was taken by a novella by Edith Wharton titled *Bunner Sisters*, probably brought to our house by Aunt Dee, which detailed the lives of two sisters who kept a shop together. In Wharton's book, the unmarried older sister, Ann Eliza, makes extraordinary sacrifices for her younger sister, Evelina, but these sacrifices lead only to the suffering and fundamental loneliness of Ann Eliza. I found the lesson bleak but reassuringly clear-eyed.

The next morning, I woke up and came downstairs to an empty kitchen. I knew the rest of the family was still upstairs sleeping, which gave me time for a short morning walk. Our house was so big that there wasn't any need to go outside. After I had ambled through the sunroom and back through the living room to the study, I took the long route through the main level bathroom and bedroom to access the back hallway.

My plan was to head down into the cellar. As I descended the stairs, I was taken aback. There was Olva. She was crouched in front of a stack of books, her back to me, and her hand was slowly tracing the spines from top to bottom. I took a further step to get a better view, and when I did, I saw Mama. She was in an identical position, crouching beside another stack.

Then it occurred to me. They must have searched straight through the night.

I crept back up two sets of stairs to my own bedroom, where I retreated beneath the covers. As I lay there, what preoccupied me was a fear for Mama. I didn't know why she had chosen to help Olva against Daddy Kratt's orders, and that kind of defiance did not correspond with what I knew of my mother. It unsettled me, and I stayed in bed until the warm breath of biscuits made its way to my room.

A rap on my bedroom door startled me from my memory.

"I am fine as I am," I called through the door.

Silence.

"I will come out in my own time!"

Silence. Another rap.

"Good grief!" I said, lifting myself from my chair and striding toward the door. I slung the door open, terribly vexed, and, when I looked out, saw nothing beyond the stale air of the hallway. A small hand emerged from the right. It was Amaryllis, holding her arm up.

"What *is* it, Amaryllis? You needn't raise your hand every time you have a question."

She composed herself, and I wondered what kind of message those cowardly adults had sent her to convey. "I'm sorry I said *pee* around the supper table," she said with great effort.

"Ah now, no matter. Perhaps you are right about why I left Sally's dinner table."

She peered at me, considering whether she should agree.

"Will you come back?" she asked. "We still have dessert." She smiled at me, and her face was like a brisk change of weather.

I returned to the table with her. The three of them were still there, locked in silence. I could tell, in the way Rosemarie's eyes were animating, that she was preparing to speak again. Olva sat braced. No one had been pleased with my story about Sally, but Rosemarie's earlier words about Charlie had made both Olva and Marcus uncomfortable. My eyes met Olva's, and we shared a moment of exhaustion over my sister. A smile hovered at my lips, and I felt the warmth of Olva's attention. These exchanges had been rare since Rosemarie's arrival. How I had relied on them and not known it!

Rosemarie turned to Marcus. "Did you know that Charlie was an accomplished mechanic?"

"I believe the skill has been in my family for generations," he replied.

Olva shifted in her seat. Rosemarie nodded, impressed, it seemed, at Marcus's knowledge of his own kin.

"Marcus," I said, "have you thought of putting those talents to use at the new plant in Spartanburg? The car manufacturing plant, I mean."

"I don't know that I have the skills needed," he said.

"You certainly do," Olva replied.

Marcus smiled at her.

Ignoring this exchange, Rosemarie said, "Marcus, I would watch Charlie repairing the elevator at the store. And do you know what my vantage point was? The majestic oak that abuts the store's east wall and offers lines of sight into nearly every window on that side of the store. I found a way to climb from the third floor out onto the tree. It was my secret getaway when Shep Bramlett would pursue me through the store." She paused for a moment. "But I was so fond of Charlie that I showed him my escape route one day."

"Marcus," I said, "is the Spartanburg plant hiring?"

"Marcus," Rosemarie said, raising her voice, "Charlie was the most talented mechanic I ever knew."

"Marcus," I said, "Olva said she ran into the granddaughter of Sterling Ray at the post office the other day. The girl mentioned they have some connection to that company. I could look into it for you."

"Marcus," Rosemarie said, and in her pause, a heartbeat of a pause, I knew what was coming. "Marcus, did you know I left town when my brother Quincy was killed?"

A silence, like wet snow, drifted across the table. Marcus lifted his water glass and stared into it as he drank.

"Do you know why I didn't come back?" Rosemarie continued. "Because I found out Charlie had been accused, that's why."

I waited. My sister had come back home after all these years to say one final thing, and I waited for it. Her face ordered itself into a single purpose, her eyes trained on me, her mouth a thin line of concentration.

"Marcus, Judith killed Quincy. She killed him, and your great-grandfather took the blame for it."

Amaryllis sat rigidly, her hand that clutched the glass rabbit resting on the table. Marcus reached over and placed his hand atop hers, and her posture softened with his touch.

Olva lowered her eyelids as if shutting her eyes would close her ears.

Ancient angers stirred within me. I felt my lungs open up like wings and then fold back down again. I took in a sustaining mouthful of air. "Much ado is made of people like you, Rosemarie, who escape the life they have been given, who refuse to look back as they tear off to explore the great wide yonder. Such a thing has never impressed me. From where I'm sitting, it takes more backbone to stay put and face the known. Daddy Kratt always said, 'Root, hog, or die!' Do you remember that? Meaning he was a survivor, like hogs set loose to fend for themselves." I turned to Marcus. "We never had hogs. It's just an expression."

Marcus stood up from his chair. "Amaryllis," he said. "Let's get your bath ready." There was less recrimination in his voice than weariness. He looked drained, as if he'd been sitting at this table his whole life.

"Don't leave, Marcus," Rosemarie said. "It's Judith who should leave."

He tapped Amaryllis's shoulder.

"No!" she cried willfully, gripping her chair. She appeared overstimulated and exhausted at the same time. "I am not done with my dessert!"

"Let her stay," Rosemarie intervened. "Olva has some news."

We all turned to Olva, whose eyes were still closed.

Olva shook her head slowly. When it was clear she would not speak, Rosemarie said, "My dear Amaryllis, you and Olva are related!"

The child dashed from her chair. "Are you my grandma?" She stood beside Olva's chair, popping up and down on her toes.

Olva's eyes opened and fell warmly on Amaryllis. "I was going to tell you on my own."

"Can I call you Grandma?"

"You may call me whatever you like," Olva told Amaryllis.

"Olva is your great-great-aunt," Rosemarie explained. "She and your great-grandfather were siblings. His name was Samuel. And Samuel's father was Charlie. I do believe I'm right in saying that Samuel's mother died in childbirth." Rosemarie turned to Olva for confirmation, but Olva would not look at her.

"Charlie!" Amaryllis said. She recognized the name. "Where is he? I want to meet him." There was such a wanting in her voice. "I don't have anybody but Daddy."

On Olva's face converged a string of emotions I could not place. She appeared to want to say more to Amaryllis, but she merely shook her head, as if convincing herself to slow down whatever thoughts were in her mind.

My sister, not noticing Olva's internal dispute, filled in the silence. "Olva and Samuel were *half siblings*," Rosemarie clarified. "They shared Charlie as a father, but the fact is that we don't know yet who Olva's mother is."

A laugh flew from my lips. "It's a good thing you don't know all the family secrets, Rosemarie. Otherwise, they would not be secrets."

Rosemarie turned to Olva. "What does she mean?"

Before Olva had a chance to respond, a knock on the front door bit through the air. Amaryllis shot up from her chair and said merrily, "I'll get it!"

We all cried "No!" at once, and the weight of the rebuff pressed the child back into her seat, where she drew her hands to her face and began sobbing. Marcus placed his hand gently on her back and then gathered her into his arms.

"I'm the one they are looking for," Marcus said, beginning to lower Amaryllis back into her chair. The child locked her arms around his neck, holding him to the spot.

"I will do it," Rosemarie said, pushing her chair back and throwing her napkin on her plate.

"Why do we have to answer it?" I asked.

"I will go with you," Olva said.

I reluctantly followed the two of them toward the front of the house. The three of us stood in front of the door for a moment. I eyed my cane, propped next to the door. Rosemarie placed her hand on the doorknob and pulled the door open in one swift, confident movement. We greeted nothing but the porch light, harsh and moth-beaten, which blinded us to what lay beyond.

"Goddammit!" Rosemarie yelled, and she leaned her head through the doorway. "Rick! We know you're there! You have no business here!"

Olva pulled Rosemarie back inside and locked the door. Noticing the windows in the living room, Olva drew the curtains. The darkness on the other side of the glass seemed alive and agitated, and I was grateful to have it concealed.

"I threatened him," Olva said.

"He deserved it," Rosemarie said.

Marcus moved into the room carrying Amaryllis. He deposited her on the sofa—our pale-gray Louis XV with silver leaf finish—and I saw that she carried with her a spoon mounded with Orange Supreme. She lay down on the sofa, sticking the spoon in her mouth at the same time, and a dollop of whipped cream fell onto the upholstery.

"Amaryllis! Look what you're doing!" I cried.

"Leave the child alone," Rosemarie snapped at me. "You are ludicrous to be fretting about a sofa at a time like this."

"Your compassion is as fickle as you are, isn't it?" I said to my sister. "You take up whatever crusade strikes you at the moment, and then you flit away when you're not the center of it any longer."

Rosemarie aimed her face at me. "At least I'm not the one who called Jolly to let her know where Marcus was."

Air shot past Olva's lips. Her hand moved to her throat, and she fidgeted with her collar. As she did, Mama's double-sided cameo came into view on her neck. The coral and gold shone brightly against her skin, and I saw that the image of the goddess Athena faced outward. Olva followed my eyes, and when she saw what I was looking at, a dead smile rose to her lips. She reached around her neck and unclasped the necklace, thrusting it toward me. "Take it!" She looked at me with such intensity, I thought she might hand over her eyes. She laid the cameo in my palm. I glanced down. The god Ares was staring back at me.

"This cameo will be suitable for my inventory," I said, casting around for anything to say. "It's a good thing my memory has not yet faded. I can recall all the stories about our heirlooms."

"You have kept your mind sharp, Judith," Olva said coldly, as if I had kept it that way expressly to have something with which to poke people. "I'm heading to bed." She glared at me. "You can draw your own bath."

Windsor chair
Wooden spinning wheel
Mahogany secretary
R. S. Prussia vase
Pie safe—Grandmother DeLour's
Butler's tray (silver plated)
Amsterdam School copper mantel clock
Hamilton drafting table
Letter opener (cut glass)

Tiffany lamp (diameter 16″; 21¾″ height)—~~broken~~ fixed

Victorian chaise longue
Octagonal Jacobean parlor table
Mahogany sewing cabinet
Westclox alarm clock (Big Ben model)
Hepplewhite side table
Watchmaker's workbench
Edwardian neoclassical brass column candleholders (10″ tall)
Abner Cutler rolltop desk (54″ × 21″ × 50″)—damaged

Riding whip—Daddy Kratt's
New York Times (Wednesday, October 30, 1929)
Peacock hat
Edwardian coral cameo (1½″ × 1″)

Highboy bureau
Butterfly tray
Cheval mirror

Glass rabbit
Persian Heriz rug
Revolving mahogany bookstand
Queen Anne chair (dusty rose)

Rococo cherub figurines
Noritake 175 Gold china
Art deco oyster plates

Silver cutlery
Waterford crystal pitcher
Crystal saltcellars
Louis XV sofa (silver leaf details)

TEN

I knew Charlie would wait patiently for my signal. He would be freezing in the shed behind the store, but I knew he would wait there. When I turned on the Tiffany lamp, he would head straight for Aunt Dee's. I needed to keep him a step ahead of both the mob and my brother.

I was the last one remaining in the store. Through the windows, the evening wind shook the branches of an ancient oak, and a few snowflakes struggled through the air. Before I locked up, the mannequins with their pursed mouths watched me creep through the millinery shop to get to Charlie's attic. I moved quietly toward the Tiffany lamp, and with the least fanfare I could muster, turned the three key switches. Light sang out of the bulbs. I stood looking, spellbound, until I remembered my duties.

Retracing my steps, I completed all the procedures for shutting down the store. Empty of people, the building had noises of its own: creaks and rattles and even a screech that sounded like a chair being pushed back from a desk. I stepped out into the cold to bolt and padlock the final door at the back of the store. I didn't dare check on Charlie in the shed—perhaps he had already fled—but stole a glance up at the Tiffany lamp blazing in the attic window.

Just as I was about to withdraw my gaze, the light in the window extinguished. I froze, my breath drawing in sharply. I studied the shed in the distance, but it was too far to determine if Charlie was there or not. Perhaps he had gone. It seemed possible. Yet the thought nagged at my mind. I decided I would go back into the store and turn on the lamp again.

Steeling myself, I unlocked the back door and tiptoed through the darkened aisles of the first floor. As I made my way up two flights of stairs, the sky tipped into full darkness outside, and through one of the large windows on the third floor, the moon cast pools of light at my feet. I was moving rapidly, hoping to avoid whomever had turned off the light, and when I stepped into the millinery shop, I gasped as one of the mannequins, turned into a gruff giant by the strength of the moonlight, wheeled at me. I screamed.

"Judith!" The voice was irritated, full of horsehair. "Shut your mouth, girl."

"Daddy Kratt!" I cried. "I thought I was the last one in the store. I had already locked up."

"You left a light on." I could tell he was studying me in the dark.

"Did I?"

"I see that Charlie fixed that lamp already."

"Oh, I suppose he did." My chest felt tight. I sipped air carefully through my mouth.

"And where is Charlie? He isn't in the attic."

I scrambled for something to say. My heart slammed against the front of my chest. I was taking too long to answer, and my father moved toward me.

"Well, he can't be too far, can he?" Daddy Kratt said, his face approaching mine. His beard was close to me. A heat seemed to come off it, and its acrid odor stung my nose.

I had sent Charlie to the shed. Had that been a mistake?

"Help me lock up."

"Yessir."

Leaving, I cast one final glance back into the millinery shop. It took all my strength of mind not to cry out. Our eyes met. It was Charlie, standing behind the mannequins, just as Quincy had when I caught him spying. I heard Daddy Kratt's footsteps moving down the stairs outside the shop.

"Charlie!" I whispered. "What are you doing here?"

"I saw the light go off," he said, his voice barely above a breath. "I saw you go back inside the store. I was worried for you."

What he had risked for me! "Stay here, Charlie," I said. "After we lock up, I will come back and get you."

Heart still jangling in my chest, my feet carried me out the door and down the third-floor flight of stairs. I heard Daddy Kratt's leaden steps echoing in the store, but then I lost track of them. Suddenly, I heard footsteps above me. Either they were Charlie's or Daddy Kratt had circled back around and ascended the side staircase.

A great commotion let loose: a crash and a cavalry of footsteps thundering in the wake of that noise. I leaped onto the stairs again, racing up to the millinery shop. I saw Charlie dart across the third floor. On his heels was Daddy Kratt. Charlie ran toward the elevator, which was broken. He would be cornered, unless he intended to barricade himself inside it.

When Charlie approached the elevator, he hurled open its

front door, jumped inside, and crashed shut the grated sliding door. The front door closed before Daddy Kratt could reach it, and my sight line was such that I could see Charlie's stricken face through the door's round window. To my amazement, the elevator heaved into motion. Charlie had fixed it! His face drifted down until it disappeared.

Daddy Kratt stopped, assessing the situation, before turning on his heels and striding past me. As he did, he nodded his head to indicate I should follow him. He expected me to help.

He lumbered down the stairs, intending to be there when the elevator door reached its conclusion. He was betting on the first floor, but he couldn't be sure. Between the third and second floors, the store swallowed the elevator from view. This occurred to Daddy Kratt, and once we reached the second floor, he whirled around and jabbed his finger toward the northeast corner, where the elevator might deposit Charlie. I was in charge of heading Charlie off there, and Daddy Kratt would continue down to the first floor.

As I waited in front of the elevator door, my arm sought the wall for steadiness, as if I'd stepped aboard a dinghy during a squall. A mechanical sound grinded cruelly. Would the elevator land in front of me? Even if Charlie wanted to redirect it back to the third floor, it would have to register a stop at either the first or second floors. If it stopped at the first, Daddy Kratt would apprehend Charlie. But what if it stopped at mine?

The elevator's noises amplified, sharp noises buried in the walls, as if the machine were arguing with itself. Then Charlie's face flashed through the small round window. I heard the sliding door clang open. It was only a beat of time, how long it takes for a moth to flap its homely wings once, but it was long enough for Charlie to lock eyes with me. His stricken face had been replaced with another expression. It was permission.

I looked up at the ceiling, where the beige paint was peeling, then down at my scuffed winter overshoes. I looked anywhere but at Charlie.

"Daddy Kratt!"

The force of my voice rocketed Charlie into motion. He flew past me, hesitated a moment on the landing, before deciding to head up the stairs to the third floor. When Daddy Kratt reached me, he was not alone. Flanking him were Mr. Burns and Mr. Aiken. At the sight of Mr. Aiken, I thought of Dovey. And where was Quincy? I hadn't seen him since he had vowed to catch Charlie himself. Then I heard Shep Bramlett call out below us, asking for our whereabouts.

"Cover the first floor!" my father yelled back to him. He turned to me. "Which way did he go?"

I swallowed, pointing back into the recesses of the second floor, the opposite direction of Charlie's flight path. Daddy Kratt nodded at me. Looking at Mr. Burns and Mr. Aiken, he said, "Just in case he sneaks back up, go to the third and fourth floors. Don't forget the attic." Then my father plunged toward the darkened aisles of merchandise—groceries, drugs, and feed—where I had directed him.

Suddenly, I was alone. Daddy Kratt had not given me a task, which filled me with apprehension. I decided, lacking further instruction, I would wait, which proved more agitating than participating in Charlie's capture. The voices of the men ricocheted through the store.

I stepped to the closest window on the east side of the store and peered out. Snow blew nomadically through the air, refusing to land on the ground but instead taking refuge on spartan, sturdy limbs of the oak that grew alongside the store. I tried to focus on the tree, grounded amid the snow staggering around it, so that I wouldn't hear the frenzied voices of Charlie's pursuers.

As I studied the tree, the limb closest to the building began to shake. I gasped. It was Charlie, climbing onto the tree from a third-floor window. His bare hands found snow-laden anchor points, and he prudently made his way down the tree. From the base of its trunk, he sprinted northward, toward the train depot and out of sight.

I pressed my eyes shut. My palms were damp with fear. I wondered if escape would be possible for him.

The next morning, Daddy Kratt summoned Quincy and me to his office. The room smelled of soap and tobacco. Our father was reviewing the store's main ledger when we arrived, and we stood just inside the door and waited for him to finish his work. The ledger was leather-bound and nearly large enough to swallow the desk. It was handsome and had cost a sum significant enough to warrant a line item in the ledger itself. Daddy Kratt's head stooped over the page in front of him, his large square thumb tracking down a list. The ledger was so stately looking, with its gold-edged pages, that next to it, our father appeared underdressed. He lacked refinement next to something so dignified.

Daddy Kratt finally looked up. He sniffed loudly, reached

into his vest pocket for a handkerchief—splotched with oil—and blew his nose. I worried about what would come next. I had been the last one to see Charlie, the last one within arm's reach before he vanished. But our father shot his gaze toward Quincy.

"Boy!" Daddy Kratt said unceremoniously. "Where were you last night? You're the one supposed to be everywhere and know everything."

Quincy didn't speak. He was struggling to keep emotion out of his face. I saw his frustration rising, but there was something else behind it, which was bringing color into his pale cheeks. Suddenly, his mouth opened, and a little breath escaped from it. It was a momentary lapse, and Quincy pulled his shoulders back and set his face to stone again. But in those few seconds, I saw that it was intense embarrassment. He had been with Dovey that night.

Daddy Kratt didn't take his eyes off Quincy. "Wherever you were, you weren't where you should've been. I'd say it's your fault we didn't catch him."

Now it was my turn to conceal my emotions. What Daddy Kratt had said was unfair to Quincy, but relief flooded my body, and I swayed on my feet. I dug my fingernails into my palms to bring myself around. Against all odds, Charlie had not been found in the night.

"I apologize, sir," Quincy responded. It beleaguered my brother, I could tell, to be blamed for something he hadn't been asked to handle in the first place. Quincy's shoulders slumped; the weight of Daddy Kratt's disappointment was profound. "I have a solution."

"And what's that?" Daddy Kratt asked. He was interested, if unconvinced.

"I will find him," Quincy said simply.

Daddy Kratt spat into his handkerchief, as if ridding himself of the taste of his own mouth. "How's it you're going to succeed at something you already failed at?"

"Give me one more chance," Quincy said.

Daddy Kratt paused before nodding his head slowly. I rocked on my heels; this was a rare concession from our father. He surprised us again by walking over to his gun case and reaching into his inner vest pocket to produce a key. I was certain my brother's jaw was clenched like mine as Daddy Kratt opened the case and pulled out a shotgun.

Immediately, I could tell it was his Purdey shotgun (side-by-side barrel at 29 inches). The Purdey brand was an old and reputable gun manufacturer. It had origins in England, and I had once heard that Queen Victoria herself bought a pair of Purdey pistols when she was nineteen, which told me volumes about her understanding of self-reliance, even though she had people watching over her all hours of the day and night. Perhaps she thought the purchase wise *because* she had people watching over her all hours of the day and night. Having Quincy as a brother, I could understand that perspective.

Daddy Kratt held up the shotgun for us to admire. It was a handsome specimen with a body of steel and a lacquered oak handle, and it was among the first items he bought to reward himself when his cotton business began to take off.

Stepping forward, Daddy Kratt thrust the Purdey into the hands of his fourteen-year-old son.

Quincy accepted it with a look of terror and thrill.

"Find him," Daddy Kratt said. "Finish it."

Windsor chair
Wooden spinning wheel
Mahogany secretary
R. S. Prussia vase
Pie safe—Grandmother DeLour's
Butler's tray (silver plated)
Amsterdam School copper mantel clock
Hamilton drafting table
Letter opener (cut glass)

Tiffany lamp (diameter 16″; 21¾″ height)—~~broken~~ fixed

Victorian chaise longue
Octagonal Jacobean parlor table
Mahogany sewing cabinet
Westclox alarm clock (Big Ben model)
Hepplewhite side table
Watchmaker's workbench
Edwardian neoclassical brass column candleholders (10″ tall)
Abner Cutler rolltop desk (54″ × 21″ × 50″)—damaged

Riding whip—Daddy Kratt's
New York Times (Wednesday, October 30, 1929)
Peacock hat
Edwardian coral cameo (1½″ × 1″)

Highboy bureau
Butterfly tray
Cheval mirror

Glass rabbit
Persian Heriz rug
Revolving mahogany bookstand
Queen Anne chair (dusty rose)

Rococo cherub figurines
Noritake 175 Gold china
Art deco oyster plates

Silver cutlery
Waterford crystal pitcher
Crystal saltcellars
Louis XV sofa (silver leaf details)

Leather ledger book
Purdey shotgun (barrel 29″)

ELEVEN

The morning after our disastrous dinner, I awoke to Amaryllis's voice. It sounded far away. I made my way down the stairs to find the front door open, heat rolling inside and sticking to everything. The child's voice again, from the yard. I braced, wondering what might be happening. Amaryllis shot through the doorway. When she saw me, her eyes widened.

I wanted to ask her where Olva was, but my throat felt parched, a dry highway from my mouth to my gullet. I wondered if Olva would ever forgive me for calling Jolly about Marcus.

"She is awake!" Amaryllis yelled at the top of her lungs. Responses rang from beyond the door. Everyone was outside.

As I stepped through the doorway onto the porch, in the shock of sunlight, I saw Rosemarie and Marcus affixing a giant bedsheet between two windows. The sheet, which they must have pilfered from the upstairs linen closet, covered part of the brick facade of the house.

"What in the world?" I said, moving toward the sheet.

"Do not take it down," Rosemarie barked at me.

"I don't even know what it is!"

"Now, ladies," Olva said wearily. Her eyes avoided mine.

When Marcus and Rosemarie finished with the sheet, they

stepped back through the bushes to appraise their work. No look of satisfaction crossed their faces.

I walked over to the sheet to examine it. No one said two words to me, but I felt the heat of Rosemarie's disapproval on the back of my neck. The edges of the bedsheet were secured to the brick lips of adjacent windows by the weight of two sturdy rocks. I gingerly placed a foot in the flower bed, between two Indian hawthorn bushes, and reached up to lift one edge of the sheet. When I peeked on the other side, I let out a gasp. Spray-painted on the sandy yellow brick of the house was a phrase.

Nigger lover.

"Who did this?"

"Who do you think?" Rosemarie said. "The Bramletts are a scourge."

I had to sit down. My head sloshed, and a flavor, like some bitter new herb, coated the inside of my mouth. I made my way to the porch, where I pressed my back into the porch chair, dumbstruck. This house was built in 1922! Sixty-seven years had passed with it standing as a monument to this town's birth and growth. Nothing like this had ever happened to me. Who would we contact about repairing the damage? Could it be repaired?

Amaryllis was suddenly peering into my face. "Are you okay?" I squeezed my eyes shut. She leaned in closer and whispered, "What does it say under the sheet?"

Before I had a chance to speak, I heard "Move inside!" from Olva, calling firmly and evenly. "Move inside now!" she directed.

Marcus was at once beside me, ushering his daughter with

words and lifting me from my chair. He escorted me inside, and we all gathered on the other side of the door.

"What on earth?" I said to the rest of them, shaking my head.

"A car passed by that I didn't recognize," Olva explained.

"We can't be afraid of everything," Rosemarie said tetchily.

"Should we not?" Olva said, her voice rising.

"I'm going on my paper route today," Marcus said, "and if you ladies would watch Amaryllis—"

"You will not!" Olva reprimanded, her voice throaty and maternal. Amaryllis began crying.

"I will not be paralyzed by this," Marcus said.

"You are hardly a man of action," Olva replied, and then a pulse of regret moved across her face.

"I've been caring for my child, haven't I?" Marcus said. "Is that not action enough for you? Or not man enough?"

"Marcus, I didn't mean—" Here Olva paused. "It's only that you must do whatever it takes as a father. You must never abandon your child."

"Well, which is it?" Marcus asked sharply. "Should I be a man of action and leave for my route? Or would that be abandoning my child?"

"Marcus, forget that I said anything." Olva looked tired and remorseful.

Marcus's face softened. He picked up Amaryllis, and into the curve of his neck she drew her head, relaxing it there as dough rests in a bowl. "Olva, why is it you never told us we were related to you? That Charlie was the link between us?"

Her mouth flattened, a little grimace of pain. Olva then exhaled deeply, and I knew what that meant. She was trying to rid herself of whatever thought she was having. Rather than press her, Marcus nodded. He looked not the least bit perturbed in the way I might have been if searching for an answer but not finding it.

It was agreed that Rosemarie would call the sheriff in York County while Marcus completed his paper route. Olva was occupying Amaryllis, and I busied myself with opening the rolltop desk and sliding out some long drawers I had not investigated recently. To my surprise, inside one of those drawers was an old and rather well-kept edition of *The Tale of Peter Rabbit*. My first impulse was that surely Amaryllis would damage the book with her curious hands. I closed the drawer, feeling the twin impulses of shame and stubbornness. What power things had over me!

On the other side of the room, Olva was now questioning Amaryllis about what kind of breakfast she might like, and the child's eyes seemed to narrow at me. I silently took my leave, walking through the dining room and kitchen and all the way out the back door.

Stepping down the back porch stairs, I decided I would take the opportunity to take a slow walk on our acreage. I felt a whisper of unease about Rick returning, but I thought it more imperative to reclaim my property. Who was he to alarm the Kratt family? He was of no importance at all.

As I walked, the morning light was too sharp for my eyes, and my breath collected in my lungs like pie weights, and I struggled to put one foot in front of the other. I didn't know if my age or my guilt over hiding the book from Amaryllis was impeding me. I made it only to the old henhouse, where I was forced to rest on the eastern-facing wall, which had crumbled enough to provide a stout seat. A thicket of peach trees sat in maturity to my left. I took a deep breath but could not smell them. My gaze wandered toward the house.

How in disrepair it looked! Not only did we need new gutters—one hung askance from the brick—but also several clay tiles of the roof were broken. My eyes caught some movement in one of the windows. It was my room. I felt a stab of concern, but because I was too out of breath to address it, I remained in my improvised seat.

I kept my eyes on my bedroom window. As I did, I remembered when my brother Quincy had once surprised me there. It was right after Daddy Kratt had given Quincy the Purdey shotgun, and I was sitting on my bed, reading. I heard Quincy's boots meeting the hardwood floor downstairs. His footfalls stopped every few moments, and I wondered what things he might be pausing to look at. The highboy bureau or the butterfly tray? The rolltop desk? The elegant Cheval mirror in the hallway?

I heard his steps again and judged he was standing in front of the study. A long mahogany table stretched beside its double doors, and on top of it sat a pair of blackamoor figures. They were an interesting pair, and I didn't fault Quincy for stopping to have a closer look. One figure was male, the other female, and they held urns above their heads. They stood on ornate pedestals and were dressed regally in reds and golds. They were a glamorous couple, very exotic and charming, and they leaned in toward one another in a rather conspiratorial way but had innocent enough looks on their faces. They had come from one of Grandmother DeLour's brothers-in-law, a world traveler who had picked them up in Venice. On several occasions, I found our maids looking at these figures with expressions I couldn't place, and they would often forget to dust them, as if pretending they didn't exist at all.

"Sister."

"Oh!" I cried. Imagining the details of the two figures, I hadn't noticed Quincy standing in my doorway. I had grown wary of him since he had taken ownership of Daddy Kratt's shotgun. How awful it was to be fearful of your own kin.

"Calm down," he said, waving his hand dismissively.

"Come in," I said, but he had already entered the room. I had not yet closed the book in my hands.

He strolled over to my dressing table and was examining the items on it. I had lined up my combs (nice ivory-handled ones from the same great-uncle who traveled extensively), and Quincy trailed his fingers across them, disturbing their arrangement.

Out of nervousness, I started reading again.

"What are you reading?" he asked.

I looked up, startled. He leaned in to retrieve the book, and I handed it over. He studied its green-and-gold binding and opened to its title page.

"*On the Origin of Species by Means of Natural Selection.*" He tilted his head as he read the subtitle. "*Or the Preservation of Favoured Races in the Struggle for Life.*"

He flipped through a few pages, and when one ripped easily under his fingers, he said, "This is an old book, isn't it?" He looked up, eyes wider. "This is the book Daddy Kratt forced Olva to search for."

"Be careful with it," I snapped. I felt his eyes on me as he turned more pages, a way to let me know he had tolerated my tone but would not forgive so quickly again.

"Ha!" he said, looking down at one of the pages. "I found a misspelled word!" He leaned in to show me the page, his fingertip pressing under the word *speceies*.

"It's just a small typing mistake."

He laughed again, and I noticed his laughter was more a man's now, as if an old engine were turning over.

"I wish I could show that to Uncle Sally," Quincy said wistfully. He shut the book and handed it back. "Will you read me a little?" he asked, his voice suddenly gentle as he sat on the edge of my bed.

This move, its seeming intimacy, troubled me. I had lost my place, so I flipped through the pages frantically, not wanting to pick an unfamiliar passage.

"Pick something!" he spat, tired of my vacillation.

My eyes landed, and I started reading without knowing what I had chosen. "'The laws governing inheritance are quite unknown,'" I began. I paused, but Quincy motioned for me to go on. "'No one can say why the same peculiarity in different individuals of the same species, and in individuals of different species, is sometimes inherited and sometimes not so.'"

I stopped again, thinking he might give me a reprieve. He stared at me coldly, and I continued.

"'Why the child often reverts in certain characters to its grandfather or grandmother or other much more remote ancestor; why a peculiarity is often transmitted from one sex to both sexes, or to one sex alone, more commonly but not exclusively to the like sex. It is a fact of some little importance to us, that peculiarities appearing in the males of our domestic breeds are often transmitted either exclusively, or in a much greater degree, to males alone.'"

I paused, closing my eyes.

"Inheritance, huh?" he said. "I thought this book was about something else altogether. He's right, though; inheritance usually favors the men. Sorry about that, Sister."

"Not inheritance in the way you're thinking," I said, unable to conceal my impatience. "He's not talking about land or money. He's talking about something deep within us, passed down generation to generation."

"I don't know, Sister. Some are just unlucky, I think." Quincy shrugged.

I held the book in the air and shook it. "This is about the struggle to exist. How difficulty is sown into life from the beginning. It's about survival. Some of us will make it, and others won't, and you hope you possess the strength of character to be one of the select few."

Quincy tilted his head thoughtfully. Then he winked at me. "The strongest man is left standing, so to speak."

"I'm sure that's how it seems to you."

"Now, Judith, don't get peevish. Survival lies in whether you stay on your toes. Whether you take advantage of whatever opportunities are in front of you at the moment. You'd like to believe there's some rhyme or reason to it, some order lent to the world that crowns a chosen few. But that's not what I've seen. Doesn't matter if you're a deacon down at the church or a criminal up in the prison, nobody gets a special turn in this world."

Apparently struck by a fresh thought, he smiled. "Now there's some comfort for you, Sister. I guess we're all in this together."

"And those who have a shotgun are at a considerable advantage," I said, thinking of Quincy's plans for Charlie.

"I suspect we're more in agreement over the matter of survival than you're willing to admit. We're both opportunists, Judith." He lifted himself off the bed. "Were you really born under such dire circumstances? Is your lot worse than the rest? God, Judith, you're the firstborn of us. Queen of the hill."

"Better to be born last," I said.

Quincy's face widened in wonder. He struggled to find words, then simply smiled. After a moment, he said, "It's been a while since I was told something I didn't already know." He laughed softly. "You think Rosemarie is somehow better off than you." He said it as if the idea were a rare, dazzling species of orchid that had chosen that instant to bloom in front of him. He shook his head lightly as if unleashing himself from its spell.

I felt exposed, and anger pushed up within me. "You punish everyone around you because Daddy Kratt never pays you any attention."

He looked disappointed, as if he had tried to create a moment between us, which I had spoiled. He walked toward the door. Before he left, he drummed his fingers on the doorframe but did not look back.

I noticed, long after he was gone, that I was still holding up the book, pointing it at the spot where he had been.

A bird's sharp and urgent call broke my reverie. I lifted myself from the edge of the henhouse wall and walked slowly back toward the house. Inside was quiet. I couldn't imagine where the others were, so I climbed the stairs, taking a deep breath after each step, and retired to my bedroom. Something new was there on my bed. I panicked, thinking it was *Origin of Species*, put there by the ghost of my dead brother. Upon closer inspection, I found it was *The Tale of Peter Rabbit*.

The child! She had taken the book from the rolltop desk but not kept it for herself. What great generosity sprang from her small body.

Now I would give her something. I leaned over and wedged my hand under my mattress, reaching until I could not any longer, until I felt on my fingertips the warmth of another book. I had been hiding it there for more than sixty years.

That evening, the darkness through the window was uncompromising. Marcus had made it back safely from his paper route, but Rosemarie's conversation with the sheriff in York had been fruitless. He had dismissed the graffiti as a prank, and she had hung up on him.

Amaryllis and I were now alone upstairs, and the others were in the cellar, looking for some kind of paint to temporarily cover the epithet until a permanent solution could be found. Amaryllis's curiosity about the message under the bedsheet had not waned, but she also appeared to intuit that we were desperate for her to remain ignorant on the matter. Because of this, her eyes held a new expression, a tart watchfulness, which aged her tender face.

Throughout the day, she had buzzed to and fro, and the

extent to which she had colonized the house with objects in a single afternoon was remarkable. Not just the few toys she had brought with her, but she gathered up items that intrigued her from every room, drawing them up into her tiny empire, which she displayed with fanatical rigor on the Jacobean refectory table in the dining room. My Victorian Dresden figurines, elegant ladies with prim details, she positioned facing one another in regiments, and when I made the mistake of adjusting one, Amaryllis swiftly corrected me.

All day long, she had begged to run outside. In an effort to distract, I had sifted through drawers and closets for things that might entice her. She had already looked at sheaves of blueprints for the house—she pored over them, tracing her fingers along the fragile paper—and before dinner, she had sat in the Chippendale wing chair, the one with claw and ball feet, and examined in her lap the antique Hammond's globe, which ordered the world in muted browns, golds, and blues. She had spun it slowly, her eyes tracking the contours of the continents.

The child's energy! We had done so much in one day, I wondered if I would have the wherewithal for tomorrow.

At the moment, while the others were in the cellar, Amaryllis was cradling the book I had just given her. It was our family's first edition of *Origin of Species*. Sitting on the sofa, she examined its cover, softened by age, and slowly flipped through the pages, which rasped under her fingertips. How tenderly she was handling it!

"Thank you for this book," she said, sinking back into the sofa with it and her stuffed bunny. Opening it, she made a soft, inquisitive noise as something dropped from the pages. I looked over and saw her regarding a small piece of yellowed paper, folded in half.

"Amaryllis! I'll take that," I said, moving toward her.

She peered at me, then back at the paper, and she was on her feet before I knew it, the sofa a barrier between us. She unfolded the paper, which she saw was two sheets.

"'Dearest Rosemarie,'" Amaryllis began to read. "'You do not understand my'"—here she paused, studying the paper—"'objectshuns'—"

"You can read," I said, incredulous, and the child shot me a wrathful look, as if underestimating her was, to date, my greatest offense.

The perceived slight only fueled her mischief. I moved toward her, around the sofa, but she skirted to the opposite end, leaving us in the same position as before. She kept a watchful eye on me as she read. "'You do not understand my objectshuns. It is true I have never done anything according to conven...'" Amaryllis brought her nose closer to the paper. "'Convenshun!'" The child flashed a triumphant smile, and I used her moment of victory to take several steps closer to her, which she ably matched, scurrying away from me.

"That is quite enough," I said loudly, and my voice sounded gaudy in my ears, desperate to be in command of the situation. The child heard it, too, and she stood her ground, daring me to advance again on her.

"'If you leave with Charlie and Olva'"—here Amaryllis paused and considered the arrival of Olva's name—"'you will never be safe.'" The child looked up at me, a request on her face, my role as pursuer evaporating from her thoughts, the contents of the letter taking hold of her. She wanted to know what it meant.

I sighed. "If you hand me the letter, I will tell you." I peered down my nose, trying to muster all the years I had on her in one searing look. Her small face, the color of a chestnut's hull, darker than Olva's skin, remained stoic. "All right," I said. "You require a better deal. If you hand me the letter, I will not only tell you what it means, but I will let you hold something else, something more dazzling."

She eyed me, fanning herself with the letter, taking her time to consider my offer. All at once, she scrambled onto the sofa and thrust the letter at my chest. I seized it, folding it swiftly into quarters. I must have been holding my breath, for a spell of dizziness caught me off guard. I pressed my fingertips to the sofa table at my right, and when I had sufficiently stabilized, I lifted my head to see the child aiming her unblinking eyes at me.

"Does the letter really matter to you?" I asked.

A throb of something like heat pulsed between us, from her to me, and while her small head balanced coolly on her body, her eyes were molten, animated in an unsettling way, and I worried she would cry out and alert the others, who would come barging in the room, wanting to know what I had done to awaken the child's outrage. The child would no doubt point to the letter folded hastily in my hand, and that I couldn't have. The pot had already been sufficiently stirred that day.

I paused to swallow. "The letter is from my aunt to my mother. My mother's name was Rosemarie—same as my sister." I gestured below to indicate the cellar, where Rosemarie and the others were. Amaryllis nodded. "Mama wanted to go away with Charlie and take Olva with them, too, but Aunt Dee objected. She thought it was too risky."

I thought of Dee, ever practical, worrying over my mother. Years ago, I had happened upon this letter, among the others I had not given Quincy after our raid of the rolltop desk. The disagreement described in the letter was why Dee had not joined us at the Easter meal over which Uncle Sally presided. It was a shame in more ways than one, including the entertainment a showdown between Dee and Sally would have provided.

Amaryllis considered what I had said about the letter. I couldn't see how she could possibly understand the import of my words. But just to be certain, I said, "Now, let's not speak about this to anyone."

Her eyes narrowed.

"If you don't speak about this," I continued, "I will let you hold that dazzling thing I mentioned. I recall that you once looked at it with interest."

"You already promised me that."

I nodded, feeling mastered by the child. "Fine," I said, waving her toward me. "Here is the tray."

She regarded me skeptically when she heard the word *tray*. Nevertheless, she joined me at the long table that flanked the sofa's back. My artifact did not disappoint. When her eyes lighted on the butterfly tray, she thrust out her hand and grabbed one of its handles, sliding it off the table.

"Amaryllis!" I cried. "Slow down! The tray is very fragile."

She was managing too many items at once, as children do. Peter Rabbit tucked himself in the crook of her left elbow, and the tray dangled from her right hand, which also clutched, I noticed, Rosemarie's glass rabbit figurine. Before I could act, the figurine dropped to the floor, and Amaryllis's hand released to rescue it. Down came the tray.

The damage was immediate and incontrovertible. The tray's back cracked, and the glass overlay shattered, buckling the layer of stiff butterfly wings, which had been shellacked upon the tray's construction or had soldered together over time. The message painted across the top of the tray—*Rio de Janeiro!*—was now indecipherable.

Amaryllis did not move, but a great thundering rose from below us as Marcus, Olva, and Rosemarie rushed up the cellar stairs.

"What's the matter?" Olva cried, panting. I quickly tucked the letter under the gathered cuff of my blouse. Olva stopped short when she saw the ruptured tray and looked up to gauge my reaction.

When Rosemarie and Marcus arrived beside her, their eyes landed on me, too. Only Amaryllis's gaze remained locked to the ground. Both of her small hands gripped her Peter Rabbit.

They were waiting on me to say something.

With no warning, Amaryllis bolted across the room and scrambled underneath the maple drop-leaf table. She began to sob in peals that flew out of her with a pitch and intensity I had not heard before. Marcus and Olva raced to her side, but she could not be coaxed from her position, wedged in the frame of the small table with face tucked and arms wrapped around her knees.

I walked over to Amaryllis's hiding place. The others watched me. Clearing my throat first, I began telling her the story of the butterfly tray.

The tray (23¾ by 15½ inches) had lived on our sofa table for upward of seventy years. Daddy Kratt set it there in 1922, the year he finished building this house and plugging it full of the finest furniture Bound had ever seen, most of it coming from Mama's family. Clad in rosewood with an interior lined with real butterfly wings, it traveled here from South America in the suitcase of one of my maternal great-uncles.

Those butterfly wings! They were wine and ochre, colors I had always considered too rich for weightless creatures. Nothing ever sat on the tray. It possessed a rather uncommon beauty, and ferrying around food and drinks on it would have been insulting.

Before Daddy Kratt earned his own wealth, he did odd jobs for the richest families in Bound and all the way out to Blacksburg. He never was a scholar, but he was clever and did his own form of research, spending time with Mama's father, Grandfather DeLour, to see how the old man conducted himself, to learn the secrets of his moneymaking. Daddy Kratt painted the DeLours' house, built their barn, tended their garden, and did anything else asked of him.

In the beginning, he probably didn't notice the toddler girl on the wooden swing who would become his wife two decades later. Once she got older, of course, he would have recognized her beauty, the kind of loveliness that glass acquires when tumbled by the ocean, muted and smooth and useless. When they married, he had not yet achieved his fortune, but he was very close, so claiming a girl from a wealthy, educated family was good business sense.

In the early days, though, when Mama was just a child,

Daddy Kratt worked to make himself indispensable to the DeLours. Grandmother DeLour, who died before I was born, was known to be a fine cook even though she rarely set foot in the kitchen. One morning, she decided she wanted to roast a whole chicken that would be basted in a sumptuous sauce, the recipe for which she had found in a French cookbook handed down from her mother. So she walked outside to consult one of the colored girls, who was doling feed to the chickens. They came to an arrangement about which hen would be suitable for the dish, and my grandmother went back inside.

Going to consult the cookbook again, she realized her ruby wedding ring was missing. She ran outside, screaming for the colored girl, who was about to wring the chicken's neck for the grand dish. She interrogated the colored girl, who I'm sure was in a panic she might be blamed herself. The girl suggested that the ring had slipped off and been consumed by one of the chickens. When they could not hazard a guess as to which bird was the thief, Grandmother DeLour screeched so hysterically that Daddy Kratt, who was about to join some of the boys picking cotton, ran to see what was the matter. My grandmother was in such a state, he had to hear the story from the girl.

When Grandfather DeLour returned home, my grandmother had been in a fit all day; she was resting in her room, where the maids were alternating cold compresses on her head with sips of whiskey, which they told her was an elixir sent by the doctor.

Daddy Kratt put his hand on my grandfather's shoulder and said, "I'll handle it." That evening, he walked outside and slaughtered every single hen and rooster the DeLours owned. After a thorough search, he found nothing.

The next morning, one of the maids found the ring stuck between the pages of the cookbook, marking the sauce recipe. This could have been very bad news for Daddy Kratt. But when he arrived back at the house, uncertain of his fate, Grandfather DeLour hailed him as a "man of action" and, from that moment, regarded my father as his pupil, teaching him everything he knew about the cotton business.

Amaryllis untucked her head slightly. I was touched by her willingness to listen. I continued my story.

Grandmother DeLour never knew her ring had been resting in the cookbook the whole time. She thought Daddy Kratt had found it in one of the chickens. As a token of gratitude, she presented him with the butterfly tray, the most unusual and exotic item in her home at the time, a gift from the same peripatetic brother-in-law who had brought her the blackamoor figures. Then she instructed Daddy Kratt to go out and buy new chickens.

Throughout my childhood, I would occasionally catch my father looking at the tray, drumming his fingers on it as if he could provoke those wings into flight. Because it was placed in such a prominent location in our home, and because Daddy Kratt was fond of it, we regarded the tray with a mixture of fear and awe. When Quincy told Rosemarie that the wings weren't from butterflies but rather tiny and helpless fairies, she avoided the tray, and when she accidentally went near it, Quincy would shriek under his breath, which would send her sobbing to her room.

I looked down at Amaryllis, worried that this last part would frighten her. She had lifted her head, and her large eyes steadied themselves on me.

"I'm glad that girl didn't get in trouble," she said.

"Which girl?" I asked.

"The girl in charge of the chickens."

"I had not thought of that," I said.

"Are you mad I broke the tray?"

I shook my head. "We still have the story. It's nearly as real as the thing. Maybe more so."

"Are you mad at us for moving in?" she asked. "Do you want us to stay?"

The child and her questions!

The others looked at me.

"Yes."

The next morning, Amaryllis beckoned me to the front porch. Marcus was in the study repairing a broken hinge on one of the cabinets, and Olva and Rosemarie were contemplating breakfast in the kitchen. I felt a bit exposed out in the open with her, but the child wore an insistence that agitated her whole body. She could be kept inside no longer. The message on the house was now covered with ochre-colored paint, and we had heard not a whisper from any member of the Bramlett family. I had agreed, then, that we could sit on the porch for a spell.

The air was silent and steady, and I was wondering where all the birds had gone when a blue jay on its twigged feet hopped onto the porch. He eyed me, that robust fellow, and I sat in the green porch chair, returning his gaze, and this seemed nearly like a prayer to me, a different sort than the starchy ones I had been repeating all my life. Amaryllis was busy building a cairn on the porch, and the morning light seemed to take notice, releasing hidden glimmers in the stacked rocks. Everything seemed to be ordering itself in the world.

The rumble of a car drew my attention. Jolly's Taurus lunged into our driveway, spilling the smell of exhaust into the air.

"Amaryllis!" I cried, bolting up out of my seat, which sent a tremor of vertigo through my body and forced me back down. From my seat, I strained to see who was driving the car.

I had never been so relieved to see Jolly herself. She emerged from the driver's side, slamming the door before her squat feet marched across our lawn.

"The mean lady is here," Amaryllis said, grasping a large chunk of blue granite in her hand. "Old Mr. McGregor."

I was pleased the name had passed on to someone else.

"Maybe you better go inside, Amaryllis," I said as Jolly approached us.

"I'm fine," the child said.

"Judith!" Jolly said, stopping a few feet short of the porch. She acted as if we were continuing a conversation already in full swing. "Your maid can't go around threatening my boy!"

"She is not the maid!" Amaryllis cried, standing up.

"A death threat is hardly something to look past," Jolly said, ignoring Amaryllis's comment. The child remained standing, the piece of granite still in her hand.

I didn't know how to respond to Jolly or how to soothe

Amaryllis, and without thinking, I did the thing that was sure to agitate them both: I pointed at the painted-over portion of the house. Jolly's eyes followed my gesture and squinted in confusion at the spot on the wall. The folds of her face slowly smoothed out in recognition.

"I am sorry about that," she said with a quietness I had never before heard in her voice. Her eyes lifted to Amaryllis, and she said, "Is your daddy here?"

I tensed, not knowing if Jolly were interested in proffering an apology or sniffing Marcus out of hiding. Amaryllis answered before I could intervene.

"Of course he is," the child said. "We live here now."

Jolly's eyes fell silent in her head. "You what now?" She turned to me. "Is this so?"

I gathered my breath. "Well, it turns out that it is."

"What on earth is wrong with you, Judith?" Jolly's voice was controlled, and in it was an earnest appeal. "Aren't you afraid that boy will steal from you?"

Amaryllis made a little noise—a deflation—and fury spun hard in my chest. The force of it lifted me from my chair, and I remained standing even though I felt light-headed. "He is certainly not going to steal from me!" I said, towering over Jolly, who stood at the bottom of the steps. "As far as I am concerned, the Bramlett family is no longer welcome at—or near—this house!"

Jolly's mouth stretched into an ugly smile, and we watched her return to her car. Walking there, she took her time, our anger not spurring her one bit. When she reached the Taurus, she paused with her fingers on the door handle. "My son is right," she said, rotating her head toward us. "This house is full of nigger lovers."

Amaryllis's feet were swift. They seemed to descend the six porch stairs at once, and before I could register what was happening, she was standing in front of Jolly's car with her right hand raised, bearing the chunk of granite. I saw Jolly's mouth softly fall open just as Amaryllis hurled the rock at the windshield. It made a crunching noise, spidering the glass where the rock had landed. It looked almost beautiful, like the shape of a firecracker. Jolly stared dumbly at the cracked windshield before her awareness snapped back. She heaved her body up, preparing to descend upon Amaryllis, with words or actions, I knew not which, but the fleet-footed child was already gone. The front door slammed as she ran into the house.

"Miss Judith?" It was Olva, voice high and strained, peeking her head out. Jolly's car door slammed, and the Taurus backed down the driveway. Olva watched it tear down the road.

I followed Olva inside. We decided the adults would have a meeting. Before we gathered, I checked that the front door was locked while Marcus checked the other doors. The number of doors in and out of this house! I reflected on those doors: the front door painted the color of Savannah clay; the glass door leading from the sunroom to the south side of the house; the back door with its shabby, chipped paint; and the cellar door, heavy on its hinges. During my childhood, some people used only the front door; others, only the back.

As Marcus was checking the cellar door, Amaryllis was bouncing beside me, full of nervous energy from her encounter with Jolly.

"Good grief," I said. "You will need something to keep you occupied, won't you?" I called to Rosemarie and Olva that I would meet them upstairs, and I devised a task for the child.

When I joined the adults, they were already in heated discussion about what to do.

"She knows I'm here now?" Marcus asked. I nodded, and he sighed. "We need to leave."

"We can't leave! You said so yourself. We have to stay and face him," Rosemarie said.

"You don't have to leave," Marcus said. In the span of half a breath—it was there and it was gone—I saw my sister's eyes tighten in resentment.

"I'll have you remember that the message on the house was directed at me," Rosemarie said. "I'm in the thick of it with you!"

Marcus let off a hot laugh, but Olva held up her hand. "Marcus is right," she said. "Rick will return."

We went around and around in conversation, arguing over when Marcus and Amaryllis should leave and how we should orchestrate their exit. Where would they go? We gathered in Marcus's room, and he absentmindedly bent down to pick up a whistle shaped like a bird from the floor. "We shouldn't pack much," he said.

"Where is Amaryllis?" Olva asked, looking at the whistle.

"I provided her a puzzle," I said. "I gave her a handful of keys, and now she's happily trying to figure out what they unlock. I thought it was quite a clever idea."

"The keys from the junk drawer?" Olva asked, a note of alarm in her voice.

"Yes. Is there a problem?" I said.

"One of those keys opens the long drawer of the rolltop desk," Olva said. She wasted not a moment before shooting out of the room.

"Judith?" Rosemarie asked.

"The Purdey shotgun," I managed to say.

Marcus beat us downstairs. We heard Olva calling frantically for Amaryllis. Then Olva's cry sharpened. When I arrived downstairs, I saw what the others saw. The front door hung open. In the doorway lay Peter Rabbit, facedown.

At the sight of the stuffed animal, my thoughts rose so sharply that I felt them as distinct pricks of pain in my head. And then I heard a wailing that soldered me to my spot. It took me a moment to understand the howl was a train, discharging its horn somewhere in the distance. I stood, immobile, until I was the last one left in the house.

I followed the others. When I emerged outside, the figures on the lawn seemed to prop dimensionless against the morning scenery as if unreal. The birds disagreed. The blue jays had taken up residence in our large water oak, and they cried their war cries and stamped their feet, a cacophony of survival. They saw what was below.

There was Amaryllis, holding the Purdey shotgun, struggling with its proportions. In front of her, at a ten-pace length, as if caught in a duel, was Rick. His carriage was slumped and perturbed, the weight of something on him that he was angry to bear.

To Amaryllis's right were Olva and Marcus, and close to the porch, on Olva's other side, was a wiry man I didn't recognize, eyes hot in his head and legs trembling with confined energy. He glanced up at me suspiciously—as if I were out of place! On the porch, Rosemarie stood alongside me.

"Hand it to me," Olva was saying gently to Amaryllis. The air seemed lighter, gaseous, as if a spark could ignite it.

"Amaryllis!" Marcus whispered in a desperate way.

But Olva put up her hand at him. "Give it to me, sweet girl," Olva said.

A small, innocent smile rose to the child's lips. Her eyes moved past Olva to land on my sister and me, and our expressions seemed to give her pause. She looked down at the shotgun. She smiled again, as if amused by the attention. Her gaze leveled at Rick, and her face was older than it had been before. A world-weariness had taken hold of her, and she blinked slowly, eyelids heavy. She stepped forward—the weight of the gun seemed to pull her forward—and just as she did, Olva matched her movements and stepped toward the child. As if they had reached a silent agreement, Amaryllis let go of the gun just as Olva lifted it from her hands.

Marcus rushed forward and fell to his knees, pulling Amaryllis toward him. Her face crumpled into tears at having done something of greater consequence than she understood. We thought it had ended, that the child's actions had sobered the adults, wringing out the madness of the moment so that only common sense remained.

But then Rick spoke.

"Good girl," he said to Amaryllis.

His friend snickered.

Olva's face emptied, and she slowly raised the shotgun toward Rick.

Windsor chair
Wooden spinning wheel
Mahogany secretary
R. S. Prussia vase
Pie safe—Grandmother DeLour's
Butler's tray (silver plated)
Amsterdam School copper
mantel clock
Hamilton drafting table
Letter opener (cut glass)

Tiffany lamp (diameter 16";
21¾" height)—~~broken~~ fixed

Victorian chaise longue
Octagonal Jacobean parlor table
Mahogany sewing cabinet
Westclox alarm clock
(Big Ben model)
Hepplewhite side table
Watchmaker's workbench
Edwardian neoclassical brass
column candleholders (10" tall)
Abner Cutler rolltop desk
(54" × 21" × 50")—damaged

Riding whip—Daddy Kratt's
New York Times (Wednesday,
October 30, 1929)
Peacock hat
Edwardian coral cameo (1½" × 1")

Highboy bureau
Butterfly tray
(23¾" × 15½")—damaged
Cheval mirror

Glass rabbit
Persian Heriz rug
Revolving mahogany bookstand

Queen Anne chair (dusty rose)
Rococo cherub figurines
Noritake 175 Gold china
Art deco oyster plates

Silver cutlery
Waterford crystal pitcher
Crystal saltcellars
Louis XV sofa (silver leaf details)

Leather ledger book
Purdey shotgun (barrel 29")

The Tale of Peter Rabbit, early edition
Bronze blackamoor figures
Origin of Species, first edition
Victorian Dresden figurines
Chippendale wing chair
Hammond's globe
Letter from Aunt Dee to Mama
Maple drop-leaf table
Ruby wedding ring—
Grandmother DeLour's

TWELVE

The morning after Daddy Kratt gave Quincy his Purdey shotgun, I arrived at the store earlier than my usual time. I wasn't there for my normal inventory duties. Walking through the front door, I was shocked to discover Olva standing beside the entrance table, both hands propped on it, as if it were holding her up. It was the same table where the strawberry shortcakes had sat months earlier. When Olva saw me, she sprang forward.

"Charlie is at Dee's!"

I grasped her arm and pulled her toward me. "Not so loud," I whispered, glancing around. The store's silence had a weight to it that made me uneasy. I leaned in. "Have you seen Quincy?"

"No," Olva said, her voice rising. "Why? Is there something I should know?"

"Shh!" I moved my eyes over the expanse of the first floor before my gaze climbed the main staircase. I saw nothing, but all the items of the store, all the things I had spent months watching over, appeared to possess a bridled energy, as though they might lunge forward if I called for them. Everything around us seemed interested in what we had to say, and even one of Mr. Burns's mannequins, wearing a maize-colored tweed coat, was angling an ear toward us.

I moved my head even closer to Olva's. I could barely hear myself speaking. "Go home. Tell Charlie I've come to pack some of his things. I'll make my way to Dee's as soon as I can."

Olva nodded and made for the front door. Before opening it, she turned around. "What does Quincy want with Charlie?"

I lifted my hand to shush her. I didn't know what to say. I communicated something, though, even if I hadn't intended to, because she nodded. Had all the listening things in the store understood me, too? The rows of canned pineapple in the bulk goods section. The prying mannequin. All the other items that had sprouted a thousand ears. Had they grasped the unspoken? Olva pressed the door open and was gone.

I swiftly made my way to the attic. On the way, I grabbed one of the leather hide suitcases from the luggage display, careful to keep my gaze trained on the path ahead rather than on the merchandise I passed. It was like making my way through a curious crowd. There in the attic, I packed the remainder of Charlie's belongings. They weren't much: a plain black comb, a small worn Bible, and a sheaf of personal papers, mostly his drawings of the internal workings of various mechanical objects. It was cold in the attic, and I rubbed my hands together and blew into them.

My eyes scanned the rest of the space. The attic stretched to nearly four thousand square feet, and beyond Charlie's workstation was a vast area where broken items, waiting for repair, were stacked against one another. Those broken things would wait indefinitely. The attic felt different, the arrangement of things altered. Were things missing? I wondered if Charlie had returned, but I didn't see how that would be possible. A mattress, which Rosemarie sometimes napped on, had been pulled to one of the far reaches of the attic, shrouded in shadows. It was barely visible from where I kneeled, and as far as I could tell, it was heaped in blankets.

The attic looked sparser, the space more exposed, and this sense of emptiness seemed to invite grandiose ideas. Unable to situate myself in this new composition, I felt a derangement take hold of me. The heap of blankets on the distant mattress seemed to shift, and I pressed my eyes shut to regain my composure.

The Tiffany lamp still sat on Charlie's desk. I looked from the lamp to the suitcase and shook my head.

"It won't fit."

The voice startled me, and I slammed the suitcase shut. When I turned, Quincy was placing the Purdey shotgun on a low bench at the entrance to the attic.

"I don't think Charlie would expect you to pack the lamp," he said, chuckling as he approached me. He peered at the suitcase. "Especially if he's getting a new piece of luggage. I suppose if you're packing for him, you know where he is."

I didn't respond.

"It's okay, Sister. You don't have to give up your secret. I already know that Aunt Dee is hiding him."

I looked at the shotgun on the bench. His eyes followed mine.

"You can't understand my situation, Sister," Quincy said, "and if you meddle, I'll tell Daddy Kratt you turned on the Tiffany lamp to warn Charlie."

I glanced down. My ear caught sound of movement in the millinery shop—the scuff of a footstep, the shuffle of merchandise, I couldn't tell. A thought both terrifying and familiar rose up, as if submerged until now, of one of the mannequins from the shop coming to life and climbing the stairs to the attic.

"What is it?" Quincy asked, noticing my expression.

"Nothing."

Quincy shrugged. "You see, it's bigger than the two of us anyhow." He took a step closer to me. "I'll tell you two things. That Charlie had an affair with—"

I held up my hand.

"You already know that," he finished. There was no anger in Quincy's voice; it was purely a transmission of information for him. "And maybe you know the second thing, too. They had a *child*."

Quincy waited for my response. My silence triggered another off-kilter chuckle from him. "You know," he said. "Of course you do. How could you not? You were always smarter. I'm not ashamed to admit that."

My gaze remained rooted to the floor. I thought of Byrd Parker. I thought of his wife, their unborn child, and the Negro who was the father of that child. All dead.

"Charlie's already a dead man," Quincy said, as if he'd read my thoughts. "I am—if you can believe it—I'm sorry about all this. You're fond of talking about survival, Judith. Well, I have to make it through this world like anybody else." A thin laugh escaped his lips. "You and Rosemarie are the mold, and I'm the gelatin that never set. Do you remember that one mechanic at Randall Clark's garage? Every time I walked by, he would peer over the black intestines of his popped hood and call out, 'Look, fellows, it's the middling!' He was talking about how I'd been born in the middle, between two girls. And I used to think about that. Because we used to call our average cotton *middling. Fair to middlin'*. It was foolish of that man to give me a name." A sly smile rose on Quincy's lips. "That mechanic called me the name until I dug up one of his secrets—oh, he was dirtier than one of his engines."

Fair to middlin'. The phrase called up a memory for me, too. Of Grandfather DeLour, Mama's father. "You are only fair to middlin'," he had once told me solemnly as I played with my dolls on the front porch steps. "But your sister, she's the finest grade there is." Everything in Grandfather DeLour's life, no matter how disparate—his grandchildren, the taste of his pipe tobacco, the fitness of his horse—he assessed in the language used to grade cotton. It brought me a strange pleasure, then, when I first heard the story of how he lost his cotton fortune. Back when Daddy Kratt was starting out, he had sold his cotton exclusively through my grandfather's company, DeLour and Sons. That is, until my father found a better deal, at which time he withdrew his product, bribed his business associates to do the same, and unceremoniously bankrupted Grandfather DeLour. I imagine it pained my grandfather to lose his son-in-law's business, but even more so his camaraderie. The DeLours had only two daughters, my mother and Dee, and so the company name, DeLour and Sons, was a misnomer. The name might have pointed to my grandfather's optimism that his wife would eventually bear him a son (she didn't), but knowing him, I'd say it was more likely evidence of his spectacular lack of imagination. Grandfather DeLour could not envision a world without a male heir to his business. I looked at Quincy. I suspect he had never felt heir to anything substantial in his life. Like me, he was vying for a better position than he'd been born into. Like me, he was searching for where he belonged.

Quincy considered me. "What, Sister?"

Now I was looking past him. Someone had emerged from behind Quincy. My brother pivoted to follow my gaze.

There was Olva, standing with the Purdey shotgun, pointing it at him.

A pebble of laughter dropped from Quincy's mouth. My breath stalled. I told myself that the shotgun was just a thing in Olva's hands. I stood up and moved toward her gently, as if walking in the midst of fragile things. Her eyes were locked on Quincy, but as I approached her, they cut toward me, and I froze.

"Is this a warning?" Quincy asked wryly. He didn't think Olva would do it. He didn't think she had it in her.

A tang of panic flushed my mouth. My mind, unbalanced by the scene in front of me, cast about for something to seize hold of, and it landed, improbably, on Uncle Sally. I recalled the conversation in which Quincy had told our great-uncle, over those thick slabs of Easter ham, the story of the stout foxes, the lean foxes, and the henhouse gate. The circumstances alone had dictated which kind of fox had survived. I couldn't help but think that whatever was allowing Olva to point a gun at Quincy might have, under different circumstances, lain hidden inside her, sleepy as a bulb buried in winter soil. But a crucible of recent events—Charlie's near lynching, Daddy Kratt's resolve to find Charlie, and Quincy's willingness to lead the manhunt—had converged with barometrical force, an ear-splitting pressure that had provoked something inside Olva and had put it to use.

Quincy looked down the barrel of the Purdey. His

expression shifted from smugness to belief, just as when I had delighted him with my jealousy of Rosemarie that day, the same day he had made me read aloud from *Origin of Species*. When he saw that Olva would pull the trigger, that she would go through with it, the very same look of satisfaction fell across his face: it was a look of wonder and ease dissolving into pleasure, a pleasure borne of the fact that the bullet about to tear through the air toward him would be something he hadn't anticipated. Quincy always knew everything that was going on around him and everything that was about to happen. It was a kind of ecstasy for my brother, at least I imagined it in this way, that in his final moments on earth, he would be taken by surprise.

Quincy's face turned wistful. "Dovey looks so pretty in blue."

Then my brother offered a final smile, this time of full recognition. Something new had occurred to him. "You are my older sister," he said to Olva. Given Quincy's belief in the despotism of birth order, perhaps her aiming a gun at him confirmed his understanding of the world.

"You are my older sister," he repeated.

Is there an instinct of survival too powerful to suppress? There in the attic of our family's store, the gunshot fractured the air, an infliction that cracked our eardrums and put the taste of lemon pith on our tongues. Sharpness gave way to a reverberation that now, these decades later, is what I hear in the hollow ache of a train's horn. The sound filled our bodies, finding a home in each of us.

My brother crumpled to the floor. The smell of blood rose from his body and met my nose as an alien odor, biological and metallic, life and not life, as if a meteor from deep space had crashed down on that very spot, bringing with it a new existence in which counting how many siblings I had would mean counting how many were dead. Olva released the shotgun from her right shoulder. As if I were watching myself do it, I walked over to her, took the gun, and gestured for her to run. She nodded, scrambling over to the opening in the attic floor where the ladder led to the millinery shop. I knew she would go back to Aunt Dee's.

I stepped toward Quincy's body, then stopped. He had fallen straight down, knees buckling, leaving him in a crouching position, and while I could not see the wound in his chest, I could see the blood, thick and dark, issuing from it, crawling away from his body, surely and steadily, as if it had been waiting to be released. I took a few steps closer but did not touch him. His body seemed leaden; no breath animated it. I thought about the chickens Daddy Kratt had slaughtered in the search for Grandmother DeLour's ruby ring. Had he twisted their necks or chopped their heads off with a hatchet? I pictured the latter: manic bodies, delivered from their heads, still whirling about the yard, frittering away the final pulses of life. But Quincy was a sleeping stone. I did not have to check his body to know he was gone.

The sound of the gunshot was still in the air. I was momentarily deaf. Because of this, I saw more clearly. Twin hallucinations cut across my mind, one toward me, one away. Quincy was suddenly striding at me, and I knew he would pursue me for the rest of my life. Floating away from me was Rosemarie, her hair moving like a golden tide, one that went out and out and would never return.

Unexpectedly, an image from my vision manifested before my eyes in a blur. It flew across the airy expanse of the attic. I felt myself pitch and reel, and a queasy sensation swept through my body, as if a child's blunt hand had spun me like a top. With a jolt—I thought I heard my brain snap against my skull—clarity was restored. It was no delusion. It was Rosemarie herself. She had dashed from the blanket-strewn mattress in the corner and was heading toward the attic's ladder, where Olva had escaped just moments before. Before she hurtled down the ladder, my sister looked back at me as I held the shotgun, a flash of horror on her face. I watched the hole swallow her head, and when it did, her hair licked back through the opening before it vanished.

Sometime that night, while the rest of us weren't sleeping in our rooms, Rosemarie slid noiselessly out of our house and escaped Bound. She was thirteen years old.

Rosemarie escaped, but I stayed. Daddy Kratt wasn't in the store when Quincy was shot. He was making his rounds at the filling station first, and I found him there alone, rotating some cans of motor oil on a shelf. Daddy Kratt had taught me early on that when I came upon a dented or scratched piece of merchandise to turn it so that the damage was concealed.

Without a word, my father followed me from the filling station. Something in my face had silenced him. "This way," I instructed as we entered the store. We moved from staircase to staircase, and the things around us felt like things again, drained of life.

When we finally climbed the attic stairs, Daddy Kratt stepped forward and crouched beside Quincy's body. My father reached down and moved my brother onto his back, exposing the blood-soaked front of the vest Quincy was wearing, the buttons he had buttoned this morning like it were any ordinary day. I stood behind Daddy Kratt, not knowing what to say or do. But then he abruptly stood up to face me. He was looking squarely into my eyes. I held his gaze. Then he turned back toward Quincy's body and knelt down in the same position as before. He reached over and carefully moved his son onto his belly again, hiding the wound from view.

Daddy Kratt exited the attic with the same stoicism with which he had entered. I trailed him, keeping my distance, all the way through the store and out the back entrance. A few feet outside the store, he stopped. I watched him cautiously from the door so that I could flee inside if necessary. My father's head tipped up. I then heard a sound so unsettling that my legs nearly folded under me. It was an ancient and unkempt howl, as if the sky had unhinged its blue jaw and let loose all the sound it had never uttered. He looked frail and deflated, but then his body reared up with a deep breath, as if gathering the sound back up. I was confused and afraid until I recognized it was a display of grief. Here was the recognition Quincy had always wanted.

Daddy Kratt whirled around toward me. "Who did this?"

I gripped the edge of the door. A woodpecker punished a tree in the distance.

"Charlie."

Without acknowledging me again, my father took off away from the store, and a thicket of trees consumed him.

The idea to blame Charlie had formed in my head the moment Olva had fired the Purdey. It was the only way I could think to preserve her. Charlie already had a bull's-eye on his head, and what would it matter if I painted it brighter? And I had saved him, too, hadn't I? I had turned on the Tiffany light and warned him. I had both saved and sacrificed him. Again, I felt as if two different versions of myself existed, crowded together uncomfortably inside me, and I wondered if I would be remembered, in the end, for the saving or the sacrificing.

That afternoon, I hurried to Aunt Dee's. I had not seen Daddy Kratt since I took him to see Quincy's body, and I had not laid eyes on Mama at all. That none of us had sought each other's company in the face of tragedy made me feel light-headed and empty, and I quickened my pace to Dee's. By the time I arrived at her house, the winter sun had grown paler and colder. I circled around to Dee's back door, where friends and family entered, but hearing me struggle through the jumble of her backyard—I had to climb through the doorless cabin of a rusted-out truck—she tore outside with her own shotgun.

"Who is it? This is my property!" she boomed.

"Aunt Dee, it's Judith!" I called out frantically, because I knew that Dee followed through on her plans, however outlandish they seemed to others.

"Get inside, girl," she said, lowering the shotgun and beckoning me with her free hand.

Dee's kitchen smelled of boiled potatoes and a sharp twang, not unpleasant, that was also the smell of my aunt. Olva turned the corner from the den.

"Olva!" I cried, and we embraced. "Where is Charlie?" I asked.

"Already gone," Dee answered. "My friends in Hickory Grove have taken him in, and he will go on from there. He may make a stop in Tirzah. I don't know. He has a son there, but they are not close."

This last piece of news caught Olva's attention. From her expression, I couldn't tell if she knew about Charlie's son. "I'm planning on joining Charlie," Olva said. Her gaze then fell on me. She looked stricken. "Is Quincy—" She couldn't finish.

"Yes," I said quietly.

Olva sat down and sobbed into her cupped hands.

I didn't know how to respond. A new emotion would be required, one not yet available to me, which could encompass the horror, the guilt, and the whisper of relief I felt. When Quincy had fallen, a great storm of sensation raged through me, only to seize up in the next moment, jolting to a stop, so that a recalcitrant numbness was all that remained.

Dee swallowed Olva with her arms. "It's not your fault, Olva. Quincy was threatening Charlie." Dee turned to me. "Judith," she said briskly, getting down to business. "You can help Olva pack."

"She doesn't have to leave," I said.

"Why's that?" Aunt Dee asked, her voice sharp and skeptical.

"Because I told Daddy Kratt..." I paused, closing my eyes. "I told him Charlie did it."

I regretted opening my eyes again. The look on Olva's face might as well have pushed me down into the earth. In that moment, she seemed to disown me, placing me apart from her.

Had I not risked a great deal for Charlie? My efforts had been rewarded with a division from Olva that felt too great to bear.

"Charlie," she whispered, as if her voice could conjure him into the room. There was something more she wanted to say, but she began sobbing again.

I wondered if it was to call him her father. I had never heard her call him that.

Dee squeezed Olva harder. "It's done," she whispered in Olva's ear.

Olva wrested herself free from Dee's arms. "They will find him," Olva said angrily.

"I have a plan," I said, moving toward them. Olva seemed to shrink from me, which made me more desperate for her to understand my idea. "Dee and I have to return to the store to get what we need." I turned to Dee. "We will need your car."

"We'll see if it starts," she said.

I felt full of action and purpose. Olva would not look at me. She was elsewhere, perhaps following Charlie's footsteps. I would bring her back.

Outside, Dee surveyed her car. It was a Cadillac Daddy Kratt had given her when he was full of familial generosity—this was early on, before he and Dee had spent any time together—and Dee had responded by letting the vehicle rot in her backyard. The passenger door seemed sealed shut, and when I pried it open, I half expected to find soil in the floorboards.

Luck or something like it was on our side. The car started. Dee drove us to the store, and I instructed her to pull to the back loading door. I scooted out of the passenger seat, telling Dee to turn off the engine and wait for me.

When I entered the store from its back entrance, I noticed that people were pulsing in and out as if it were a normal workday. I didn't see Daddy Kratt, which was a blessing, but I saw the coroner from York and several of the boys loyal to my father. I shuddered; they were probably there to clean up. Every man in good standing in our town seemed to be there, in fact, and I wondered if Daddy Kratt would speak to them in his office, devising a plan of his own. I pushed the thought out of my mind.

As I picked my way through the crowd, Mr. Clark, the car mechanic, timidly tipped his hat at me, which startled me into thinking he knew why I was there. But he was just paying his respects. I had lost my brother.

I traveled to the third floor, avoiding people's gazes most of the way, and when I got to the millinery shop, I stopped. The coroner and his assistant had already navigated the ladder up to the attic, and they were fluidly guiding a stretcher through the room of mannequins. On it was Quincy's body, covered in a white sheet. I moved to the side as they brought him through the doorway. Busy with their grim work, they didn't acknowledge me, and I focused on their hands, gripping the stretcher. I had thought that when my brother's body passed me—I braced myself for it—I would feel him next to me, just like the hundreds of times we had crossed paths in the store during our young lives. But when the coroner and his assistant went by, the body on the stretcher gave no sense of my brother. Whatever had animated Quincy had abandoned his body. He was just a thing they carried now.

Once they moved toward the elevator, I stepped into the

millinery shop. I pulled back my gaze when it wandered to the opening of the attic. Biting down on my tongue to renew my focus, I found a bolt of fabric and got to my task. When I had my load secured to a shop cart, I pushed it to the freight elevator. I steadied my breath, thinking of Charlie's last ride on the elevator and whispering a thank you to him for fixing it. His escape and my plan would not have been possible without his mechanical genius.

When the elevator landed on the ground floor, I backed my cart out and continued toward the rear exit. With the store brimming with people, how I would make it back to Aunt Dee's car, I was not sure. But people averted their eyes as I passed through. Their discomfort with grief gave me passage.

When Dee and I returned to the house, Olva was waiting for us on the porch. Beside her sat Mama. Mama wore a long-sleeve, button-up dress, and several of the buttons were off-kilter, her white slip showing underneath. Olva's torso was draped across Mama's lap, and Mama was stroking Olva's back with her hand in long, fluid movements. They were lost in shared pain. I was grateful when Dee called out, rousing them from their poses, but my relief was spoiled as I watched Mama stroke the air two more times, even though Olva had moved. Mama's gaze floated in front of her, as if she were looking at everything at once or nothing at all. I wondered if the image of her son rose before her, and if so, was he alive or dead in that vision? Or was she thinking of Charlie? I was suddenly very angry with her for bringing this disaster down on our heads.

Dee was looking at me. I stepped forward and began talking. I explained to them what we were about to do. We worked through the rest of the day and the night, even Mama, whose movements were dreamy and ponderous, as though governed by an invisible tide she had surrendered to.

The next morning, Daddy Kratt's Cadillac swayed to a stop in front of Aunt Dee's house. Aunt Dee and I watched from the window. Mama and Olva hid in the Indian's tepee about a hundred yards from the house. I prayed that my father would not cut the engine.

The prayer was unanswered. Daddy Kratt, his work boots on, thrust himself out of the car and paused, glaring into the distance where the east side of the house broke out into flat acreage—the beginning of a neighbor's cotton plot—with a few sturdy red maples on the periphery. Daddy Kratt squinted into the sun, his jaw working. He stayed there, deliberating on what he saw.

He then bulldozed his way toward the house, knocking over one of Aunt Dee's empty pots. It broke in two, the larger piece rocking on its side. As if on cue, Dee pushed me aside and flew out the front door.

"Isn't the damage done?" she yelled at him, her voice full of rage and despair. She was brandishing her shotgun, but Daddy Kratt didn't seem to notice. He stood in front of the Cadillac and appraised his sister-in-law's ravings. Then he looked to the east again. We knew what he was looking at. A body hung from one of the maples.

"Cruelty!" she screamed. She seemed not to have control

of her voice. That was unusual for Dee, and it frightened me. "On *my* land? This is low, even for you, Brayburn." The shotgun bobbed in her arms. "Charlie was a good man, and you are a vile fool."

Daddy Kratt strode toward her.

Aunt Dee stood to attention. "You stop right there," she said. "He's on my land, and I'll dispose of the body my way." My father took another few steps forward, and Dee aimed the shotgun at him. "You know me, Brayburn," she said, her voice now disciplined.

He stopped.

I held my breath.

Daddy Kratt hoisted a wad of phlegm into his throat and spat onto the cold earth, wiping his mouth with the sleeve of his olive-colored work coat. He pivoted slowly and walked back to the Cadillac. It was the walk of a man who had gotten his way. My breath released. Suddenly, he turned his head back toward the tree in the distance. His jaw pulsed. He looked for a final moment before returning to the car's driver's seat. Dee stood alert, her shotgun raised, until his car disappeared into the amber haze of the morning road.

Olva crept out from the tepee, helping guide Mama out, and I joined Dee outside.

"I hope that worked," Dee told us.

"How could it not?" I asked.

Her laugh was brittle. "For one thing, Brayburn might want to know exactly who did it. And when he starts asking around, he may get suspicious if no one lays claim to the deed." She paused, seeming to absorb what we had done. "The lynching."

"Daddy Kratt is not prone to snooping," I said. "That was Quincy's job." We fell silent at my brother's name.

"Will Mr. Burns miss his mannequin?" Dee asked.

A weight fell from my throat to my stomach. It was something I had not considered. "How could I have missed that?" My mind felt dull, useless. "He adores his mannequins."

"We will return it, then," Dee said.

"We will bury him," Olva replied. She held the horizon with her eyes. "We will bury him, and there will be no more discussion of it."

We nodded. There was no more discussion of it.

Olva took off toward Dee's shed, and we followed her. We gathered our supplies in a wheelbarrow: several stout shovels, hedge clippers, and a small ladder. Over her right shoulder, Dee heaved the bolt of fabric I had brought from the milliner's shop.

"Here we go," Dee said as we set back out. Her face was grave and businesslike.

As we crossed the field away from Dee's house, my cold fingers wrapped around the handles of the wheelbarrow. Our breaths were icy plumes, revealing the secret of the air around us. The morning sun had grown more severe, silhouetting the maple so that it loomed as a colossus before us. Its roots knuckled into the earth, and its immense branches expanded in orchestral drama. I wondered what that red maple had seen over its lifetime. How had time filtered through its spired leaves? What night skies had cascaded above, a blinding rush of stars, and how had the hot earth simmered underneath? Had its branches bent with the weight of a body before? Eras of memories, locked into the bark.

Approaching the mannequin with measured steps, we slowed our breathing and tucked our voices in our mouths. It hung long and limp. To disguise its female form, we had dressed the mannequin in Charlie's hat and clothing, which he had left at Aunt Dee's when hiding at her house. Although the face was featureless and smooth, the body seemed to carry the weight of a real person when suspended. It was tall, too, like Charlie. And the hands! The hands wilted to its sides so delicately and with such human desolation that I felt a wild urge to fill them with mine. But I was afraid to touch them.

I looked over at Olva, and where I thought I might find gratitude or relief, I found something bitter there, a tightness around her jaw, even as her eyes streamed with tears. She reached out and took the mannequin's smooth hand in hers for a moment. Then Dee unrolled the shirt cuffs to hide the color of the mannequin's skin.

In silence, we went about our duties. Dee sliced the rope with the clippers, and she bore the weight of the mannequin, not letting it touch the ground. We rolled it as best we could in the bolt of fabric, and even Mama managed to help. Olva and Dee carried it, one of them stationed at its head, the other its feet. We decided to bury it by Dee's wild strawberries, not too far from her house.

We dug for hours, until our hands ached and our bodies strained to remain upright. It was winter, so no flowers could be found, but Olva collected handfuls of red berries from a holly bush. Olva handed Mama some berries, and the subtle weight in her hand tipped something inside my mother. Mama collapsed next to the wrapped body and began sobbing, her slight frame barely able to contain the coarse, uneven breaths that heaved in and out of her mouth. She lurched violently; no one could approach her, though Dee and Olva tried. A heat rose from her rocking body. The air smelled of crushed berries.

When Mama stopped crying, the cold swept in again, more biting than before. Dee dropped to her knees beside Mama. "Go with Charlie now," Dee said. "Take Olva!"

Mama shook her head, and one side of her mouth curled up. "You always said it was unsafe."

"What is safe or unsafe any longer?" Dee said. "I thought if you were here, I could protect you. I was naive. Go—be with him. I can send word to my friends that you and Olva are coming. They'll take care of you. They'll shepherd you to your next place."

Mama looked at the wrapped body in front of her. I thought she would fall into tears again, but her gaze straightened, and she lifted her spine. "Where is he now?" she asked Dee.

"Hickory Grove."

"So close!" Mama cried.

"He leaves there in the morning," Dee said.

Mama turned to Olva, and I could see Mama's profile, the profile of her beautiful face, and the silhouette was like carved stone, strong and erect, sacred and powerful. Mama's self-possession made Olva's eyes grow calm, and the two sat looking at one another, settling on a decision between them, their eyes working it out, making the arrangements, steeling one another's courage.

"Don't leave!"

My words had come out like begging. But it was anger I

felt first, a blood beat hammering at my temples. Anger at the thought of their escaping this calamity, leaving the rest of us to clean it up. Anger at the thought of Mama abandoning one family for another. And on the day of her son's death! Mama and Olva turned to me. In their faces, I saw immediate resignation. They would stay. Now I was flush with both relief and shame. It was anger, yes, that had pushed the words up from inside me, but I also wanted Mama and Olva to stay because of how I felt that day in the attic with the two of them and Charlie, those moments crisp in my memory, the warmth of the room still resting in the center of my palms.

"We should lower the body," Dee said, breaking the silence.

Before we let it down into the space we had made, Olva leaned over, and around its neck, she hooked the cameo Mama had given her.

"No," said Aunt Dee, retrieving the cameo for Olva. "Keep it. Keep it as yours."

Olva held it in her palm, curling her fingers around it.

Mama did not attend Quincy's funeral. Aunt Dee had made the decision, and Daddy Kratt, less despotic than usual, didn't stop Dee from gathering her sister in the early, fumbling hours and whisking her back to her kudzu-wrapped home. Quincy was dead, Charlie was gone, and Rosemarie was nowhere to be found: the torment that daily visited my mother was plain to see. When I dashed Mama's final hope to be with Charlie and Olva, I had extracted what remained of her. She became a long, solitary coil of smoke escaping a snuffed candle. Her facial expressions seemed off cue, as if she couldn't quite keep up with conversations any longer or else she was reacting to different conversations in her mind.

Daddy Kratt insisted we hold the funeral service in our home. It was three days before Christmas, and our maids had hastily taken down the holiday decorations put up a month earlier. Time did not afford replacing our everyday decor, so the house had an austere feel, as if it, too, were in mourning, wearing simple and somber attire appropriate for the circumstances. With the mantel bare and side tables undressed, the unfamiliarity troubled me. As I look back, I wonder what made our house a home for me. Was it my family? Or was it the things in their proper places?

In the living room, the furniture had been shifted further so that Quincy's casket could sit in the same spot as the sofa. Four boys from the church carried it inside and placed it atop a long table, outfitted with a simple black skirt. It was kept closed at my father's insistence. I would have to account for the casket in my inventory of the store; it had come from the first floor, near the back, next to a small light-filled room that acted as our plant nursery. You could buy a casket and step a few feet over to buy the flowers to plant on top of it.

I stood for a long while there in the living room. As I studied the glossy wood, I felt a delicate movement of emotion inside me, as a teacup sets down on a saucer. I had outlived my brother.

Funeral guests trickled into our house, hugging the outskirts of the room to keep a wide orbit from my brother's body. As the eldest daughter, people directed their condolences toward me, especially when they realized Mama, poor, ephemeral Mama, wasn't fit for company. I was praised for my stalwartness, how much I was putting my family before myself by keeping my head on straight during these difficult times. Yet their remarks did not go much beyond that. The people who had worked for my father for years upon years did not convey their sorrow. Instead, I sensed relief in their slight handshakes and tepid condolences. What gossip about them had been laid to rest with my brother?

The exception was the Sullivan family. I watched through the living room window as Lindy Sullivan—the girl I had once forced a shower upon, along with her sisters—approached our door on careful feet. She didn't come inside for the service, but instead, she set by the door a persimmon crumble, still warm. Our cook, Ima, walked outside to pick up the crumble and thank Lindy, but the girl had already hurried off, not requiring any gratitude in return. It meant a good deal to me, because the Sullivans, poorer than anyone, wouldn't have come by flour or sugar easily. Their kindness filled me with the sour ache of sadness.

I greeted Pastor Cunningham when he walked into our house. The pastor was hefty but meek, a gentle manatee of a man, floating along the currents without any will of his own. When he saw me, his face—neck folds, jowls, and all—lifted up into a consoling smile but also as if he were bracing against a pain he hoped would be over soon. I gathered that Daddy Kratt had requested a meeting, at which time the pastor would be given threatening but opaque directions about what the sermon should convey. As he entered our house, Pastor Cunningham's anxiety was plain to see. His gaze avoided the casket in the middle of the room.

Rosemarie did not come back, not even for her brother's funeral. At the time, though, I didn't know she had left Bound. I assumed she was off somewhere avoiding life, or in this case, avoiding death, picking wild honeywort in a field or wading shin-deep in a river even though the trees clacked with ice. Later, when it was clear she had fled town, Daddy Kratt dispatched some of his loyal boys, a search party meant to find her, as if she were a filly run off from the stable, but they returned, their faces as empty and untroubled as their hands.

After Pastor Cunningham's arrival, Daddy Kratt finally walked down the stairs wearing his finest suit, and he did not want to look anyone in the eye, I could tell. His beard sat entirely still under his chin. It was, I now understood, how grief looked on my father.

The service was short. Pastor Cunningham had elected to say very few words, owing to his nervousness, and those he chose were mild and dull. In attempting to avoid conflict, the pastor might well have created for himself another problem, and time would tell just how much Daddy Kratt had found the sermon lacking. The pastor seemed to sense this, because afterward, when we were all moving into the study for some light food and beverage, there was no sight of him. It was ludicrous, and a bitter laugh rose to my lips, but I restrained myself out of respect to Quincy. What was it about our family that made desertion people's first instinct?

I'd grown tired of people telling me how well I was handling things. What had sounded like praise two days ago now sounded like a ruling on my lack of feeling. When I entered the study, its double doors opened wide, I considered how Daddy Kratt had built this house with a study twice the usual size. My father had not come from an educated family, nor did he possess much formal education of his own, but his ambitions were more expansive than anyone's. In front of me, people nibbled politely at their food. Mr. Burns and Mr. Aiken were arguing over President Hoover, who was still assuring the nation that the economy was foundationally sound.

As they argued, Dovey cried quietly beside her father. She then crossed the study and stepped into the living room. I followed her. She took a few tentative paces toward the casket and paused, gazing at it, just as I had earlier. Moving forward, she touched it with her fingertips. This was too much for Dovey, and her chin dropped to her chest, tears running onto her black smock, which gathered at her ribs and widened down to her shins. A hand trembled at her temple. The other hand, the one that had touched the casket, dropped to her belly, where her palm landed and gave an almost imperceptible press, there and gone in a fragile pulse of time. But I had seen it. The slight rounding of her belly. A capacious dress to hide it.

The room seemed to lose its edges around me, everything blurring, but the hard voice of Dovey's father from the study revived me, tightening my vision so quickly that I felt a sharp tap of pain behind my right eye.

I hurried back to the study. Others were listening to Mr. Aiken, too. "What's more," he was saying to Mr. Burns, "we've got our own problems right here in Bound. Brayburn's being stubborn as ever." Mr. Aiken was complaining that my father was continuing to hoard his ginned cotton because the prices were still astonishingly low. Mr. Aiken wondered how long our cotton would sit there and how this might damage Bound's local economy. Talking business at my brother's funeral! And yet perhaps Quincy's death was part of that business: some secrets buried with him, other secrets, the ones he protected, that might now see the light of day. I wondered if Mr. Aiken knew about his daughter.

Suddenly, Mr. Burns, gesturing with his coffee cup, was announcing loudly to Mr. Aiken, "The world may indeed be going to hell in a handbasket, but what concerns me right now is that somebody has stolen one of my mannequins."

Daddy Kratt, who had been standing nearby, tilted his head toward the conversation. His jaw began working, his beard coming alive. He took a few steps toward Mr. Burns, and then he changed course and stepped haltingly toward the food table. He made it nearly to that table when he turned on his heels and moved toward the door. He looked almost to be stumbling. Suddenly, the room was silent except for a few loud voices, guests who had not yet noticed my father's behavior. Those voices stuck out raggedly against the silence of the room but were quickly chastened.

Shep Bramlett strode forward. "Brayburn, let's sit down a moment," he said. He was jocular, trying to overshadow my father's behavior.

Daddy Kratt just blinked at his business partner with an empty look on his face.

Someone behind me whispered, "Where is Mrs. Kratt?"

When my father heard this, his shook his head lightly, as if having a secret argument with himself, and then his body moved toward a group of people who stood near the door. As he moved toward them, they parted, as though his body let off a kind of magnetic pulse that had edged them aside like iron shavings. He left the room, and we heard his footsteps stamp toward the front door. Everyone scurried to the windows to watch him double back and take off behind the house.

It was the first time I had ever seen my father flee a room. The others noticed it, too, and when they started to collect their coats and hats, the murmurs picked up in the house, and when they graduated to a steady drone, I could feel something happening. I felt the change as if a string had been gently strummed within me, and I was powerless to dampen its reverberations, leaving a feeling of seasickness hovering at my throat.

Guests exchanged glances with one another. I saw faint smiles lingering behind their confused looks. No one could articulate it, but everyone felt Daddy Kratt's diminished presence. His body had not taken up the space it normally did as he had parted the crowd. He had run from them, the way they normally ran from him.

I stood numbly in the study. I had meant to look for Dovey again, but she was gone with the others. I was now alone, save Ima, who had come in to retrieve the uneaten food. She stood behind me a long while before she spoke.

"I am sorry, Miss Judith," she said, and her words were like a warm hand on my shoulder. I didn't know if she was offering sympathy for my brother's death or my father's erratic performance, but I needed shelter from both.

Clop clop clop.

Ima and I whirled our heads to the study doors. It had to be my father: the hard clip of his shoes hitting the wood floors, walking from the rear of the house to the front. Ima hurried out the back entrance of the study.

The footsteps stalled just shy of the study's entrance. I took a deep breath and walked through the doors. There was Daddy Kratt, waiting for me.

"We need to head down to the cemetery," he said. His tongue seemed to sit more thickly in his mouth.

In his face was the echo of what had happened in the study. A lone nerve twitched the skin of his right eyelid. His jaw was fixed. I studied him, trying to figure out if he had discovered our deception with the mannequin.

My gaze swept across the living room. During the reception in the study, Quincy's casket had been noiselessly removed from our house and taken to the grave site. Daddy Kratt had stipulated that his son's casket would be released into the earth only in front of family members. Which meant the two of us—my father and me.

The day after the funeral, I arrived early at the store. Ice drew down the branches of the oaks that flanked the building. I was on the second floor, completing my inventory and pondering our slipping sales, and the store was more silent than usual. I listened for a sound from my father's office—a chair scraping, a lone cough—but there was nothing.

Then I heard rustling above me. I left my daily ledger on the foot of the staircase and made my way toward the noise. It was coming from Mr. Burns's office. Sweat began to pearl on my body as if it were the middle of summer, and my sweat reacted with the wool of my coat, making me itch at the back of my neck.

I swallowed hard, heading toward the millinery office. A low hum was coming from the door to the office, and when I rounded the corner, I found Mr. Burns, dressing one of his mannequins in a long, brown trench coat.

"Oh!" he said, quickly regaining his self-possession. His lips flattened into an insincere smile. "How can I help you, Miss Kratt?" He continued to fuss with the mannequin's coat, scrutinizing and then pulling off a stray string.

"Are you still missing one of your mannequins, Mr. Burns?" I asked quietly.

His eyebrows lifted and fell. "Indeed I am," he said curtly.

"I don't think you are, sir."

"Excuse me?" A single note of laughter hopped from his lips.

"I think you found your mannequin in the storage room, where you had accidentally misplaced it."

A sputter of air escaped his mouth. "Miss Kratt, I most certainly did not misplace my mannequin. You may be aware that there have been some rumors," he said, eyeing me.

I looked down at my hands.

"Mr. Burns," I said, steeling myself as I lifted my gaze, "I know some rumors of my own. Where do you suppose Mrs. Greeley is this morning?"

He stood taller. "How in the world should I know?" he said, his voice high.

"I've noticed you spend a good deal of time with her. My late brother, Quincy, noticed it, too." I stepped toward him. "I wonder if Mr. Greeley has noticed."

Mr. Burns let out a strained laugh. "I don't know what you're talking about," he said, busying himself with some drawings on his desk.

"If you don't *find* your misplaced mannequin, I will pay Mr. Greeley a visit. Business matters, of course."

Mr. Burns lifted his head, staring out into the middle of the room. He sniffed. "All right, then."

I stepped backward toward the door, not wanting to take my eyes off Mr. Burns but wanting to make my exit as quickly as possible.

"Good," I said. "I don't think my father has come into work yet. I'm going to retrieve him from our house. I need you to speak with him sometime today, Mr. Burns. Tell him you merely misplaced your mannequin. It was never missing in the first place. And you need to spread the word about it. Do you understand?"

He gazed down, lifting one of his hands feebly in acceptance of my plan.

I turned on my heels and shot out the door. A wave of euphoria carried me down three flights of stairs and outside. I stuffed my hands into the pockets of my coat and leaned into the bitter air, shrugging my collar over my ears.

On my way home, I passed the tree that had always held my sister. It sat bare and silent against the cold December morning. If Mr. Burns managed to be convincing, Daddy Kratt would believe Charlie had indeed been hanged. I wasn't sure what Daddy Kratt would do if he discovered the truth about how we had used the mannequin. Mama and Olva were still at Aunt Dee's and had planned to stay there until the storm settled. And Charlie—hopefully, he had flown far away from Bound.

When I arrived home, I mounted the steps just as Daddy Kratt was opening the front door. "Are you heading to the store?" I asked. I tried to sound nonchalant.

My father seemed distracted, and he nodded gruffly.

As he stepped onto the porch, we both stopped. Shep Bramlett's Plymouth was crawling down the road. My father and I watched it, and I was shocked when it didn't pull into our driveway. It continued on, at its snail's pace, which gave us an opportunity to study who was inside.

Daddy Kratt let off a rough noise as if he had been sucker punched.

Shep was driving, but in the passenger seat was Byrd Parker, Daddy Kratt's one-time business rival, the one for whom life was a litany of distress mumbled across parted lips. I still remembered—it had the ability to produce a fresh shock—when Quincy had broken the Tiffany lamp while showing it to Byrd. Sitting in Shep's car, Byrd turned his melancholy face toward us. In his expression lurked no retribution, even though Daddy Kratt had blackmailed Byrd, taking his cotton gin in the wake of his wife's drowning in the unnamed lake.

At that moment, Daddy Kratt knew he had lost his standing in Bound. Quincy wasn't around any longer to wield his secrets in our father's favor. Shep Bramlett had found another business partner, and curious as it was, Byrd Parker, who had suffered his own disgrace, was the one Mr. Bramlett had chosen to pluck from the mud and reinstate into the community. Perhaps it was somewhat promising that scandals did not stain eternally, but as I studied my father's face, sapped of all expression, that was cold comfort now.

Daddy Kratt's breath got quieter and quieter. We both stared at Byrd. Mr. Bramlett was going slowly because he wanted us to see. The look on Byrd's face, riding there in Shep's Plymouth, was a salute, solemn in nature, as if paying his respects to my father's own misfortune. Not only the loss of his son, but also his diminished position in Bound, a town on which he had laid siege—and enjoyed the spoils—ever since his arrival almost half a century ago.

Not long after we watched those two men parade by that day, Daddy Kratt sold his cotton gins to Byrd Parker, including, of course, the one that had been Byrd's in the first place. He held onto the store for a few more years, but ultimately, he was forced to sell the Kratt Mercantile Company to the Bramlett family. Until he died, Daddy Kratt worked at his filling station, which he had sold to Mr. Clark, and he spent most of his time there, mainly drinking. After Shep Bramlett ran our store into the ground, he didn't even have to sell it, because he had weaseled it out of my father's hands for such a cut rate. Every day on Daddy Kratt's walk to the filling station, he could see the store he built from nothing sink back into nothing again.

After Quincy's death, Mama and Olva spent most of their time at Aunt Dee's, although Olva would come visit me in the house from time to time. Under the care of Dee and Olva, Mama regained some of her vitality before she went quietly in the night by way of a stroke, her gentleness in life extending to her death. After that, Daddy Kratt became a wisp of himself, running the filling station poorly and spending the day drinking with his loyal boys, who weren't loyal any longer, until he died from tuberculosis. Mr. Aiken came to pay his respects to me at the house after Daddy Kratt died, and he called tuberculosis the "poor man's disease," which would have killed my father if he hadn't already been dead.

When Mr. Aiken visited, I didn't dare ask him about Dovey, who had gone to stay with an aunt in Atlanta shortly after the funeral. Dovey never returned to Bound. I heard nothing more about her, whether there was a baby, how she was faring. If there was gossip, my ears were spared it. There was nothing to substantiate she had given birth to Quincy's child, another Kratt, a possible heir. Because of this, I told no one, not even Olva.

I was alone in the house for many years until Olva agreed to move in after Dee died. Like Mama, Dee suffered a stroke. She asked to be buried in her own garden, upside down and only to her hips so that her leg bones could be used for tomato ladders, a request we very nearly honored. Who knew Dee would outlive all the men of her age in Bound, just like she said she would? Who knew my sister would come back home? Who knew Olva's kin, Marcus and Amaryllis, would move in? Who knew Olva would raise a shotgun at a man for a second time in her life?

I had not even known these were the questions to ask.

THIRTEEN

Rick glanced at his friend. We were all standing in our same positions, frozen in a terrible tableau. Olva was pointing the Purdey shotgun at Rick. Her arms were fixed, tireless. The next time I blinked, I saw Quincy where Rick was standing, and I squeezed my eyes to quit the hallucination. Opening my eyes again, I found just Rick, his jaw hanging slackly, some mixture of amusement and insolence there.

Behind Olva was Jolly's Taurus, which I now saw was parked half on the driveway, half on the lawn, in a reckless and presumptuous way. Rick's friend was still the closest to me, and when he smiled uncivilly, I saw that his two front teeth were gray. He reminded me of the Sullivan sisters, who used to hide their neglected teeth from me with mysterious, pressed-lipped smiles.

"It's not even loaded," Rick said to his friend, chuckling.

With a sober, practiced fluidity, Olva whipped the barrel open to show two shells and snapped it back shut. Rick's face fell quiet. How was he to know that Olva had once fired this very shotgun at someone? I was the only living person who knew.

No one said a thing. Olva stood there aiming the gun. Amaryllis clung to the backs of her father's legs. I wondered if Marcus would do something, but his feet were planted solidly, as if sheltering the child was the most important thing he could be doing at that moment. I thought we all might stand there forever. Rick spoke first, in a way that signaled he thought he held the right to speak and be listened to.

"No reason for you to get involved," he said to Olva. He was relaxed, confident. His friend's mouth twitched. Rick turned to Marcus. "It's you who started this whole thing. You thought you could slide by without paying your rent—"

"You raised our rent—"

Rick held up his hand. "I don't want to hear it. You think I make squat down at my store? Property is my livelihood now, and people like you are always thinking you can cheat the system to take more than the rest of us."

"You're the cheat," my sister interjected.

Rick didn't even look in her direction. "How I see it," he said, "is that you call your grandma off or Tommy and I will get that gun from her the hard way. Nobody ever gave me a handout, but that's all you want. We're just living our lives, and you go on making problems for us." Rick looked over at his friend. "You're making Tommy tense. Can't you tell?"

Tommy's face quivered.

Olva's laugh was swift and metallic. "Tense?" she said. "His tension? Yours?" She kept the gun steady. "I will tell you a thing or two about tension. I will tell you that we did not create it. You did. You merely have not felt it until now. Understand this—for me, for Marcus"—she nodded toward Amaryllis—"for that child, tension lives under the surface of everything. We feel the itch of it under our skin. But we will rise from that tension. Agitation is what sheds the snake of its skin, what shucks the moth of its cocoon."

Rick and his friend Tommy exchanged glances. Rick's face held a slight smirk.

"The last time I pointed a gun at a man," Olva continued, and this got Rick's attention, "I knew that pulling the trigger would mean making some things worse, even if it might make other things better. But it was the only way I knew to protect my family. It was the means I was given at that moment. And as I stand here before you, I can tell you that Marcus and Amaryllis are my family, and I'll make things worse to make them better if I have to. I'm not afraid to do that."

Rick and Tommy looked at each other again. Rick then seemed to motion with his eyes, a signal for Tommy.

"It's time for you to leave now," Marcus said to them, as gentle as if he were coaxing his child to go to bed. He gestured for Amaryllis to join Rosemarie and me on the porch. The child came to stand to my left, above the gray-toothed man. Marcus then positioned himself close to Olva, his long body standing with hers.

Rick brought his hands to his face and cradled his head for a moment. He seemed to be wrestling with something in his mind, and it was unsettling the way he was letting us watch him. All at once, his contemplation veered to action. Events rushed forward at a cruel velocity, thread unspooling irrevocably from a bobbin. Rick lunged at Olva, knocking the gun from her hands. As Rick and Marcus scrambled for the weapon, Tommy charged Olva's back. Time thinned out, became brittle, and, for a moment, no noises arose from the fray, no sounds at all, just bodies moving around and around, chasing survival, arms and legs interwoven, inseparable. Time broke. A ferocious wail shot through the air, seizing our eardrums. The birds screamed and shook the trees. Amaryllis, still wailing, soared off the porch—clear over the hedges—and alighted next to Tommy. Her body had the force of an ungovernable wind. As she landed, she threw her weight at Tommy's knees, pushing him down. Fear and pride converged on Olva's face when she saw what Amaryllis had done. As Tommy fell on his side, Rick wrenched the shotgun from Marcus and stepped back to clear a space for its long barrel. He aimed the shotgun at Amaryllis.

Olva let out a noise that sounded halfway between life and death. Marcus said hoarsely, "Please don't." His eyes, wild with terror, seemed trapped alive in a body gone dormant. He swayed gently on his feet.

Tommy looked up from the ground. His face twitched violently. He got to his feet and stumbled backward. "I'm done helping you," he said to Rick. "You're on your own." Rick did not watch as his friend staggered past the car and took off running down the road.

Amaryllis leveled her eyes at the barrel of the gun in Rick's hands. "Go away!" she screamed.

Rick stared at her. His skin was thick, veiled in sweat, and it seemed to sit more heavily than before on his face. His expression was protean. It shifted before our eyes in a disquieting way, rearranging with each new thought, and I wondered if he had control of what was happening, thoughts scrambling and slipping in his mind, each vying for ascendancy. And then his expression settled into the shape of recognition. Recognition, it seemed to me, that Amaryllis was a child. He took a few slow steps back. He did not look at anyone. He carried the gun with him to the edge of the driveway, where he laid it down on the grass before yanking the door of the Taurus open. He started up the engine and reversed heedlessly, almost slamming into our brick mailbox. The car careened away.

Inside, we locked the front door. We could hear one another panting. Olva peered out the window. Marcus held Amaryllis on the sofa, and she cradled her Peter Rabbit, which she had rescued from the doorway.

"He didn't do it," I said, feeling both grateful and bewildered. "Rick spared her."

Olva turned from the window and gave a dark look. "He hasn't earned my respect for one moment of mercy."

Rosemarie was walking in circles. The emergency had awakened a frenetic energy in my sister. "Holy God, Olva! When you had the shotgun, I thought you would really shoot him!"

I could tell my sister was entertaining with feverish delight a scenario: Rick, shot dead on my front lawn. My tongue pressed to the roof of my mouth. For here was my sister who had not been living encircled by the heirlooms in this house. My sister, who had breezed in with all her easy emotion about it. Who had gone out to get some fresh air for sixty years.

Rosemarie was speaking again. "You should have shot him! He pointed a gun at Amaryllis!" Rosemarie's forehead creased.

"Wait, when did you ever point a gun at a man? You said that to him."

Olva turned toward her. "I shot Quincy."

"Is that a joke?" Rosemarie said with a jumpy laugh.

Olva, mouth set, shook her head.

"That's not possible." My sister was silent for a moment. "I was there," she said quietly. "When Quincy was killed, I was there. It was Judith." An old rage emerged in her eyes, but she wouldn't look at me. Her voice rose. "I saw Judith. I smelled the rose water she used to wear. The smell makes me sick now."

"I did it," Olva said.

"No, I saw *Judith*," Rosemarie insisted. She was tracing the same path in her mind, around and around. "Judith was holding the shotgun."

"She had taken it from me," Olva said.

Rosemarie stepped toward the wall and steadied herself. "No. Quincy even said it himself. *You are my older sister.* He said that right before she shot him."

"He was talking to me," Olva said. "I'm his older sister, too. We share a mother, Rosemarie."

"What?" my sister said, her face a squall of confusion.

"I'm your half sister. I'm Mama and Charlie's child."

Rosemarie's gaze scattered and refocused. "Mama is your mother?" Her eyes lashed toward me. "Did you know this? Am I the only one who didn't know?" She steadied herself again. "Olva—before we searched, did you already know who your parents were?"

"Rosemarie, let me explain—"

"Why did we go to Hickory Grove?" Rosemarie asked,

livid. "Is that why you asked me to play with Amaryllis and that dog so you could talk to the preacher alone? So you could keep secrets from me?"

Olva spoke calmly. "I have known since my childhood that Charlie and Mama were my parents. I decided it was time to tell Marcus and Amaryllis how I was related to them." She looked gently at the child, who smiled. "I had never tracked down the records. I wanted to show Amaryllis most of all. I could tell her I was her great-great-aunt, but I wanted her to see that someone wrote it down. Someone cared enough to document it. All these years, the black church in Hickory Grove kept the real history of the births and deaths of the area. What brave custodians they were. All those stories of men and women and children who could not claim their own lives." Olva looked at me. "I suppose that is another type of inventory, one in defiance of the inventories from a generation before that sought to erase the existence of a whole people by turning them into possessions. It's a question of what we own. Do you own your own life? If you have never had to ask that question, you are fortunate indeed."

Rosemarie was still shaking her head in bewilderment. "Why did you invite me here, Olva? If you already knew the details of your birth?"

"It was time you knew the truth about Quincy's death," Olva said. "For you. But also for me. I needed it to be known by everyone. All these years, Judith was the only one who knew."

Here, she looked at me pointedly. I glanced away.

At the mention of Quincy's name, Rosemarie's face

contracted. "Quincy always protected me. It was why I left when he died."

My sister stood in silence for a few moments, rocking back and forth, and I wondered if she were testing out her new footing. Our family's story sat on a different foundation than she had once thought. She turned to Olva. "How could it be?"

"When Mama became pregnant with Olva," I explained, my voice finally available to me, "she stayed at Aunt Dee's. Daddy Kratt didn't notice, because he was building his local empire. Then Mama traveled with Dee away from Bound so that she could give birth to Olva."

Rosemarie shook her head. I hadn't answered the right question. She turned her eyes at Olva. "You cared for us so thoroughly. Even if you were our sister"—here, she paused, absorbing her own words—"you cared for us as if we were your children. You were always so"—her mouth sought the word she wanted—"selfless."

Olva's face contorted, and I said quickly, "Olva was trying to protect Charlie."

Olva let out a solemn breath before her voice rose. "I killed a man! I killed my brother! Every dawn I am blessed to see greets me with that fact. It is like a ringing in my ears I cannot stop." She lifted her palm. "And I allowed my *father* to be blamed for my actions. All these years, I have been too ashamed to tell Marcus and Amaryllis."

I could see the back of Marcus's head, which straightened when he heard their names. I could not see the child, who was still folded in his lap on the sofa.

Olva's voice sank to an accusing whisper, and she looked at me. "I have always been afraid you would tell them."

"I kept quiet about it!" I cried. "Rosemarie was the one to tell Marcus and Amaryllis you were related to them. I kept quiet about that, too!" My attempt to shift the blame to my sister felt feeble. I lifted my fingers to my eyes, rubbing them, which triggered small bursts of light against the backs of my eyelids. I did not feel well at all. "I did the best I could," I said to Olva. "I helped Charlie escape. I silenced Mr. Burns. Pointing a finger at Charlie was to save you. But you have never forgiven me for that decision."

"Decisions are a luxury," Olva replied. Her voice was hard.

"Charlie would have been dead if I had not thought to string that mannequin up in a tree. But you never saw it that way, Olva." I was exhausted. A sensation of nausea began to flip-flop gently in my throat; I stepped to the Windsor chair and lowered myself into it. I tried to steady my breath. "It was the last time in my life when I resolved to act. After that, I went back to watching."

No one said anything, and I couldn't bear to look over to gauge Olva's response.

Rosemarie made a soft noise of disgust. "So Charlie wasn't hanged after all."

"Wasn't he?" It was Marcus's voice from the sofa. The words sat in the air. He stood up, lifting Amaryllis with him. She tucked her head in the crook of his neck. Marcus did not appear shocked, as I thought he would be, to hear that Charlie had not been hanged. Instead, his expression was steady. "I have carried the memory of my great-grandfather strung up in a maple—a maple I pass every day on my paper route. To me, Charlie swung from that tree, even if you say he really didn't. I have felt the weight of him hanging inside me as long as I can remember. Like I've been housing two bodies in this one my whole life. And the outside world hasn't been any easier. It was part of my family's history that my great-grandfather killed a white man. And a Kratt no less. People in this town don't forget things like that. Over the years, it drove the rest of my family away from South Carolina. But I'm the one who stayed. I'm the one who kept my family here despite everything. Do you know how careful we had to be? How invisible we had to make ourselves? How *selfless*?" Marcus looked at Rosemarie. Then he took a few steps toward me, the child dwelling in his arms as if part of him. He looked squarely in my eyes. "And wasn't it convenient for you that you could hold Quincy's death over Olva's head for all these years?"

"It wasn't like that—it isn't like that! Tell them, Olva!"

Olva said nothing.

Marcus kept talking. "You held it over Olva's head. So don't tell me that wasn't Charlie's body hanging. So many things hanging in the balance. No wonder Olva and I found each other. All our lives, this place has bound us."

Olva walked over to the sofa to gather Amaryllis from Marcus's arms. The three of them stood together—a unit—and then the child followed Olva and Marcus wordlessly up the stairs. I didn't know if they planned to take a rest or pack their bags and leave.

"Olva! Don't leave me!"

Halfway up the stairs, she turned around, and the silence was agonizing. I counted my heartbeats throbbing in my ears.

She finally spoke. "Judith, I have no plans to leave you."

Rosemarie and I remained in the living room long after Olva, Marcus, and Amaryllis disappeared upstairs. I felt no triumph but was relieved beyond measure by Olva's words.

I looked at my sister. Her right hand rested on the sofa, index finger absentmindedly tapping the gray fabric, and in her face was an agony of confusion. She had left Bound when she was thirteen years old with a false story about our family. Her eyebrows moved up and down; expressions skittered across her face. I saw that nowhere had ever felt like home for her. Perhaps she had thought coming back to Bound would soothe that restlessness, even now in the dusk of her life.

"Your husband," I said. "Sounds like he was a decent fellow."

Her finger continued to tap the sofa. "He was," she said distantly. By degrees, her expression returned to the room. She laid her eyes on mine. I felt it was the first time she had truly looked at me since her return. "You should have met him."

I nodded. "If I had, I'm sure I would have found fault with him."

Rosemarie's eyes widened, and then her jaw fell open, spilling loose and ragged laughter into the air, driving the tension from the room. I joined her, and for a few moments, we could hardly breathe, so urgent was our laughter.

FOURTEEN

The next morning, Rosemarie was gone. For a second time in her life, she had fled Bound. I knew she had departed before I entered her room. Her few belongings were missing (the ratty duffel, her man's shoes), but more conspicuous was the absence of her voice. That laughter, too, which pursued you until you succumbed to it.

The night before, after Amaryllis was in bed, Marcus and Olva had returned to the living room and stayed up late, the murmurs of their conversation sifting upstairs to my bedroom. After drawing myself a bath that afternoon, I had pulled out Alfred Lord Tennyson's long poem *In Memoriam*, in which Tennyson mourns the death of his friend Arthur Henry Hallam. I was reading the stanza in which a hand offered at the beginning is finally taken at the end. How well Tennyson understood grief. How hard it was to reach out and take the hand. But in the end, the hand is taken. The hand is taken!

That night, I tried to tame bouts of fitful sleep, a failed experiment that left me more agitated than before. I had a nightmare about Amaryllis and the shotgun. Then another about Olva and the shotgun. In actuality, Olva had hidden the weapon. She said she had buried it by the stunted peach trees, but she wouldn't say exactly where. We couldn't give the thing away. It was indelibly ours, and we could not relinquish ownership. It would always have its hold on us, in our waking hours and in our sleeping hours.

As the weeks passed, we didn't speak about Rosemarie's departure. We hardly spoke at all. Amaryllis asked the most questions, but Marcus and Olva would only answer her when I was out of the room. Olva saw Jolly at the post office, but the two ignored one another. Jolly looked embarrassed, Olva said.

Marcus kept his paper route, and he went back to his occasional work of repairing items around town. After the altercation with Rick, Marcus was hired by the staff of Grace Baptist, the local black congregation, to restore the church's faulty electrical switches. Marcus seemed pleased by this. Yet I was careful not to pretend I knew what Marcus and Olva were thinking. The situation was like something freshly painted, and I was careful how I proceeded in its midst.

One morning, it was early October, I found Marcus working in the study at Daddy Kratt's desk. The desk (80 by 51 by 30 inches, mid-nineteenth-century English, burr yew wood, satinwood and ebony inlay) was a partners' desk, with an opening on either side meant for business associates to work opposite one another. It had been Grandfather DeLour's, and he had purchased it, one would imagine, with the intention of one day working across from his son (the longed-for son of DeLour and Sons). When Daddy Kratt ruined his father-in-law's company—a feat equal parts calculating and devil-may-care, my father in a nutshell—the desk fell into his possession, too. I would often peer into the study to find him seated there, scratching out his signature on eviction notices or swindled land purchases, and he had the habit of abruptly glancing across the desk and then chuckling, as if it gave him great unceasing pleasure to see the other side of the desk empty.

When I entered the study, I saw that Marcus had taken apart a small clock, its innards organized in neat piles on the desk. He was working on it with a long instrument, as if he were a dentist, cleaning the clock's teeth.

"You look just like Charlie when you do that," I said from outside the double doors.

Marcus regarded me with a polite smile before returning to his work.

I lingered at the doorway. "I have a question for you." Marcus looked up again, and I stepped into the room so that I might have the courage to ask it. "Will you take me to Rock Hill? I need to see a lawyer to have some business matters handled."

His instrument hovered above the open mouth of the clock. "Right now?"

I hesitated. I did in fact want to go at that moment, but he seemed busy. "Whenever you are ready."

He nodded. "I'll meet you out front in an hour."

I retreated from the room to gather some things for the trip, and when an hour had passed, I found Marcus standing beside his Pontiac.

"I thought we would take my car," I said, motioning toward my Cutlass as I shielded my eyes from the sun with my other hand. "You can drive me."

"We'll take my car."

His voice held no invitation for debate, so I climbed into the passenger's seat of his Pontiac.

"No one can say you didn't prepare for the trip," Marcus said, surveying my large leather bag, which was an old, distinguished piece of Daddy Kratt's luggage.

"Well, yes," I said, a bit embarrassed. I was certainly not going to tell him what was inside. I had packed pickled okra (one jar), Wray Little's rum apple butter (one jar, already opened), a sleeve of saltines, four butterscotch candies, my social security card, and an antique brass teacher's bell, which I thought would be useful in an emergency.

As Marcus pulled the car onto the road, my breath felt tight in my throat, and it became increasingly difficult to usher air in and out of my lungs. I suppose I sounded quite terrible, because we had not even made the next turn when Marcus swerved the car to the side of the road and stopped.

"Are you all right?" he asked, alarmed.

I managed to collect breath back into my lungs. "I am fine."

Marcus looked at me, then my bag. I was clutching its smooth handles for support. "Judith, when is the last time you left your house?"

It took me a long while to speak, but Marcus was patient. I was thinking of Mrs. Clark, wife of our mechanic, who had become a shut-in when we were children. The stories we had spun about her! In our later teenage years, she had been found dead, splayed out on her back porch steps, her walking cane a few feet in front of her. It was dreadful: her first breaths of fresh air in decades had been her last.

"I have not left my house for sixty years. Since my brother's death."

Marcus made a sound, a surprised but not unkind one. He

didn't say another word about it. My nose stung with gratitude. He didn't ask why we were going to Rock Hill, so I nestled into my seat and watched the scenery outside. Soft rain began to settle onto the windows, making the world outside hazy and faraway. I was thankful for the obfuscation, because the rate at which the landscape between Bound and Rock Hill had changed was distressing. Land that had once supported lively communities was now a smattering of barns gone to seed, and railroad tracks, halfway demolished, sat at odd angles in heaps on the ground. Kudzu hung from the trees like hanks of hair, and trailers outnumbered homes.

This was the world I had relinquished. A few months after Quincy's death, Rosemarie long gone, I had given up my duties at the store and simply stopped leaving the house. My sister had gone to make her way out in the world, but I would defend my small corner of it.

"The world has changed," I said.

"It has," he replied, and his voice went up, as if he were moving forward in his mind.

When we arrived at my errand's destination, Marcus accompanied me inside, settling into a chair in the waiting room. The receptionist, chewing gum as if it were her job, eyed Marcus. The lawyer, when he retrieved me, did the same thing. My appointment was fairly straightforward, despite that the lawyer seemed to find my plans ill-advised and spent a few moments asking me all manner of silly and unrelated questions. When I realized he was testing my mental faculties, I made him aware of the Kratt family's legacy in Bound. I saw that the desk in his office was cheaply made, and I explained to him about our

Abner Cutler rolltop desk, adding for good measure the story of when we as children plundered that desk in the dead of night. The lawyer suddenly became quite economical with our time.

Before I rose to go, without giving the lawyer too much detail—what was it his business?—I asked him if Olva's claim to the house might be threatened if some new family member turned up and how I might guard against that. He seemed not to hear me at first but then dryly said "These documents are binding" and pushed them across the table.

I returned to the waiting room, and Marcus and I prepared to leave. The receptionist's eyes followed him all the way out.

The rain cleared for the ride home, and we sailed past tobacco farms that lined the highway. When Marcus cracked the windows, the musky smell of fertilizer swept into the car.

"Why did you ask us to move in?"

"Oh," I said, startled. "Rosemarie asked you."

"But you knew she'd leave. You could have said no."

Here was a pause. On the radio, turned low, a man's voice, maybe a preacher's, moved up and down with a kind of self-assured joy, certain of the things he was saying.

"I care for Olva," I said.

Marcus nodded, and I looked out the window at the next exit, which curved away from the highway before disappearing into a stand of pine. "And I care for you and Amaryllis."

"You don't have to stand arm's-length away from everyone," Marcus said. "You know that, right?" He could be as direct as his daughter! He waited for a response.

In the cedar-smelling cabin of his Pontiac, there was no pretending I hadn't heard him. "I will take the advice under consideration." I turned my gaze out the window. I felt a familiar sternness inside me. Why was it so hard for me to accept a hand extended? As we passed more shorn fields of tobacco, a great insistence materialized in my mind. Before I knew it, words were escaping my mouth. "I'm sorry I blamed Charlie, Marcus. I didn't know what else to do to save Olva, and Charlie seemed… He seemed…" I paused, not able to locate the words. "He seemed…"

"Available to you?"

I paused again. "Yes." Another pause, my thoughts gathering in my head like a thundercloud. "I should have…" I had never uttered what I was about to say. Releasing the words to the air would have given them breath, and I had not wanted to allow them life, allow them to grow and mature into regret. Living was burdensome enough as it was. I steadied my thoughts. "I should have let Mama escape with Olva and Charlie. To leave and be a family with them. She had wanted to do that all along. She told us as much when we buried the mannequin. But I begged them not to leave. And their pity for me paralyzed them. I'm sure the decision was against every instinct they possessed. But they carried that pity—so dutifully!—like a rock through a river."

Marcus studied me. I felt neither reproach nor forgiveness from him. We fell into silence. After a few minutes, he turned up the volume on the radio, the preacher again, a black one I could now tell, and he was quoting Isaiah. *Behold, I will do a new thing; now it shall spring forth; shall ye not know it? I will even make a way in the wilderness, and rivers in the desert.*

When we arrived home, Marcus and I found Olva sitting on

the sofa. She was reading a book. When I saw its cover, I knew which book it was. The soft room of my mouth went dry.

"You went somewhere!" Olva said. Her face was wide with wonder.

"She did," Marcus said.

"Yes," I confirmed. "I did." I could still surprise myself, even after all these years.

Olva saw I was looking at the book she held. "I found this book many years ago under your mattress," she said. "But I figured you had good reason for keeping it there. Every so often, I would slide it out and read a little, returning it before you noticed. I didn't find it that one night when Mama and I searched, though. You had hidden it too well from us."

"I wanted it to be mine alone," I confessed. "I had hidden it even before you were forced to look for it." It pained me to admit my selfishness. "I have given it to Amaryllis," I said, hoping Olva would see my contrition. "In my younger years, it helped me understand some aspects of survival."

"Survival," Olva said, drawing in a breath. She held it for a long while before driving that breath from her body. She lifted herself from the sofa and walked over to face me. "Do you remember when your great-uncle used to come around during the holidays? I remember after every meal, he would push his chair back from the table. His short arms would be resting on his round belly, and he would pontificate on Darwin's ideas, or what he thought he knew of those ideas, which it turns out was not much. He knew your family had taken me in. I remember that Easter meal as well as you do, when he invited me to the table with the rest of you. It was the first time I'd been invited to that table—in my own mother's house!" She fell silent. When she resumed, her voice had lowered. I held my breath so I could hear her. "Sally went on and on about how God favors certain traits and how those traits are favored in nature. How the strongest and most deserving humans would be separated from the rest. And the rest—he's looking right at me as he says this—the rest would perish. *Perish.* How's that something to say to a child? So yes, I have thought often and hard on the matter of my survival. I survived by taking care of people my whole life. I used to think it made me a stronger person, how there's strength in sacrifice, but now I see that even if I found wisdom there, it came by way of force."

Olva considered the book again, giving its cover a firm press with her hand before she set it down on the sofa table. "Everything turns into something else, now doesn't it?" she said.

Perhaps I'd been reading that book the wrong way my entire life.

I took a step closer to Olva, placed my documents on the table next to the book, and stuck my arms out straight from my body.

"Oh," she said, and it took a moment for her to settle into my awkward embrace. I could feel Olva's gaze meet Marcus's over my shoulder.

"Well then," I said, releasing Olva. "I'm going to rest in the sunroom on the divan. I'm a tad dizzy and don't care to take the stairs to my room."

The next morning, I woke with a start. Fumbling for my glasses on my bedside table, my hand fell through space when it found nothing. I rolled to one side, feeling a pressure on my face. My glasses! By degrees, I realized I was in the sunroom, where I had fallen asleep the day before and slept through the night. Light pressed in through the wide windows, and the house was already stirring. Someone had covered me in a wool Black Watch blanket.

With some difficulty, I lifted myself from the divan, not calling for Olva's help as I usually did. I made my slow way toward the kitchen, and when I pressed my hand against the sideboard in the dining room to rest, there was Amaryllis at the entrance to the kitchen, tapping her foot. Her rabbit dangled from her hand. I winked at her, and she squirmed away, laughter curling off her like whitecaps as she trotted into the kitchen.

I sat down in one of the chairs at the kitchen table. She twirled around and suddenly was right beside me, our old wooden tray in her rabbitless hand. "What's this?"

"Good morning, Amaryllis. That is a wooden tray. Just a plain wooden tray. We use it for carrying our water glasses outside or sometimes even out in the yard when Olva is gathering vegetables from her garden."

Amaryllis kept her eyes on me. "What is this?" She held up the tray again.

"Amaryllis, go get the butterfly tray. It's not past repair. It's a true antique. I will tell you that story."

"You already told me that story," she said, pushing the wooden tray at me. "What is *this*?"

Children and their need for repetition! Looking at her face, which did not waver, I remembered a story about the tray she was holding.

I gestured for her to sit down with me at the table, and she placed the tray between us. "This has been around a long time. It was probably from Grandmother DeLour's house." I placed my hand over one of the tray's handles, which was a simple oval carved into its side. As I did, Amaryllis crawled her fingers to grip the other handle. We looked as if we were completing a circuit of some kind.

I told her that, during my childhood, the tray was a workhorse, as it is now, doing all manner of odd jobs because we did not worry about spoiling it. But once, it was used in a way that was startling to us. It was the only time Charlie ever called on our house, or at least the only time I knew of. (Amaryllis perked at hearing Charlie's name.)

Daddy Kratt was away with Shep Bramlett at a trade show in Charlotte, and Mama must have thought that we children were dispatched across town. Yet it was a rare afternoon in which we were all three upstairs, reading in our rooms, but when we heard grown-ups in the living room, we clustered out of sight on the landing between the stairs.

Hearing Charlie's voice, we crept down the stairs farther so that we could see what was happening. What Mama and Charlie said was very boring, not amounting to more than small talk, but I recall they sat closer on the sofa than I deemed appropriate. Mama then did something unusual. She withdrew to the kitchen and returned with this wooden tray, on which sat two cups of tea in Grandmother DeLour's Noritake china, along with sugar and cream—such delicacies! She served Charlie from the tray, taking his instructions about how many spoonfuls of sugar and how much cream. He laughed and protested at first, but then he grew quiet and serious and let her do it. They were silent after that, just looking at each other, and we retreated up the stairs as they sipped their tea.

"Are we related?" Amaryllis asked.

"Oh," I said, surprised my story had prompted that particular question. I considered it. "Well, Charlie is your great-great-grandfather on your father's side, and Charlie and my mama were—Well, Charlie and Mama were the parents of Olva."

The child waited.

"That makes us—" I paused, and she searched my face. What word was there? "That makes us—"

"Friendshipped," Amaryllis said, her grasp on the wooden tray relaxing. Her eyes swept across the kitchen. "I'm hungry."

I laughed. "Go out on the porch, and I will bring you your breakfast."

She hopped from her seat and bounded toward the front door. I picked up the wooden tray and began my duties. For her drink, I would fetch chamomile tea.

Later, I sat in the sunroom. The day was on the decline, and after serving Amaryllis breakfast, I had not moved very much.

"Let's go down to the train depot," I said to Olva, who had walked in to check on me.

"They are tearing it down."

The unused tracks were a nuisance for whoever owned the land now.

"Let's get our last look then." I noticed her expression. "My bones can manage it!" I croaked, which made us both laugh.

She nodded and left the sunroom, returning with my shoes.

"Tell Marcus and Amaryllis to join us," I said.

"They are taking a walk of their own."

"Perhaps we will see them on our way."

We maneuvered down the stairs with Olva guiding me. She steadied me with her arm. "Are you sure you're all right?" she asked.

I knew what she was thinking. I had not been out of the house since my ride with Marcus.

"You needn't conquer the world so quickly," she said, but she capitulated when she saw my resolve.

We helped each other down the porch stairs. Well, she mostly helped me, and we made it all the way down the drive-way before I had to rest. I squinted back at the house.

"Is it satisfying to have a place to call your own now, Olva? Marcus and Amaryllis will never want for a home."

Olva turned to appraise the house. "We'll have to decide what to do with it."

"What on earth do you mean?" I cried.

She said nothing, a ghost of a smile rising to her lips.

"Will you stay?" I asked. I was wondering who would turn down a house given freely but kept the thought to myself.

The silence was keen. So I asked the question again.

"Will you stay?"

She studied the road ahead of us for a long while. She didn't answer. We began moving again, and I tried to keep my mind on each footstep rather than what was behind me.

On our journey to the depot, we stopped frequently, giving me time to rest but also to survey what Bound had become.

Many of the old homes, which were small but solid in their day, had given way to double-wide trailers. The yards were curious spaces, more dirt than grass and cluttered with all the wrong things: cars, forsaking driveways, in various stages of disrepair, and dirty pieces of furniture—sofas flattened from use and hulking mastodon recliners—all of which sat empty, save for the occasional sleeping mutt. A lone child was rapping a stick on a patch of dirt. He wore a Lone Ranger mask and dirty underwear. His eyes followed me.

Our trek to the depot was a slow one, but it was eased by the fact that autumn had finally soothed summer's heat. We passed the former site of the Kratt Mercantile Company, where my father judged himself a world maker. He was alone in that judgment now. The store, what was left of it, looked like a deserted sanitarium, its windows pockmarked by rocks and the paint hanging off the front door in long tufts, as if the building had been in the midst of shedding its skin before relinquishing the effort. We moved on.

We passed the old home of the Sullivan girls, who paid me a marble each to walk through our house. I stopped in my tracks when I heard laughter jostling through one of the windows that opened to the street.

"Do the Sullivans still live there?"

"Yes indeed," Olva said. "Those five girls had too many babies to count. And then those babies had babies."

Suddenly, the front door swung open, and two gray-haired women stepped out onto the porch. One was bobbing an infant in her arms to calm its cries. They didn't seem to mind us watching them from the road. I thought the one with the child looked like Lindy, who had tried to steal a glimpse of our spinning wheel those years ago. Who had brought a persimmon crumble to my brother's funeral. She wore a long gray house robe, and her hair was unkempt. I lifted my hand to wave just as she shifted her focus back to the baby. Yet she glanced back up again, and seeing my hand still raised, stole one hand from the child's bottom to acknowledge me.

Olva and I continued to walk along the edge of the road, where the wild grass collided with the blacktop like seaweed hugging a shoreline. We passed a few bald spots of land where I remembered houses had once been. We passed someone's garden, where the butternut squash had abandoned its rectangular plot of land and soldier-crawled all the way to the road. We passed a tract of land Daddy Kratt used to own. Someone had built a ramshackle hut on it, not amounting to much. We passed two kinds of birds I didn't recognize.

In the distance, we saw the outlines of Marcus and Amaryllis strolling through one of the old cotton plots. The child ran ahead of her father and then back to him, and he raised her up. They were laughing, or so it seemed to me. He lifted her all the way onto his shoulders. They kept walking like that. Together, they stretched long and lean into the sky, and from where we were standing, it looked as if Amaryllis could drag her fingertips across the clouds if she wanted.

When we arrived at the depot, I was too tired to stand any longer, and we found a bench. To the right of the depot was evidence of its demolition. Giant pieces of equipment sat abandoned until the next workday, their long yellow arms collapsed to the ground at severe angles. They looked like grand creatures from another era, but who could tell at which end of life they were poised, if they were coming or going, if we had caught them rising up from the elements or surrendering to the earth.

I saw a speck in the sky. I blinked, and it was still there. A red-tailed hawk! It glided above us, making a languid circle. With no warning, it dropped from the sky and grazed the earth before climbing back up again. *Nature, red in tooth and claw.* My head was a tad dizzy, and the sensation moved to my chest, then expanded to my limbs. It was like the passing of the seasons in my body, the tight budding of spring in my chest and the flush of summer, followed by the release of fall and the shutting down of winter.

"What will become of Bound?" I asked. A kind of desperation had seized me. I urgently needed to know.

When Olva didn't answer, I turned to look at her. Her expression was unfamiliar. I couldn't place it.

She studied the depot. "No," she said. "No, I don't believe we will."

I was confused at first by her answer, but then I understood. Under my skin, I felt my heart chattering. She was answering my earlier question, the one she had left unanswered.

Will you stay?

We made it home from the depot. The nearest bedroom on the main floor was Olva's. I said I would rest there for a spell, if she didn't mind, because I knew I would not make it upstairs to my bedroom. Inside the room, Olva's bed was made, watertight, and the air held the faint scent of rose water. It was the perfume from our childhood; it didn't remind me of myself any longer. It now belonged entirely to Olva. I lowered into a peach-colored parlor chair of Grandmother DeLour's that was positioned in the corner. By degrees, I felt better, and when my head had settled, I was able to focus on what was around me. I seldom visited Olva's room.

There was much to see. A stained-glass angel was propped against the window, its colors muted in the twilight. Beside me, atop Olva's bureau, sat a wooden owl that still bore the marks of someone's knife. Next to that was a silver tray with edges tarnished by unknown fingerprints. I had never before seen these objects. Everywhere I looked was a new curiosity, unknown to me: a stout forearm of driftwood; a jar of cream-colored ribbon; and a vase, its wisp of a neck stretching up elegantly like a heron's. Paintings stacked against a wall, the one facing outward an oil portrait of a woman I didn't recognize, her smile shimmering. There was more. An old pair of binoculars, missing one lens. A bowl of marbles so shiny, they looked wet. These things, their relationship to one another, seemed to structure the room. The variety of objects was remarkable. Before me was a complex system, as intricate as the natural world outside, with its own exchanges and hierarchies and dependencies. The things in the room seemed to be having conversations with one another as clearly as birdcalls might fill the afternoon air. I seemed to hear them, and I felt their eyes, too, looking at me, returning my gaze. On the table beside me sat a notepad and pen. I grasped the pen and wrote a few things down. My inventory felt complete.

Everything turns into something else. This is what Olva says. It occurs to me that objects experience evolution, and not only are they shifting over time on their own, creeping from one state to another, but their significance to us is also transforming, stirring toward different directions in our minds, a permutation that happens whether it suits us or not. And even if objects were possessed of an obstinacy that allowed them to remain unchanged, we should not be fooled into thinking we could approach them in the same ways, because nothing less than our existence, it seems to me, reminds us that this is impossible. We enter this world curling our tiny hands around our mother's fingers, and we exit with those same hands cinched by arthritis. How could we pretend our grasp, clutching onto life from opposite ends, stays the same?

How had I not known about the items in Olva's room? My stomach felt like a metronome tipping. The full weight of recognition hit me. Just as the items in my inventory told a story about the Kratt family, these things in Olva's room told a story about her. It was a story I hardly knew.

I slowly lifted myself up to slip something onto Olva's bureau. Returning to the chair, I sat a while longer. I felt in the left pocket of my trousers for the newspaper clipping I always kept there. Finally, I closed my eyes, and in my lap, I laid my hands, one palm stacked gently within the other like a crescent-shaped bowl.

Everything turns into something else.

Windsor chair
Wooden spinning wheel
Mahogany secretary
R. S. Prussia vase
Pie safe—Grandmother DeLour's
Butler's tray (silver plated)
Amsterdam School copper mantel clock
Hamilton drafting table
Letter opener (cut glass)

Tiffany lamp (diameter 16″; 21¾″ height)—~~broken~~ fixed

Victorian chaise longue
Octagonal Jacobean parlor table
Mahogany sewing cabinet
Westclox alarm clock (Big Ben model)
Hepplewhite side table
Watchmaker's workbench
Edwardian neoclassical brass column candleholders (10″ tall)
Abner Cutler rolltop desk (54″ × 21″ × 50″)—damaged

Riding whip—Daddy Kratt's
New York Times (Wednesday, October 30, 1929)
Peacock hat
Edwardian coral cameo (1½″ × 1″)—Olva's

Highboy bureau
Butterfly tray (23¾″ × 15½″)—damaged
Cheval mirror

Glass rabbit
Persian Heriz rug

Revolving mahogany bookstand
Queen Anne chair (dusty rose)
Rococo cherub figurines
Noritake 175 Gold china
Art deco oyster plates

Silver cutlery
Waterford crystal pitcher
Crystal saltcellars
Louis XV sofa (silver leaf details)

Leather ledger book
Purdey shotgun (barrel 29″)—buried

The Tale of Peter Rabbit, early edition
Bronze blackamoor figures
Origin of Species, first edition
Victorian Dresden figurines
Chippendale wing chair
Hammond's globe
Letter from Aunt Dee to Mama
Maple drop leaf table
Ruby wedding ring—Grandmother DeLour's

Burr yew wood partner's desk (80″ × 51″ × 30″)
Brass teacher's bell
Wooden tray
Parlor chair (peach upholstery)
News clipping—York Herald, December 21, 1929

What Olva owns

On Thursday, October 5, 1989, Judith Kratt of Bound, South Carolina, passed away at the age of 75 years. She is survived by two sisters, Olva DeLour and Rosemarie Kratt Anderson, and friends Marcus and Amaryllis Watson. A private memorial service will be held for Judith.

Judith lived in Bound her entire life. She stayed, and that is something. She died in her home, surrounded by those who loved her.

Obituary, *York Herald*, October 7, 1989

November 5, 1989

Dear Amaryllis,

This morning, you brought your father and me bread and jam on the front porch. Two slices for each of us. You called me Grandma, which I love. You used the old wooden tray to transport the contents of our breakfast, and you shared a little story about the tray. You said Judith had taught you that story. I do believe she would have been proud of the way you told it.

As you know, Judith wrote an inventory of the items in this house. It grew into much more than that. It is my intention to pass along that inventory to you, along with this letter, when you are older. In Judith's inventory, you will find stories about your great-great-grandfather Charlie. And of your father. And me. You might be interested to find yourself in its pages, too. Perhaps you will read it. Perhaps not. Or you might put it in a junk drawer until you are ready to read it. I have come to believe that the odds and ends in junk drawers are no less distinguished than the Waterford crystal in the cupboard.

Judith left everything, even this house, to you, your father, and me. Only a month has passed since her death, and you have handled this busy time, full of decisions and angry speculation by others, with poise beyond any six-year-old. Every person who paid his or her respects to Judith also challenged our right to stay here. We would invite them in, make them some coffee, and show them her last will and testament, properly signed and notarized. They drank their coffee a little more strenuously after that.

Jolly Bramlett was the first to make an appearance. Her sister, Vi, the more decent one, was not with her. Someone told me they had a falling out, which doesn't surprise me. It is an illusion to think siblinghood is immutable; it has its cycles just like everything else. Jolly sauntered in as if nothing had ever happened involving our family and her son. Rick's actions became a part of history, just as easy as that. Too easily, in my opinion. That day is a sore in my mind, and every one of my thoughts aggravates it. Yet I assume Rick has had his own share of troubles since then. I have seen him only once: he was sitting in his truck, eating his lunch alone, a faraway look on his face. I wonder if loneliness is not a constant companion for him. Bound is no easy place to live, after all. It can make people want to reside in the past. Jolly demonstrated that herself: when she strolled inside this house, it appeared her chief interest was getting an eyeful of the Kratt family's heirlooms. That would have pleased Judith immensely.

None of the visitors has understood that this house has always been every bit ours, even before a piece of paper named it so. It did not rattle me, then, when I read about Dovey's pregnancy, a potential heir, in Judith's inventory. What of it? Our ancestors maintained this house, the whole town when you think on it. They labored in the fields, cleaned the houses, and cared for most of the children in Bound. The tending, the mending, the very upkeep of life. We did those things. We keep doing them.

We have decided to sell the house, to move on. You know this, of course. As young as you are, you feel as if you've worn through this town, too. We officially own the things around us, and because of that, we may do what we like with them. We have decided to sell most of them. Judith would be greatly saddened by that news, but we will take this inventory with us, and I believe that would mean something to her. Rosemarie returned for Judith's memorial service. Before she left again, hardly two days after the service, we asked her if she wanted anything from the house. The only thing she requested was a copy of Judith's obituary. Rosemarie had written it herself.

The things we have found while packing have not ceased to amaze us. The Tiffany lamp was in a box in the attic. We will take that with us. Just yesterday, I found Mama's double-sided cameo on my bureau. The goddess Athena shone up at me. Judith had left it there. That is a kind of grace, I think. In the cellar, we found a resplendent peacock hat, and I realized at once it was the one that caused Rosemarie so much pain. I hesitated to let you play dress-up in it. You are quite grand when you wear it, though. I like to think you are showing it how a happy memory begins.

The night after Judith and I visited the train depot, she left this earthly world. The trip to the depot was hard for her, and she wasn't ready for another outing so soon after the one with Marcus. I should have kept her home. But she was more determined than usual that day, and it was time to let her begin caring for herself. A stroke delivered her into the Lord's hands. Deep in her body, unknown to her, she had been following the bloodline of the DeLours, a genealogical link between her and the generations before. She collected on that inheritance in a devastating way.

I miss her, you see.

On that trip to the depot, Judith kept asking me if we would stay in the house. I was reluctant to answer. Finally, I told her we would not. She was silent, so I can't know whether she accepted that. It would not have mattered either way. We are bound for something beyond this house. We will choose what we take with us.

My wish is for us to make a long trip in the car

before we settle down somewhere. I want us to reach farther than we have been allowed in the past. I mentioned this to the preacher in Hickory Grove—Reverend Bell—when we visited him. He is my age, and he was stricken. "Olva, pardon my saying so," he counseled, "but floating from place to place is not a luxury we can afford. People will wonder why you are traveling and what you are running from. They will not accept you have a right to go wherever you wish. The open road is no place for us." I placed my hand on his arm but could not erase his fear.

The other day, Marcus mentioned applying for a position at the new car manufacturing plant in Spartanburg. I want to be supportive, of course, but it is my hope we will leave this area for good. If Marcus takes my advice, he will use the money from the sale of the house and the auction of the things inside it to start his own business. Your father is gifted with the ability to repair broken things—and to repair other wounds. I've always known this about him, a gentleness that makes him seem more like a woman than a man. I'm sorry to say I made him feel ashamed of that quality over the years. But I'm not too old to accommodate new ideas. I've rid myself of a few things to make room.

Throughout my life, I wondered why Charlie never tried to come back and get Mama and me, to rescue us, even if it might have endangered him. Or why he didn't reunite with his only son in Tirzah, Marcus's grandfather, and make us all one big family. Charlie never mentioned his son to me. I can't know what created a rift between the two of them. I hope I wasn't the cause. If Charlie's son had discovered I was his half sister, I can imagine it might have been difficult to know how to feel about that, what with my being raised by one of the prosperous white families of Bound. It made me angry to think of Charlie abandoning the idea of his son, then abandoning Mama and me, too, when he fled. I wanted him to *do something*, even though it took me my whole life to set my story straight. And, of course, if we had left with Charlie, if all these imaginings had come to pass, I would never have met you, my dear Amaryllis.

There is something I have not told you and your father yet. Reverend Bell shared some information in confidence, away from Rosemarie's ears, when we saw him. He found record of someone he thought might have been Charlie. The man lived on Johns Island, along the South Carolina coast. This man had changed his name, the documents indicated, and while his old surname was unknown, his new name was Charlie Delour.

Reverend Bell's records also showed that Charlie Delour had three children on Johns

Island. Probably those children had children. That he started a new family—it stings, I must admit. But perhaps he took the long view, building a circuit that we might complete later. When the three of us set out on our road trip, I will steer us first to the coast. Wouldn't it be something else to find our kin there? Aunts and uncles. Cousins. Brothers. Sisters. To be able to say, of my own accord: *Sister, I am coming home*, or something very nearly like it. Whoever or whatever we find there, it will be our choice whether we stay or leave. At the very least, I doubt you will object to visiting the ocean. We will have to get a little life vest for Peter Rabbit, now, won't we? You have experienced far too much for your age, and you carry it quietly. In my mind, in the place where my deepest wishes reside, I see you running along the shore, simply looking like a child.

That last trip to the depot, Judith and I shared the most extraordinary sunset. The earth was both affirming its vastness and reflecting the sprawling wilderness of our souls. Right in front of us, the clouds broke, and the westerly sun asserted itself. It had been waiting behind the depot and, given the opportunity, reached long arms of light straight through the abandoned building, undeterred by two sets of murky windows, until it assembled that light in golden planks on the ground in front of us. I reached over and took Judith's hand in mine. We would rest our eyes on that place until we couldn't any longer. We would watch. We are watching. Before us, a house of light is being built, one that will be gone tomorrow.

Yours,
Olva

READING GROUP GUIDE

1. How would you describe Judith? What are her virtues? What are her flaws?

2. Why does Rosemarie's return compel Judith to begin writing her inventory? In what other ways does Rosemarie disrupt Judith's life?

3. How would you characterize Judith and Olva's relationship? Is it one of equals? How does their relationship change throughout the novel?

4. In the first chapter, Judith compares the concept of memory to a letter opener made of cut glass: "held to the window, it produced a different color for each of us." How do Judith's memories shape the way she tells her family's story?

5. Olva has her own take on memory. She says to Judith, "Memory and history are bound up with one another. Where does one end and the other begin?" What do you think Olva means by this? How might the relationship between memory and history be an especially charged one in the South?

6. Quincy describes siblinghood to Judith in this way: "You and Rosemarie are the mold, and I'm the gelatin that never set." Judith weighs in, too: "This was the way of siblings, how my existence, my very selfhood, grew partly from what Quincy was not. And from what Rosemarie was not." How has birth order influenced the experiences of the Kratt children and the choices they've made? Do you think your life has been affected by the decisions and actions of your siblings? If you are an only child, do you think you would be a different person if you had had siblings?

7. This novel teems with objects. Judith records items in her inventory, but other inventories materialize, too, such as the merchandise in Daddy Kratt's department store, the gifts left for Rosemarie, and the collection of unfamiliar belongings in Olva's bedroom. What additional inventories can you find in the book? Why does Judith organize life into lists?

8. Which object in the book do you believe is most significant and why? In your own life, do you have an object that you value above others?

9. What do you think Judith covets most in her life? Is it a thing?

10. Daddy Kratt and his associates pursue Charlie in the book's 1929 timeline. The Bramlett family searches for Marcus in the 1989 timeline. How are these two pursuits related? How do the two men's circumstances impact their relationships with their families?

11. This novel explores the power of ownership. Olva says to Judith and Rosemarie, "Do you own your own life? If you have never had to ask that question, you are fortunate indeed." What do you think she means by this? How might questions about ownership be especially critical to ask in the context of the South's history and legacy of slavery and racial injustice?

12. When Judith begins her inventory, what is her purpose? How has that purpose changed by the end of the novel?

13. Is Daddy Kratt a villain? What about Jolly Bramlett and her son, Rick? What do these characters struggle with?

14. What do you make of Olva's decision to sell the Kratt house and most of the heirlooms within it? Why does the possibility of a Kratt heir—Quincy and Dovey's potential child—not faze her?

15. Has the relationship between Judith and Amaryllis shifted by the end of the book? If so, how, and which objects play a role in this shift?

16. Why does Rosemarie leave Bound for a second time in her life?

17. Why does this novel end with a letter from Olva to Amaryllis?

FURTHER PROJECTS

1. Judith provides a list of novels containing spinsters like herself. She includes Jane Austen's *Emma*, Charles Dickens's *Great Expectations*, Henry James's *The Bostonians*, George Gissing's *The Odd Women*, and Edith Wharton's *Bunner Sisters*. Read one or more of these novels. Is Judith similar to those spinsters? Is her commentary accurate: "It is true some of these fictional heroines have challenging personalities, but defects of character are often an outcome of circumstances, are they not?"

2. The author reveals in her Q&A that this novel began as a retelling of a story from her family's history. Is there a story from your family's history that is intriguing? An heirloom that has a tale to tell? Start with writing a paragraph. Then write another paragraph. Then another. That's how a book begins!

A CONVERSATION WITH THE AUTHOR

Where did the idea for *The Last List of Miss Judith Kratt* come from?

The book was inspired by a real murder that occurred in my family two generations before me. (You'd think this news would produce a fresh shock for me each time I mention it, but in my family, we discuss the details of the incident so frequently and at such length that they have been rendered ordinary.) Early drafts of the manuscript were my attempt to tell the actual story of my great-uncle fatally shooting his own brother, but eventually, I freed myself from retelling that specific event. Characters shifted; plotlines changed. Yet the heart of the story—a Southern family haunted by a brother's murder and the chilling allegation that a sibling may be to blame—remained the same.

The story of the Kratt family is told from the perspective of a first-person narrator, the Southern spinster Judith Kratt. How did you make that decision?

The voice of Judith is based on my unmarried great-aunt. She was the sister of the two brothers mentioned above—one shot the other—and I chose to adopt her point of view because I was interested in following the path of a character's mind as she absorbs and recounts a family tragedy. That, and I've always been drawn to compellingly flawed narrators, especially in the first person. Judith is our guide through the novel, but we see her limitations, and that gap between her telling of events and what we otherwise sense to be true, mainly through other characters' reactions, provides a rich interpretive space, not only for witnessing Judith's growth, but also for examining how memory and perception color a person's outlook.

Why did you choose for Judith to narrate the story through an inventory of objects?

I grew up in a Southern house crowded with family heirlooms. I'm fairly certain the stories about those heirlooms took up twice the space of the actual items. I wanted to tell a story through objects in part because I'm fascinated by how possessions can evoke starkly different memories—and thus meanings—for different people. For families, inheritance can be a thorny subject, to say the least. For Southerners, our willingness to engage with the fraught history of objects in our region—for example, the problem of Confederate monuments—is critical.

Do you have a favorite character? If so, who and why?

It's true that I'm obsessed with Judith's voice. I'm interested in the moments in which she surprises herself and, even more, in her mistakes and misjudgments. But my heart is with Olva. She checks Judith's vision of the world when it narrows, and over the years, she has had to provide a tremendous amount of emotional labor for Judith. I often wonder about Olva's life after the final pages of the novel. As the book ends, she finds herself closer in birthright to the Kratts, but also, to some extent, free of them. What will she do with that new awareness? I'm enthralled by that question.

Who are your favorite authors and why?

The novels of George Eliot—*Middlemarch*, in particular—taught me the value of applying a sympathetic imagination to my characters. Anything written by Virginia Woolf is a master class in the magic of language. As for contemporary writers, Marilynne Robinson and Elizabeth Strout are literary giants to me. Both authors can coax staggering truths about the human condition from a scrupulously observed insight about a character or the delicate arrangement of images within a sentence. Honestly, the syntax alone of some of their sentences can have me in fits for weeks. I pore over the works of Kazuo Ishiguro, especially how he develops the voices of his first-person narrators. And the poets! William Butler Yeats, Walt Whitman, Seamus Heaney, Eavan Boland, Rita Dove, Mary Oliver, Naomi Shihab Nye, and Kimberly O'Connor. My ritual is that I read a poem before I begin writing each day.

What is your most treasured family heirloom?

I have a poem clipped from a newspaper that was found in my grandfather's wallet when he died. Even more remarkable, the poem's subject is death.

ACKNOWLEDGMENTS

Like Judith Kratt, I'm a list maker. Here, my list of happy debts is long, as writing a novel is not done in isolation, though it often feels that way. I thank my lucky stars for Kerry D'Agostino, my agent. She's a joy to work with and is not only a tireless advocate and a discerning editor, but also a kind, thoughtful person. My heartfelt gratitude goes to Shana Drehs, my editor. Her perceptive questions, as well as her enthusiasm and trust, were instrumental in helping this book mature. I'm grateful, too, for Kaitlyn Kennedy, my publicist, for her unflagging efforts in getting the book into readers' hands.

Thanks to Dominique Raccah and the whole Sourcebooks team—Lisa Amoroso, Sabrina Baskey, Margaret Coffee, Stephanie Graham, Heather Hall, Kelly Lawler, Lizzie Lewandowski, Danielle McNaughton, Heather Morris, Valerie Pierce, Brittany Vibbert, and Heidi Weiland. Warm gratitude goes to Dawn Bourgeois for the cover photograph. I'm happy our two works of art found each other.

I hope my great-aunt Jean would be pleased to learn that she inspired the character of Judith Kratt. From both Jean and my mother, I inherited published and unpublished histories of York County, South Carolina. Those texts were central to my research, and they include Jerry L. West's *Sharon: The First*

Fifty Years 1889–1939; Doris M. Thomas's *Remembering Sharon, 1889–1989: Fact and Fiction* (1989); and J. Edward Lee and Jerry L. West's *York and Western York County: The Story of a Southern Eden* (2001). In some cases, I moved around or conflated minor historical details for the needs of the story.

Support from the James Jones First Novel Fellowship kept this project going (thanks in particular to Kaylie Jones, Laurie Loewenstein, Taylor Polites, and Nina Solomon). Rebecca Mahoney blessed the book as an ongoing editor, and our alligator walks in Florida were a lifeline. Without Lighthouse Writers Workshop in Denver, this novel would not be out in the world. I'm especially indebted to a revelatory workshop there with Tiffany Quay Tyson. One more Lighthouser: my friend Kimberly O'Connor, a gifted poet and an unflagging believer in my teaching and work, even back when I didn't have the courage to call what I was writing a novel ("that long document filled with words").

To thrive as a writer, you need your wolf pack. I'm lucky to have found mine. Paulette Fire, Windy Lynn Harris, Rachel Luria, Ainsley McWha, Twila Newey, Roberta Payne, Julie Comins Pickrell, and Natalee Tucker—collectively known as the She-Thugs—make me a better writer and a better human.

Bill Aarnes and Nancy Whitaker set me on this path. Ann Bortz reminded me, again and again, that everything turns into something else. Tracey Lanham and Heather Lindemann helped me find my voice after a period of dormancy. Victor Luftig refined my thinking in an earlier chapter of my writing life, as did Steve Arata, Alison Booth, Karen Chase, Brian Glavey, Neil Hultgren, and Kate Nash.

Amy McKeehan is my creative partner. Kim Braxton taught me how to imagine. Ali Sweeney provides a light in the fog, and Maria Gabriela Guevara will drive through a snowstorm with me for the sake of literature. Margaret Mitchell and Tiffany Putimahtama hold me up with their unwavering friendship. Kim Clark, Heather McRae, Rusty Miller, Susan Peck, Christina White, and the whole Furman crew are there for me no matter what. Zabrina Aleguire speaks my inner language. Donna Heider is a beloved mentor. Dana Bobotis taught me the delights of narrative by writing and illustrating stories for me about my stuffed animals. And Frank and Margaret Bobotis put storytelling in my bones.

Words won't do justice for these next two. Jason Heider is my foundation, my champion, my love. Our daughter, Abby, animates the world we walk through. Finally, my first and best review of the book is already in. When Abby was six years old, before publication was in sight, I let her read some of the manuscript. Later, I found this note on my desk:

Dear Mom, I love you! I like the stories you write about Olva and Rosemarie!

Love, Abby

xoxo and a 1000 more

ABOUT THE AUTHOR

Andrea Bobotis was born and raised in South Carolina and received her PhD in English literature from the University of Virginia. Her fiction has received awards from the Raymond Carver Short Story Contest and the James Jones First Novel Fellowship, and her essays on Irish writers have appeared in journals such as *Victorian Studies* and the *Irish University Review*. She lives with her family in Denver, Colorado, where she teaches creative writing to youth at Lighthouse Writers Workshop. *The Last List of Miss Judith Kratt* is her debut novel.